DRAGON LADY

The throne-like chair on which she sat had been carved into a writhing mass of snarling dragons. "My husband said you might need to be convinced of the sincerity of his message—In such an event, he gave me certain instructions.' She said something in Chinese and the two men with guns moved a step towards me.

"You will find these gentlemen to be most persuasive." She rose and moved to the door. "I am not quite sure how they will go about convincing you. I really don't care. Goodnight." She opened the door, said something more to the two men, and left.

"What did she say?" I asked.

"She told them to mind the furniture."

Avon Books by Ross Thomas

THE COLD WAR SWAP
CAST A YELLOW SHADOW
THE SEERSUCKER WHIPSAW.

ROSS THOMAS

THE SINGAPORE WINK

AVON
PUBLISHERS OF
DISCUS • CAMELOT • BARD

AVON BOOKS
A division of
The Hearst Corporation
959 Eighth Avenue
New York, New York 10019

First Avon Printing, October, 1970

To
Frances Phillips

CHAPTER I

He was probably the only man in Los Angeles wearing spats that day, pearl grey ones that peeped out from beneath the uncuffed trousers of a grey suit so dark that it seemed almost black. There was a white shirt and a neatly knotted pale grey tie that blossomed a trifle before it ducked behind a vest. There was a hat, too, but it was only a hat.

If either of the two men who came in out of the rain were a customer, it would be the other one, the big man with the tightly cropped grey hair and the left arm that stuck out at an acute angle as if he couldn't straighten it all the way. He circled the car slowly, opened a door and slammed it, beamed at the satisfying thunk, and then said something to the medium-sized man in the spats who frowned slightly and shook his head.

The car was a cream-colored 1932 Cadillac V-16 roadster that became all mine after its owner, a plunger in the commodity market, made a disastrous guess about sorghum futures. The bill for the restoration of the car amounted to $4300 and the commodity plunger, gloomy and depressed, had apologized for an hour about his inability to pay. Three days later he had sounded optimistic, even cheerful, when he phoned to assure me that a deal had almost jelled and that soon everything would be worked out. It was, around five the next morning, when he poked the barrel of a .32 revolver into his mouth and pulled the trigger.

The Cadillac, with a $6500 price on it, was now the centerpiece in the showroom, flanked by a 1936 Ford four-door convertible cabriolet and a 1938 SS 100 Jaguar. I was asking $4500 for the Ford and the Jaguar was tagged at $7000, but any reasonably neat stranger with a clean shirt, a checkbook, and a driver's license could have had his choice for an offer of $500 less.

The big man, really big, well over six-three, lingered by the Cadillac, not quite ignoring the growing impatience of his friend in the spats. The big man wore a double-breasted blue blazer with gold buttons, grey flannel slacks, a white turtleneck polo shirt, and the ecstatic expression of a crap shooter who has just hit his seventh straight pass. I decided that he was too old for both the expression and the clothes.

The man in the spats frowned again, said something, and the big man took a last, savoring look at the Cadillac before they started back towards my corner office, a glassed-in cubicle that held a desk, a safe, three chairs and a filing cabinet. The big man came in first and he didn't bother with the amenities.

"How much you want for the Caddy?" His voice didn't go with his size. It was high, almost piping.

Because he might be a customer, I took my feet off the desk. "Sixty-five hundred."

The smaller man, the one with the spats, wasn't listening. After he gave me a quick glance he let his eyes wander around the office. There wasn't a great deal to see, but he looked as if he hadn't expected much.

"This used to be a supermarket," he said. "An A&P."

"It used to be," I said.

"What's the sign outside mean—*Les Voitures Anciennes?*" He did better with the French than most.

"Old cars. Old used cars."

"Why don't you say so?"

"Then nobody would ask, would they?"

"Class," the big man said, staring at the Cadillac through the glass office wall. "Real class. How much you actually take for the Caddy, no kidding?"

"It's completely restored, all parts are original, and the price is still sixty-five hundred."

"You the owner?" the smaller man asked. His r's gave him away; so did his t's. He was from the East Coast, either New Jersey or New York but it could have been a long time since he had lived there.

"One of them," I said. "I have a partner who handles the mechanical side. He's in the back."

"And you sell them?"

"Some days," I said.

The big man turned once more from his lingering inspection of the Cadillac. "I had one like that once," he said dreamily. "Except it was green. Real dark green. Remember it, Solly? We drove it down to Hot Springs that time with May and that other doll, the one you had, and we run into Owney."

"That was thirty-six years ago," the man in the spats said.

"Christ, it sure don't seem that long."

The smaller man turned to one of the chairs, took out a white handkerchief, flicked it over the seat a couple of times, put it back in his hip pocket, and sat down. His movements had been neat, precise and unhurried. He leaned back in the chair, produced a thin gold cigarette case and took out an oval cigarette. Or perhaps the case was so thin that it mashed his cigarettes into ovals. He lit it with a gold Zippo.

"I'm Salvatore Callese," he said, and I noticed that his suit jacket had no pockets. "This is my associate, Mr. Palmisano."

He didn't offer to shake hands so I merely nodded at both of them. "Are you interested in some particular car, Mr. Callese?"

He frowned at that and stared at me with dark brown eyes that curiously seemed to have no sheen. They looked dry and dead and I almost expected to hear them rustle when they moved. "No," he said. "I'm not interested in used cars. Palmisano here thinks he is, but he's not. What he's really interested in is thirty-five years ago when he could still get it up and he thinks maybe the Caddy out there would help. But you don't get that back with a thirty-six-year-old used car, although I'd say that a lot of your customers might think so."

"Some of them," I said. "I sell a lot of nostalgia."

"Nostalgia," he agreed. "A secondhand nostalgia dealer."

"I just like the car, Solly," Palmisano said. "For Christ's sake, can't I even like a car?"

Callese ignored him. "You're Cauthorne," he said to me. "Edward Cauthorne. It's a nice name. What is it, English?"

I shrugged. "We were never much on tracing the family tree. I suppose English will do."

"Me, I'm Italian. So's Palmisano. My old man was a greaseball; couldn't even speak English. Neither could Palmisano's."

Both of them were in their late fifties or early sixties and Palmisano, despite the left arm that jutted at an odd angle, looked fit and lean and as if he still wouldn't mind a day or two of hard physical labor. He had a long, spade face with a thick-lipped mouth that seemed too wide for the piping voice that came out of it. His nose hooked nicely towards a strong chin and his black eyes were shaded by long grey lashes that blinked a lot, as if in perpetual surprise.

"Are you selling something," I said, "or did you just come by to get in out of the rain?"

Callese dropped his cigarette on the floor and carefully ground it to shreds with a neat black shoe. "Like I said, Mr. Cauthorne, I'm Italian and Italians put a lot of stock in family. Uncles, aunts, nephews—even second and third cousins. We're close."

"Tightly-knit," I said.

"That's it. Tightly-knit."

"Insurance perhaps? It's only a guess."

10

"Hey, Palmisano, you hear that? Insurance."

"I heard," Palmisano said and almost smiled.

"No, we're not selling insurance, Mr. Cauthorne. We're just doing a favor for a friend of mine."

"And you think I can help?"

"I think so. You see, this friend of mine lives in Washington and he's getting on in years. Not old, but he's getting up there. And just about all the family he's got is this godson."

"It's all he's got," Palmisano said.

"That's right," Callese said. "It's all he's got. Now this friend of mine over the years has built up a fine, legitimate business and naturally he's looking to leave it to somebody close, like a relative, but the only thing he's got like a relative is this godson and the godson can't be found."

Callese stopped talking and stared at me some more with his powder-dry eyes. He had a slice of a mouth that turned abruptly down at the corners, even when he was talking. Two deep creases ran down from his nose to form parentheses around the mouth and a thin, white scar wandered from his right eye, down his cheek, and back to the lobe of his ear.

"Am I supposed to know the godson?" I asked.

Callese smiled; at least I assumed it was a smile. The corners of his mouth turned up instead of down although he kept his lips together as if he felt that his teeth weren't much to look at.

"You know him," Callese said.

"Does he have a name?"

"Angelo Sacchetti."

"What about him?" I said.

"You know him then?"

"I knew him."

"Do you know where he is?"

I put my feet back up on the desk, lit a cigarette, and tossed the match at the butt that Callese had ground out on the floor.

"How much have you dug up on me, Mr. Callese?"

The man in the spats made his shoulders move in an

expressive Italian shrug. "We checked here and there. We learned a little."

"Then you must have learned that I killed Angel Sacchetti two years ago in Singapore harbor."

CHAPTER II

It was no news to either of them. Callese took out his gold case and lit another of his oval cigarettes. Palmisano yawned, scratched himself in the crotch, and turned to resume his inspection of the Cadillac. I glanced at my watch and waited for one of them to say something interesting. After a few moments Callese sighed, blowing out a stream of smoke.

"Two years ago, huh?" he said.

I nodded. "Two years ago."

Callese decided to inspect the ceiling. "How'd it happen?"

"You know how it happened," I said. "If you've done any checking at all, you found that out."

He gave me a wave of his left hand. It was a disdainful, rejecting motion. "Newspaper stuff," he said. "Secondhand information, just like your cars out there. I'm not much on secondhand anything, Mr. Cauthorne."

"Just tell his godfather that he's dead," I said. "Tell him he can leave everything to the Sons of Italy."

"You got something against Italians maybe?" Palmisano said, turning towards me.

"Nothing at all," I said.

"How, Mr. Cauthorne?" Callese said. "How'd it happen?"

"It was a pirate picture," I said and my voice seemed to belong to somebody else. "We were shooting second unit. I was stunt coordinator and Sacchetti

12

was number two. The scene called for a cutlass duel on a Chinese junk. The junk was anchored out in the harbor where there happens to be a tricky current. Sacchetti and I were on the stern of the junk, hacking away at each other. Sacchetti was supposed to jump to the rail, grab a line, and lean out over the water while parrying. He didn't parry when he should have and my cutlass sliced the rope. He fell overboard and never came up. He drowned."

Callese had listened carefully and when I was through, he nodded. "You know Angelo well?"

"I knew him. I'd worked a few pictures with him before. He was a top fencer, but better with the épée and foil than he was with the cutlass or saber. He rode well, I remember."

"Could he swim?" Callese asked.

"He could swim."

"But when the rope was cut, he didn't come up." It wasn't a question the way he said it.

"No," I said. "He didn't."

"Angelo could swim good," Palmisano said. "I taught him." The big man was watching me as I put my feet back on the floor, rose, and started to reach into my inside jacket pocket for my wallet. I never made it. Palmisano was suddenly right next to me. His big right hand clamped on my wrist and jerked it down, over and behind my back where he could easily snap it if that turned out to be a good idea.

"Tell him to get his goddamned hand off me," I told Callese in what turned out to be an almost conversational tone.

"Let him go," Callese snapped.

Palmisano shrugged and released my arm. "He could have been going for it," he said.

I stared at Callese. "When did you let him out of the attic?"

"He's been away for a while," he said. "Now he looks after me. It's his first job in a long time and he wants to make good at it. What were you reaching for, Mr. Cauthorne, your wallet?"

13

"That's right," I said. "It has a card in it."

"What card?"

"A card with a name on it. It's the name of the man who can arrange for you to see the film that was shot when Sacchetti went over. If you want to see how he died, it's all there in living color."

"No," Callese said. "I don't think so." He paused for a moment. "What—uh—what happened to you, Mr. Cauthorne, after Angelo didn't come up?"

"I don't follow you."

"I mean did the cops investigate?"

"Yes. The Singapore police. They ruled it an accident."

"Was anyone else interested?"

"There was a man from the embassy. He asked a few questions, and then, back in the States, there were Sacchetti's creditors. He seemed to have had a lot of them."

Callese nodded his head, apparently satisfied. Then he stared at me again. "What happened to you?"

"I don't seem to be following your questions too well."

Callese let his eyes wander around the showroom and then shrugged. "I mean, no more movie work?"

"I retired," I said.

"Because of what happened to Sacchetti?"

"That might have had something to do with it."

Callese's shoulders moved again in another expressive shrug. "So now you're selling used cars." He made it sound worse than it was, but perhaps not much worse. Certainly no worse than running an abortion mill.

There was a silence for a while. I picked up a paper clip from the desk and straightened it out. Then I began to bend it back into its original shape which is more difficult than it sounds. Both Palmisano and Callese watched me with what seemed to be interest. Then Callese cleared his throat.

"The godfather," he said.

"There is a godfather?"

"He'll want to see you. In Washington."

"Why?"

"So he can pay you twenty-five thousand dollars."

I went on bending the paper clip. "For what?"

"For finding his godson."

"There's nothing left to find."

Callese reached into the inside breast pocket of his jacket, took out a plain white envelope, and tossed it over on the desk. I opened it and took out three photographs. One of them had been taken with an old Polaroid and was beginning to yellow. Another seemed to be a blowup from a 35 mm. camera, and the last was square in shape, possibly the product of a Rolleiflex. The subject in each picture wore dark glasses and sported a new mustache and the hair was longer, but there was no mistaking the profile in the Polaroid shot. It belonged to Angelo Sacchetti who had always been proud of that profile. I put the pictures back in the envelope and handed it to Callese.

"Well?" he said.

"It's Sacchetti," I said.

"He's alive."

"So it seems."

"The godfather would like you to find him."

"Who took the pictures?"

"Different people. The godfather has lots of contacts."

"Then tell him to get the contacts to find his godson."

"That won't do."

"Why not?"

"It's a delicate matter."

"Tell him to use some delicate persons."

Callese sighed and lighted another cigarette. "Look, Mr. Cauthorne. I can tell you just three things. First, Angelo Sacchetti is alive. Second, there's twenty-five thousand in it for you when you find him. And third, the godfather wants to talk to you in Washington."

"Then there's more to the story?" I said.

"There's more. But the godfather's got to tell it to you. Look at it this way, you find Angelo and you clear your name."

"Of what?"

"The accident rap."

"I can live with that."

"Why don't you just talk to the godfather?"

"In Washington," I said.

"That's right. In Washington."

"He'll tell me what it's all about?"

"Everything." Callese rose and stood there as though it were all settled. "You'll go then." There was no question in his tone.

"No," I said.

"Think about it," he said.

"All right. I'll think about it and when I'm through doing that I'll still say no."

"Tomorrow," Callese said. "I'll call you tomorrow. Same time." He started for the office door, paused, and looked around again. "You got a nice little business here, Mr. Cauthorne. I hope it makes a lot of money." He nodded as if satisfied with a good day's work, turned, and walked across the showroom towards the street door. Palmisano started after him, but stopped and spun around quickly to me.

"What's your final price on the Caddy?"

"To you, six grand."

He smiled, apparently considering it a perfectly splendid bargain. "I used to have one just like it except it was green. Real dark green. What do you drive?"

"A Volkswagen," I said, but he was already walking across the showroom for another close look at the Cadillac and I don't think he listened. I don't think he really cared.

CHAPTER III

When the Great Atlantic and Pacific Tea Company finally decided that the dog-eared supermarket it had located near La Brea and Santa Monica was a loser, probably because of urban blight and excessive pilferage, it emptied the shelves of a couple of hundred varieties of breakfast food, loaded up the meat case and the cash registers, and moved out to some distant suburban shopping center where the customers were more honest and where there were twenty acres or so of convenient parking.

The land on which our establishment rested was part of a complicated lease-buy-back package which I never fully understood other than that the real estate man who handled the property was willing to give us a five-year deal dirt cheap if we agreed to a stipulation not to "engage in the retail sale of foodstuffs." We agreed to that and none of the neighbors objected when we opened *Les Voitures Anciennes*. The neighbors consisted of a Cantonese carryout, a car wash, a sheet metal firm, and three bars.

We kept the remodeling of the building to a minimum and it managed to keep its aura of cat food, vienna sausage, and Clorox. We moved the interior wall that divided the store closer to the plate glass windows, built the cubicle of an office around a safe that the A&P thought was too much trouble to remove from its cement cage, and used almost four-fifths of the floor space for the paint, body and mechanical shop. We kept three or four cars in the display area to sell, and to show the odd passerby what we could do

17

in the way of the house specialty, which was the restc ration of any car built prior to 1942.

Despite the firm's rather chi-chi name, supplied by my partner in a rare moment of aberration, our balance sheet was surprisingly profitable almost from the first. My partner was Richard K. E. Trippet who, in 1936, had been a member of England's fencing team at the Berlin Olympics. He had placed third with the foil, losing out to a gentleman from Costa Rica. After having his hand shaken by both Hitler and Goering, Trippet had gone back to Oxford to brood about the state of the world. The next year he joined the Loyalists in Spain, became fascinated with the Anarchists, and now claimed to be chief poohbah (chairman, I suppose) of all the Anarcho-Syndicalists in the eleven western states. Not counting Trippet, I believe there were seven of them. He was also chairman of his Democratic precinct in Beverly Hills and seemed to grow offended when I sometimes accused him of political dualism.

I had met Trippet and his wife Barbara at a Sunday afternoon cocktail party given almost two years before by perhaps the most obnoxious couple in Los Angeles, which takes in a great deal of territory. The couple was Jack and Louise Conklin. Jack was a film editor, one of the best, and Louise was one of those actresses in television commercials who go into a kind of sexual ecstasy over new brands of detergent, furniture polish and floor wax. When they weren't working, the pair of them liked to cruise the supermarkets in their 2 + 2 Jaguar on the lookout for young, grocery-laden matrons who needed a ride home, but who wouldn't mind stopping by for a drink at the Conklins'. Once home, Jack and Louise would both put the make on the young matron, and, according to Jack, they got them into bed, or onto the dining room table, or wherever they did it, seventy-five percent of the time. But then Jack Conklin was a confirmed liar and I cut his estimate by twenty-five percent at least. He was also a loudmouth, a bore, and for all I knew he cheated at cards. The reason I was at his cocktail party that Sunday afternoon was

18

that I had no place else to go which, I am convinced, is the only reason anyone ever goes to a cocktail party.

Conklin must have been born a cuckolder. Once he and his wife had made out with a young matron, she and her husband went on the guest list for the next cocktail party. Conklin liked to talk to the husbands; Louise liked to relive old memories with the wives. That Sunday I was on my third drink when I wandered into a discussion held by my future partner, Richard Trippet, his wife, Barbara, and a rather drunk pediatrician who, I suspected, was one of the husbands that Conklin liked to talk to. The pediatrician, a short man of about fifty with a pink shaved head that did nothing for his small face, was force-feeding the Trippets the details of how he had just bought a 1937 Plymouth coupe for $250 and was planning to spend $2,000 more in New York to have it restored to what he described as "mint condition."

"You know where I found it?" he asked, his left hand wrapped around a highball glass and his right hand slicing the air for emphasis. "I found it in an ad in *The New York Times*. I picked up the phone, called the guy in Delaware, and airmailed him a check all in the same day."

"How interesting," Barbara Trippet said, which was a more polite comment than I could think of.

Trippet, however, seemed fascinated by the pediatrician. He placed a hand on the doctor's shoulder, leaned forward, and in a low, intimate tone confided: "After careful consideration, I have decided that although there were a great many models manufactured in the United States in the 1930's, none could match the 1937 Plymouth for either vulgarity or inadequate workmanship."

The pediatrician considered that carefully, took another gulp of his drink, and came back with: "You think so, huh? Vulgar, huh? Well, just tell me one thing, buddy, what kind of car do you drive?"

"I don't," Trippet said. "I have no car."

A look of what I felt to be true commiseration ap-

peared in the eyes of the pediatrician. "You don't hav
a car—*in Los Angeles?*"

"No car. I usually walk."

"Sometimes we hitchhike though," Barbara Trippet
said.

The pediatrician shook his head sadly and swayed
towards me. "How 'bout you, mister? You got a car,
don't you?" He seemed to be almost pleading. "Your
friend here with the funny accent doesn't have one.
Not even one."

"Motor scooter," I said. "A 1947 Cushman."

By now the doctor was visibly moved. "You ought
to get yourself a car. You know, save up enough for
the down payment. I got a Continental and my wife's
got a Pontiac and my two kids have both got Mus-
tangs, and now I'm going to get that little 1937 Plymouth and I'm going to love that little car more'n all the
rest of them put together. You know why?"

"Why?" Trippet said and I was surprised at the genuine interest in his voice.

"Why? I'll tell you why. Because in 1937 I was
going to college and I was poor. You guys must know
what being poor's like."

"Not really," Trippet said. "I've never been poor."

For some reason, I believed him.

"Well, you're lucky, fella," the doctor said, obviously convinced that a man who didn't have a car in
Los Angeles probably was not only poor, but destitute.
"I was church-mouse poor. I was so poor that I got
kicked out of my room one night because I couldn't
pay the rent. So I was wandering around the campus
and I see this car, this thirty-seven Plymouth, that belonged to this rich kid in one of my classes. Biology
class. So I crawled in and went to sleep. Christ, I had
to sleep someplace. But this rich prick (excuse me
lady) comes out about eleven o'clock to lock his car
and finds me in it. And do you think that son of a
bitch would let me sleep in it for the rest of the night?
Hell no, he wouldn't. Not on your life. He said he was
afraid I'd get it dirty. Well, you know what I promised
myself right then and there?"

"That some day," Barbara Trippet said, "you would earn enough money to buy one exactly like the one your friend had." She smiled sweetly. "The rich prick in biology class."

The doctor looked at Mrs. Trippet with approval. "Right," he said. "That's exactly what I promised myself."

"Why?" Trippet asked.

"Why what?"

"Why did you promise yourself that?"

"For Christ's sake, mister, I just told you."

"But what are you going to do with it? The Plymouth, I mean."

"Do with it? What do you mean, do with it? I'm going to *own* it."

"But you already have four other cars," Trippet said. "What possibly useful purpose will it serve?"

The doctor's pink, shaved head became a shade pinker. "It isn't supposed to be useful, damn it! It just has to be there—sitting out there on my driveway so I can look at it. Christ, I can't talk to you people. I'm going to get another drink."

Trippet watched the doctor weave his way through the crowd. "Fascinating," he murmured to his wife. "Absolutely fascinating." Then, turning to me, he asked: "Do you actually have a motor scooter?"

I didn't have the chance to answer because Jack Conklin, Los Angeles's number one cuckolder, slammed what he thought was a hearty hand against my shoulder blade. "Eddie, boy! Good to see you. Getting any?"

Before I could reply he turned to the Trippets. "I don't think we've had the pleasure. I'm Jack Conklin and I'm the lad who's footing the bill for this little get-together." Conklin really talked like that.

"I'm Richard Trippet and this is my wife, Barbara. We came with some friends, the Ramseys, but I'm afraid we didn't have the opportunity to be introduced. I hope you don't mind gate crashers."

Conklin applied a heavy right hand to Trippet's back and encircled Barbara's waist with his left arm.

She edged away. Conklin didn't seem to notice. "Any friend of Billy and Shirley Ramsey's a friend of mine," he said. "Especially Shirley, eh?" and this time he dug an elbow into Trippet's ribs.

"To be sure," Trippet murmured when he was through wincing.

"If you want to meet anybody, just ask old Eddie Cauthorne here. Old Eddie knows everybody, right Eddie?"

I started to tell him that Old Eddie didn't know everybody and didn't want to know everybody, but Conklin had moved off to use his ever busy hands on other guests.

"I believe," Trippet said, turning to me again, "that we were talking about your motor scooter. Do you actually have one?"

"No," I said. "I drive a Volkswagen, but I have twenty-one other cars. Would you like one?"

"Thank you, no," he said.

"All pre-1932. Prime condition." As I said, I was on my third drink.

"What in the world for?" Trippet said.

"I inherited them."

"What do you do," Barbara Trippet asked, "drive hither and yon?"

"I rent them. To studios, producers, ad agencies."

"That makes sense," Trippet said. "But the gentleman we just spoke to—the one with the 1937 Plymouth. He's afflicted, you know."

"If he is, so are thousands of others."

"Really?"

"Sure," I said. "Take those twenty-one jalopies I have. I keep them in a warehouse way to hell and gone out in East Los Angeles—past 190th. Nobody sees them; they're not advertised; my phone's unlisted. But I get at least one or two calls a day from nuts who want to buy a particular car—or even all of them."

"Why not sell?"

I shrugged. "They produce an income and I can use the money."

Trippet glanced at his watch, a gold affair that was

22

hicker than a silver dollar, but not much thicker. "Tell me, do you like cars?"

"Not particularly," I said.

"How splendid. Why don't you join us for dinner? I think I've just had a perfectly marvelous idea."

Barbara Trippet sighed. "You know," she said to me, "the last time he said that we wound up in Aspen, Colorado, with a ski lodge."

After escaping from the cocktail party, we had dinner that night at one of those places on La Cienega which seem to change owners every few months. Barbara Trippet was a small, bright brunette of about my age, thirty-three, with green eyes and a wry, pleasant smile that she used often. At fifty-five, Richard K. E. Trippet just missed being elegant. Perhaps it was the way he wore his clothes or the manner in which he moved. Or it could have been what at first seemed to be a totally languid carriage until you noticed that actually he held himself fencepost straight and that it was the grace of his movements that gave him that curious air of blended indolence and energy. His hair was long and grey and it kept flopping down into his eyes as we talked over the steaks. He was not in the least reticent about himself, and most of the things he told me that night were true. Maybe all of them. I never found otherwise.

Not only was he an Anarcho-Syndicalist in theory and a registered Democrat in practice, but he was also a naturalized U.S. citizen, a top-grade fencer, a saxophone player of merit, a specialist in medieval French, and had been, at one time or another, a captain in what he described as "a decent regiment," a racing driver-mechanic, a skiing instructor and ski lodge owner (in Aspen), and finally he was still—now—a person of "independent means."

"Grandfather made it all in Malaya, you know," he said, as if everyone else did. "Tin mostly. When he came back to London to retire he couldn't abide the climate and died within a fortnight. My father, who knew absolutely nothing about business and had no intention of learning, simply looked up the most conservative bankers he could find in the City and told them to take care of things. They still do. Barbara's also rich."

"Wheat," she said. "Thousands of acres of Kansas wheat."

"I feel like Tacky Tom at Rich Rollo's party," I said.

"Not to worry," Trippet said. "It's just that when we get to my perfectly marvelous idea, I want you to rest assured that we can handle the necessary financing."

That brought us up to the coffee and brandy, but it still took a while to get to the point.

"That chap at the party with the Plymouth," he said.

"What about him?"

"Pathetic case really. Yet typical."

"How?"

"Most middle-aged Americans, I've noticed, attach an inordinate amount of sentiment to the first car that they owned. They may not remember their children's birthdays, but they can tell you that first car's year, model, color, even date of purchase, and exactly what they paid for it down to a dime."

"Probably," I said.

Trippet took a sip of his brandy. "My point is that there is scarcely an American over thirty whose life hasn't been touched in some meaningful way by a particular make and model of car—even if he only lost his virginity in it despite an awkwardly located gear lever."

"It was a 1950 Ford convertible and the gear shift didn't seem to bother anything," Trippet's wife said. "In Topeka."

Trippet ignored her. "Snobbery, greed and status play an important role, too. I know of a lawyer in Anaheim who is actually hoarding five 1958 Edsels. Hoarding, mind you, waiting for their price to rise. Another chap I heard of retired at thirty-five from whatever he was doing, something profitable, I'd venture, and began to collect Rolls-Royce. Why? Because

24

he liked 'big things,' big houses, big dogs, big cars. Such temperaments are perfect for exploitation."

"Here it comes," his wife warned me.

"I'm braced," I said.

"What I propose," Trippet went on, not in the least perturbed, "is that we establish one of the nation's most useless, unneeded businesses."

"Something like the ski lodge?" his wife said.

"To the young," he continued, "we become vendors of snobbery and status. To the old and middle-aged we cater (or rather *pander,* don't you think?) to their nostalgic yearning for the past. We provide them a tangible link with yesterday, with that time when not only their cars were simpler, but also their world."

"He does talk pretty," I said to Barbara.

"He's just warming up."

"How do you like the proposition?" Trippet asked.

"Interesting, I suppose. But why me?"

"Obviously, Mr. Cauthorne, you don't care a fig about cars—no more than I. You have a most presentable appearance and you also have twenty-one sturdy relics safely garaged in East Los Angeles which we can use for bait."

"Bait for what?"

"For suckers," his wife said.

"For future clients," Trippet said. "My idea is that we establish a garage—no, not a garage. That's too plebeian a word. We establish a clinic. Yes! We establish a clinic that specializes in restoring junkers to their original, pristine condition. Note that I stress the word 'original.' For instance, if a microphone to the chauffeur's speaker were needed for a 1931 Rolls, we would not settle for a microphone that was used in—say—a 1933 Rolls. No, we would scour the country, indeed, the world for exactly the right part. Only the 1931 microphone will do. Guaranteed authenticity will be our motto."

"Unfortunately," I said, "I'm not of independent means."

Trippet waved my objection away. "We'll capitalize

your twenty-one cars. That will do nicely and I'll manage the rest."

"All right," I said. "Now I understand the why me. What about the why you?"

"He wants to get out of the house," his wife said.

Trippet grinned and brushed the hair out of his eyes for the twenty-third time that evening. "Can you think of a better method to study the decay of the system than by establishing a useless business that charges exorbitant fees to foolish persons for services and products that are absolutely unneeded?"

"Not offhand," I said. "But I really don't think you're serious."

"He's serious," his wife said. "It's the only time he gets serious—when he comes up with a nutty one like this."

"Of course I'm serious," Trippet said. "While trafficking in sentiment and snobbery, I strike another blow at the underpinnings of the system and at the same time turn a neat profit. I'm not above that, you know. Must be some trait I inherited from grandfather."

"Let's suppose we're in business," I said. "Who does the work—you know, the kind where you get your hands dirty?"

Trippet looked surprised, then offended. "I do, of course. I'm really quite good with cars although I no longer have a liking for them. Prefer horses, actually. Naturally, we'll pick up a couple of bodies to train and to perform the more menial tasks. By the way, just what is it that you usually do when you do something?"

"I'm an unemployed stunt man."

"Really? How fascinating. Do you fence?"

"Yes."

"Excellent. We should have some jolly times together. But tell me, why unemployed?"

"Because," I said, "I lost my nerve."

In the two years that followed it worked out much as Trippet had predicted that night in the restaurant on

La Cienega. He discovered the A&P building near La Brea and Santa Monica, supervised most of the remodeling, bought the necessary equipment, arranged for the legal papers to be drawn up, and then counseled me to have my own lawyer go over them. When everything was ready Trippet set out to restore a 1930 Packard which was part of my legacy. The car was a straight eight Model 7/34 boat-tailed speedster with a high-ratio rear axle that enabled it to do one hundred miles per hour on the straightaway if its future owner were so inclined. Trippet gave the car fourteen coats of handrubbed lacquer, reupholstered the interior in glove-like leather, supplied it with a new top and white sidewall tires, including those in the fender wells, and then instructed me to sell it for $8,000.

"Not a penny less," he warned.

The first day that the Packard went on display, twenty-three persons came in to look at it. The twenty-third was a seventy-year-old retired cowboy singer who now lived in Palm Springs. He walked around the Packard twice and then came back to my office.

"Does it run?" he asked.

"Perfectly," I said.

"How much you asking?"

"Eight thousand."

He grew a canny expression. "Give you seven. Cash deal."

I lifted an eyebrow and smiled what I hoped was a chilly smile. "I'm sorry, sir, but we do not haggle."

The ex-cowboy singer nodded at that and went back out to look at the Packard some more. Five minutes later he was back in the office writing out a check for $8,000.

I thought about some of this, but not all, after the man in the spats had left, trailed by his outsized companion. If they were a problem, so was the rain that splashed against the plate glass windows. Then the rain finally stopped and I picked up the phone and dialed a number. A voice answered on the third ring and I made an appointment for later that evening. I had

27

some questions about the man in the spats and the man I was to see that evening might have the answers And then again, he might not.

CHAPTER IV

The rain had started again, a thick, grey downpour that slowed homeward-bound traffic on Wilshire Boulevard to a fitful crawl and made drivers champ their jaws in unison as they cursed the idiot ahead. There was an opening in the curb lane and I slipped into it, turning right some two or three blocks past Doheny. Behind me a horn blasted out of pique or jealousy or both. A few blocks and a turn or two later I parked next to a fire hydrant, deciding that if a cop left a dry patrol car to write out a ticket in that rain, I no doubt deserved it.

The apartment house that I parked in front of was a fairly new two-story garden-type structure, built in a U around a swimming pool, and coated with pale yellow stucco that the rain had wetted down so that it looked like tapioca. I sat in the Volkswagen for a while, smoked a cigarette and watched the windows grow steamy. At six-thirty I draped a raincoat around my shoulders and made a dash for the shelter of the building. There were some pale pink roses growing near the outside staircase that led to the second floor, but the rain had knocked most of their petals to the ground. I was only slightly wet when I went up the stairs, turned right, and rang the bell of Christopher Small. There was a light scraping sound as someone inspected me through the security peephole. Then the door opened wide.

"Come on in, Eddie. How are you, wet?"

"Not too bad. How're you, Marcie?"

"Fine."

Marcie Holloway was a tall black-haired girl with blue eyes, a wide mouth with an attractive overbite, and a nose that could have been just a little snub and perhaps a trifle shiny if you worried about such things. She carried a drink in one hand and a cigarette in the other. Her narrow plaid slacks seemed to be part of a suit and she comfortably filled the white blouse that topped them. She had been living with Christopher Small for almost three years which, in that town, may have been some sort of a record.

I made another inane comment about the weather, she asked if I would like a drink, and I said that I would.

"Chris'll be out in a minute. Scotch and soda okay?"

"Make it water."

Marcie disappeared through a door with my raincoat and I sat down on a green divan and studied some of the photographs that almost covered the opposite wall. There seemed to be more of them than I remembered. They ran from the ceiling to near the floor, were framed by thin, black molding, and shielded by glareproof glass. They portrayed Christopher Small and friends and he seemed to have a lot of them. The room also had a built-in bookcase that held six books, some crockery, and a collection of china cats and kittens. There was a color television set in one corner, a stereo unit in another, and twin speakers were strategically placed at ceiling height in opposite corners. The rest of the furniture looked as if it came with the apartment.

Those who have eyes good enough to read the "and featuring" credits on the late show might recognize Christopher Small's name. He had earned a comfortable living in Hollywood for more than thirty years by playing minor roles in films that called for a cab driver, a reporter, a tough sergeant, a bartender, a number two cop, or—most often of all—a number three or four gangster, the one who gets queasy about the entire setup and takes off in the getaway car before the rest of the gang has had a chance to clean out the tellers' cages.

By his own rough estimate, Small had appeared in more than five hundred feature films and television productions, but he is probably best remembered for a picture that earned him a brief vogue during World War II. The film had the members of a New York mob deciding, for God knows what reason, that the Germans posed an even greater threat than the cops. The mob enlisted *en masse*, went overseas, and apparently won the war—only to gulp back their tears at the film's end as they crowded about their mortally wounded chief while he took his own sweet time to die in Small's arms, muttering something unlikely about brotherhood, democracy, and peace.

Small's brief moment of fame occurred in an earlier scene in the film which required him to burst into a farmhouse, his Thompson submachine gun at the ready, and capture what appeared to be the entire German high command with the line: "Freeze the mitts, Fritz!" A radio comedian picked it up and for a while it became a popular saying around high schools and colleges. In the mid-sixties some Merry Andrews at an Eastern university decided to hold a Christopher Small Festival, but nothing ever came of it other than a press release.

Small came through the door that led to a bedroom, shook hands with me, and asked how business was. I told him that it was fine.

"Marcie getting you a drink?" he asked and lowered himself into a green overstuffed chair that matched the divan.

"Yes."

He turned his head and yelled back at the kitchen: "Make it two, Marcie."

There was an answering yell which I assumed to be one of assent. Marcie and Small yelled at each other a lot.

"Doing anything?" he asked and I knew that he was talking about the stunt business.

"Nothing," I said.

"And you're not pushing either."

"No, I'm not pushing."

"You could get something if you pushed," he said.

"There's not much demand."

"The hell there isn't."

"Let's just say that I like what I'm doing."

Marcie came in from the kitchen carrying the drinks on a hammered aluminum tray. She served them and then curled up on the other end of the sofa, one foot tucked under her rear in what has always seemed to me a most uncomfortable position.

"You getting the usual lecture, Eddie?" she asked.

"Chris still seems to think that I'm neglecting a promising career."

Small stretched out his legs and crossed his ankles. He wore tan, wide-wale corduroy slacks, a yellow short-sleeved shirt, and brown loafers. He had let his hair go grey and his stomach pushed a little at the front of the knit shirt, but his face was still the same: lean and long with a pointed chin, hollow cheeks, a strong thin nose, and deepset dark eyes that he could make crafty or frightened or cruel, depending upon what was called for by the script.

"Well," he said, "you have to admit that you invested a hell of a lot of time to get where you were. Now it's just going to waste. Your old man would be goddamned sore."

"He's dead," I said.

"He's sore wherever he is. I remember when you were just a brat—no more than five or six. He used to tell me then how someday you were going to be top stunt man."

"Sure," I said, "and for my tenth birthday I got fencing lessons. Just what I always wanted."

My father had been a stunt pilot, one of the first of that strange breed who descended on Hollywood in the twenties, willing to attempt anything that the writers could dream up for ten dollars and a place to sleep. He never got over the fact that he had flown with Frank Clarke in 1927 when the dogfight for *Hell's Angels* was filmed over San Francisco Bay. It was still the highlight in his life when, heading for yet another flying assignment at age sixty-one, he crashed into the tail end of a seven-car freeway pileup, went through the windshield, and bled to death before they got him to the hospital. He left me the twenty-one pre-1932 cars, a house full of furniture, and some odd memories. But as Small said, my father had always wanted me to be top stunt man. He taught me to drive at twelve, fly at fourteen, and by the time I entered UCLA I was an accomplished rider, fencer, gymnast, boxer, member of both the Stuntman's Association and the Screen Actors Guild, and working regularly.

"I can put in a word for you at a couple of places," Small said.

"No thanks. It just wouldn't work out."

"You ought to try once more anyhow," he said. "It's such a damned waste—all those years you spent at UCLA in their film school."

"Just three years," I said. "I was a dropout."

"You ought to try anyhow," Small said again.

"Maybe he likes what he's doing," Marcie said. "Maybe he just doesn't want to go around falling off horses anymore."

"I'll think about it at any rate," I said in an attempt to mollify Small and end the lecture.

"Let me know if I can help," he said.

"Well, actually you can."

"Just name it, kid."

"I need some information."

"About what?" he asked.

"Not what, who. A couple of guys."

"Okay, who?"

"Salvatore Callese and somebody called Palmisano," I said.

Small made his face go blank. There was absolutely no expression on it—no surprise, no warmth, no anything. He looked at Marcie. "Go see about something," he said.

"What?"

"Christ, I don't know what. Anything. Go cook something."

32

Marcie rose quickly and started towards the kitchen. Then she paused, and turned to Small. "How about some fudge?" she said nastily.

"I mean for dinner, for God's sake!"

"Fudge for dinner," she yelled, and disappeared into the kitchen and started to slam some pots around.

His name really wasn't Christopher Small. It was Fiore Smaldore and he had been born in East Harlem on 108th Street and by the time he was fourteen he was running numbers after school. His older brother, Vincent Smaldore, had risen quickly in the gangland hierarchy and seemed destined for a brilliant career until one October morning in 1931 when somebody dumped his body out at the corner of 106th Street and Lexington Avenue, a casualty of the bitter feud between Joe (the Boss) Masseria and Salvatore Maranzano. The older brother of Fiore Smaldore (soon to become Christopher Small) had insisted that the youngest member of the family finish high school, but the seven bullets in the body of Vincent convinced the younger brother that safety lay elsewhere. Los Angeles was as far as he could get before his money ran out on Christmas Day, 1931. He drifted into motion pictures, first as an extra and then as a bit player when they discovered that he had a voice that recorded well. It satisfied him, and his friends and enemies back in New York, inveterate movie-goers all, liked to punch each other in the ribs whenever they saw him on the screen. They also thought that it was nice to know a motion picture actor who could show them around Hollywood even if he weren't a real star. There wasn't much Small could do about it, and over the years he had served as tour leader for a large number of those who made their very good livings on the darker side of the law in such cities as New York, Cleveland, Chicago, Detroit, and Kansas City.

"It wasn't so bad in the forties and the fifties," Small once told me. "We'd go to places like Ciro's and the Derby and Romanoff's and we'd get our pictures like you see over there on the wall took. But now you know where they got to go? Disneyland, that's where.

33

Christ, I must have been to Disneyland fifty times." The pictures, I once noted, were all signed and bore such salutations as "To Chris, a swell guy, from his pal, Nick," or "Thanks for a swell time, your buddy, Vito."

Small was now leaning towards me, his elbows on his knees, a look of apparently genuine concern on his face. "What do Callese and Palmisano want?" he said.

"You know them?" I said.

"I know them. What do they want with you?"

"They want me to see a man in Washington."

"What man?"

"The godfather of Angelo Sacchetti. They say that Angelo isn't dead and that his godfather wants me to find him."

"Where?"

"Christ, I don't know where."

"Why you?"

"I don't know that either."

Small rose and walked over to the bookshelves and picked up one of the china kittens. "Marcie collects these things, you know," he said.

"I know. I gave her a couple."

"Salvatore Callese," Small said to the kitten. "Or The Yellow Spats Kid as they used to call him a long time ago in Newark."

"He still wears them," I said.

"What?"

"Spats. Only they're pearl grey now."

"He'll always wear them. You want to know why?"

"Okay. Why?"

"Because his feet are cold. You want to know why his feet are cold, even on a warm day in Los Angeles?" Small turned from the collection of cats and kittens, leaned over the back of the green overstuffed chair, and stared at me with eyes that seemed almost haunted.

"Okay," I said again. "Why are his feet cold even on a warm day in Los Angeles?"

"Because about thirty-seven years ago when he was just a punk the 116th Street boys caught him screwing

34

one of the guy's sisters. So you know what they did? They had a party. They got a washtub full of ice and dumped some rock salt in it to make it good and cold and then they put the beer in and they also took off Callese's shoes and socks and put his feet in the tub so that they'd cool off. They kept them in there for about three hours until all the beer was drunk up and then they took him back to Newark and dumped him. He damned near lost both feet and they've been cold ever since and that's why he wears spats and that's why they used to call him The Yellow Spats Kid."

"What happened then?"

Small walked around the chair and sat on one of its arms. "He waited. He waited until he could walk again and then he started. One by one he picked them off. Some got run over, some got cut up, and some got shot. He was thorough. That's one thing you can say for Callese, he's thorough. He did such a good job that they finally moved him over to Manhattan, downtown, and then when Siegel got it, they sent him out here to help look after things. He's been doing it ever since."

"What about Palmisano?"

"Him." Small sniffed as if he smelled something bad. "Giuseppe Palmisano, alias Joe Dominoes. He's fresh out of Atlanta where he did a straight six for conspiracy to violate the narcotics laws. No parole, no time off for good behavior. An ordinary soldier and not too bright. You want to know why he's sometimes called Joe Dominoes?"

"Why?"

"You notice how his left arm sticks out funny—like he can't straighten it out?"

"I noticed," I said.

"Well, they caught him one night, four of them, and they busted his arm in four places. Each one got to bust it once. Then they cut his throat and left him to bleed to death, only he didn't, but they nicked his vocal cords or something and that's why he talks so high and that's why he wears turtleneck sweaters—he was wearing one, wasn't he?"

"I thought he was just trying to be stylish."

Small shook his head. "No, he's always worn them, ever since they cut his throat."

I took another swallow of my drink and waited. Small was staring at the floor now, his own drink held in both hands. I doubt that he still knew I was in the room.

"All right," I said. "Why do they call him Joe Dominoes?"

Small snapped back from wherever he had been with a slight start. "Why? Well, all this happened about the time that Wallace Beery had just made *Viva Villa!* You ever see it?"

"I've seen it."

"You remember the scene where Beery decides to save ammunition and he lines—what was it—three or four prisoners up in a row? Then he uses one bullet to pass through the bodies of the three or four prisoners he wants executed. Well, Palmisano, after he got well, saw this flick and he decided that it seemed like a good idea. So the story goes that he caught up with all four of them at once, lined them up in a row, and used one 30.06 slug from an old army rifle he had to kill all four of them and they just fell over like dominoes. That's what they say anyhow and that's why they call him Joe Dominoes."

"You know some nice people," I said.

"You know why I know them."

"Yes, you told me. What about the godfather of Sacchetti? Do you know him?"

Small was silent for several moments, staring at the carpet again. Then he said, "I think I'll have another drink. You want one?"

"No thanks."

He rose and disappeared into the kitchen, returning a few minutes later with a drink that was darker in color than the one he had had before. He took a long swallow of it and then lit a cigarette.

"The godfather," I said.

"In Washington."

"That's right, in Washington."

"You remember that I once told you about my

brother and how he wanted me to finish high school and all."

"I remember."

"I didn't tell you why though, did I?"

"No."

Small sighed. "Well, believe it or not I was taking a college preparatory course. You know, so I could get into college. Can you imagine that—in East Harlem?" He laughed, but there wasn't any humor in it, just a certain amount of bitterness. "There were only two of us taking that course, me and the other guy who's the godfather of Angelo Sacchetti."

"You've lost me," I said.

"A long time ago, about seven or eight years before you were born, they had a meeting in Atlantic City."

"They?"

He gave me a disgusted look. "You want a name for it?"

"Does it have one?"

"Why don't you ask J. Edgar Hoover?"

"I don't have to. He calls it the Cosa Nostra."

"*La* Cosa Nostra is what he calls it."

"Is that its name?"

"No," Small said, "but it's always good for a few laughs. So let's get back to the meeting."

"In Atlantic City."

"That's right. They were all there, Costello, Luciano, Vito Genovese, even Capone and his brothers. Anybody who was anybody. They got together at this meeting and decided that they needed to reorganize their operations. They were going to lay out territories, cut out the wars, and improve their image, although nobody was using that word then you understand. They just wanted to get more respectable and one of the ways they decided to go about it was to send some of the younger, brighter punks to college. So they went around the room to find out if there were any candidates. My brother was there and he put in my name and promised them that he'd break my neck if I dropped out of high school. Costello said he knew a young kid who he'd do the same thing to, so out of

37

that entire crowd they could only come up with two they could send to college, me and this kid that Costello nominated."

Small paused and took another long swallow of his drink. "Well, the other kid made it. You know what happened to me—I already told you that. But they got a tutor for the other kid and he not only finished high school, but they got him into Harvard and they put him through in style. I mean he didn't lack for anything. Then when he got through Harvard, they sent him down to the University of Virginia's law school. I hear he breezed through that."

"And this is the man in Washington who wants to see me?" I said.

"He's the one."

"How did he get to be Sacchetti's godfather?"

"Because Angelo Sacchetti was Sonny from Chicago's kid and Sonny from Chicago once saved this guy's life."

"You lost me again."

Small sighed, this time more deeply than before. "I shouldn't be telling you all this. It's just going to get you in trouble."

"From what you've said, I'm already in trouble."

He thought about that for a moment and then seemed to come to a decision. Or perhaps he was just acting it all out; I could never tell.

"All right," he said finally. "This Sonny from Chicago, nobody ever found out his real name, showed up in New York one day with a one-year-old kid on one arm and a violin case in the other." He paused and looked at me skeptically. "You think I'm kidding about the violin case, don't you?"

"You're telling it," I said.

"Then keep your looks to yourself."

"Go on."

"Well, it seems that this Sonny's wife was an ex-hooker who had got into some trouble with one of the Chicago outfits and they dumped her into Lake Michigan. I don't know what kind of trouble it was. So this Sonny takes his violin case and takes out seven of the

38

guys who he thought were responsible for it and he brings his kid and his Thompson down to New York. Well, by this time the kid I went to high school with is through with law school and he's back in New York and running a few errands for Costello. He meets this Sonny from Chicago who's also gone to work for Costello and they start palling around together. You know why?"

"I couldn't even guess," I said.

"Because this Sonny from Chicago looks nice, you know, neat—just like a college kid. He speaks well, dresses conservatively, and this kid I went to high school with has turned into something of a snob because of his education. You follow me?"

"So far."

"Well, the guy who's gone to college gets into trouble—not with Costello, but with somebody else, it doesn't matter who. But it's bad trouble, very bad, and Sonny from Chicago and this kid get caught in a fight down in the Village. Somehow Sonny saves the kid's life and the kid promises that he'll make it up to him."

Small gave me another of his long pauses. "Well?" I said.

"Well, they catch Sonny from Chicago trying to cheat in a crap game two weeks later and they just nail him to the wall and leave him there. The college kid hears about it, so he takes this one-year-old baby of Sonny from Chicago's to raise. He becomes his godfather."

"And the baby was Angelo Sacchetti."

"That's right."

"Why the name Sacchetti?"

"I don't know, but somebody once told me that he got it off a box of noodles."

"What happened to the college kid—the godfather?"

"They sent him to Washington."

"Why?"

"Why does anybody send anybody to Washington? As their lobbyist."

"I'd say he forgot to register."

"Don't kid yourself."

"What does he do?"

Small managed a pained expression. He did it very well, I thought. "Let's just say he looks after their interests."

"And this guy reared Angelo Sacchetti?"

"He tried to anyhow. Maybe you don't know it but Angelo had about nine governesses and maybe as many tutors. He was kicked out of four prep schools and three colleges. The only thing he ever liked was sports and that's how he wound up out here."

"His godfather put the word in?"

"Right," Small said.

"Does the godfather have a name?"

"It used to be Carlos Colanero. Now it's Charles Cole, and in certain circles it's even Charlie the Fix."

"You seem to know a lot," I said.

Small gestured at the framed pictures on the wall behind him. "With a few drinks in them they sometimes talk a lot—to one of their own kind."

"Why does Cole want me to find Angelo?"

"I don't know," Small said. "Angelo hung around sometimes, but not much. Then he was dead for a couple of years and nobody seemed to go into mourning. Now you say he's alive."

"And they want me to find him."

"Not they. Charles Cole does, and when you meet him you'll have gone about as high as you can go."

"You think I'll meet him then?" I said.

There was still another pause. Finally Small said, "Cole does and Cole usually gets his way."

"Any advice?"

"Sure. Change your name and disappear. This isn't just a search for the missing heir. It's some kind of big mess or they wouldn't send Callese out on an errand-boy's job and he wouldn't go on one. Somehow, they've got you all wrapped up in it."

I thought about that for a moment while Small watched me intently. "I think I'll say no," I said.

"They don't understand what it means."

"There isn't much they can do."

"There's just one thing," Small said.

"What?"

"They can make you wish you'd said yes."

CHAPTER V

Someone had done a thorough job. All four tires on both the Jaguar and the Ford were slashed, the canvas tops were in shreds, and two empty gallon cans of Karo syrup stood on the floor at the rear of the two cars near their open gasoline tanks. The Cadillac was untouched.

Trippet was walking around the Ford when I arrived the next morning, his hands thrust deep into his trouser pockets as he gave instructions to Sydney Durant, one of our long-haired young employees who looked as if he were about to cry. I could tell that Trippet was upset, too; otherwise he would never have had his hands in his pockets.

"We had some night visitors," he said.

"So I see. How bad?"

"The tires and the tops obviously, but those can easily be replaced. I was hoping that we could drain the tanks, but they jumped the ignition on both cars and let them idle until the syrup had the opportunity to do its work. Syrup is worse than sugar, you know."

"I didn't," I said.

"Bastards," Sydney said.

"Take a look inside," Trippet said.

"The upholstery?"

"Quite."

I looked. A razor or a sharp knife had been used to slash the soft leather that covered the seats of both cars. Someone had taken his time. After neat vertical cuts had been made every two inches or so, they were followed by similarly spaced horizontal slits. It was as fine a job of professional vandalism as one could hope to see.

"What about the office?" I said.

"Nothing touched, nor was the Cadillac."

"No, they wouldn't touch the Cadillac."

Trippet looked at me quizzically and then turned to Sydney. "Be a good chap and go fetch Jack and Ramón and push these into the back."

Sydney shoved a long blond hank of hair from his eyes, glowered out at the street as if he expected to find the vandals with their noses pressed against the plate-glass windows, and then muttered something about what he was going to do when he caught up with the sons of bitches.

"We'll help," I told him. "But let's get these two off the floor first. They're not very good advertising."

Sydney headed for the back shop and Trippet said: "You don't seem too surprised."

"I think someone wanted to give me a message. Everything considered, they were more polite than I could expect."

"Who?"

"I don't know who did it," I said, "but I probably know who ordered it done."

"Friends of yours?"

"Newly found acquaintances. Let's get a cup of coffee and I'll tell you about it."

We walked around the corner to a short-order cafe that afforded fairly good coffee and after the waitress had served us in a booth I told Trippet about Callese and Palmisano and who they were and what they wanted me to do.

"What they did to the Ford and the Jag was just a friendly nudge," I said. "If I keep on saying no, they might blow up the place or burn it down or something equally unpleasant."

"And if you still said no?"

"They could get more personal—maybe a broken arm or leg."

42

"You wouldn't be of much use to them then."

"I wasn't talking about my arm or leg, I was talking about yours."

"Can't say I fancy that."

"No, I didn't think you would."

"I suppose we should ring up the police."

"I suppose so," I said.

Trippet poured a small container of cream or milk into his coffee and then reached for the one that belonged to me and poured that in, too. He added three teaspoons of sugar and then stirred it all up together.

"What would they do, take fingerprints?" he asked.

"I don't know," I said. "Probably ask around the neighborhood to see whether anyone noticed something unusual about three o'clock in the morning—such as somebody hacking away at the tires with a sharp knife."

"Sounds rather useless," Trippet said. "But we'll have to call them so that the insurance people will be happy."

"That's true." I sipped the coffee and it seemed better than usual. "I'll probably be getting a visit or a call about three o'clock this afternoon from Callese. He'll be wanting to know what I've decided."

"What will you tell him?"

"No. Or do you have some other suggestion?"

Trippet leaned against the back of the booth and inspected his coffee spoon carefully. "I'm not unduly upset about the wanton destruction of our private property, Edward. That's the risk that any entrepreneur takes who ventures into the commercial jungle." He put the spoon down and looked at me steadily. "I don't like it, of course, but I'm not outraged—as Sydney is. However, I will not be coerced."

"Then you agree that I should say no?"

"Absolutely no."

"Okay. When we go back to the office we'll call the police and the insurance company."

"I'll take care of it," he said.

"There's one other thing you might do."

"What?"

"Check to see whether our fire insurance premiums are paid up."

The call came from Callese at 3:05 P.M. I remember writing the time down because I thought it might be important. I also took notes on the conversation. I needn't have bothered; Callese didn't have anything to say that I couldn't remember.

"You can pick up your ticket at the United desk at the airport, Mr. Cauthorne," he said by way of greeting. "The flight leaves at ten-fifteen tomorrow morning, first class, of course. There'll also be an envelope with further instructions and some expense money."

"I won't be needing it."

There was a brief pause, and then something that sounded like a sigh. Or perhaps it was just Callese exhaling smoke from one of his oval cigarettes. "My job is to get you to Washington to see a man," he said. "You can say no in Washington."

"I'll say it here."

"I must not be too good at persuasion."

"You're fine," I said. "I found your message this morning. Very neat work."

There was a pause and then he said, "I suppose now I'll have to think up something that will persuade you."

"Don't bother," I said and hung up.

I pushed a button under the desk that rang a klaxon horn in the shop. Trippet came in, dressed in his white siren suit with *Les Voitures Anciennes* stitched across its back in green Old English letters. Our crew of three wore similar ones. I think they even wore them on their dates.

"He called," I said.

"And?"

"He said he was going to think up something that will persuade me."

"Any notion of what it may be?"

"None."

Trippet produced a box of *Senior Service* and

44

offered me one. He always offered them and I always refused. He was extremely polite.

"I seriously doubt that he'll try anything here tonight," he said.

"Why?"

"The police. They said they'd keep an eye on us for the next few days."

"They say anything else?"

"They wanted to know who did it—you know, perhaps a disgruntled customer. I, of course, told them that we had no disgruntled customers."

When the police came I had been out to lunch with a prospective client, a man who owned a string of drive-ins that featured twenty-cent hamburgers. He was anxious for us to restore a 1933 Stutz DV-32 Bearcat that he had found in somebody's garage in San Francisco. We passed one of his drive-ins on the way to lunch and I had a moment of apprehension when he slowed down, but it was only to check the volume of business. We ate at Scandia's on Sunset and while we were waiting to be served he showed me some snapshots of the car. I looked at them, nodded politely, and handed them back.

"Can you do it?" he asked.

"Probably," I said. "But we'll have to see the car."

"I'm having it trucked down next week."

"If you like, we'll look at it then."

He nodded happily at that. "How long will it take?"

His name was Fred Cooper and he called his hamburgers Cooperburgers. I had yet to try one, but quite a few million other persons had, enough so that he could eat at Scandia's and play around with old cars.

"That particular model had a straight eight engine with thirty-two valves," I said. "It also had one of the best hydraulic brake systems ever built, plus automatic lubrication, and it retailed for about $5,000 in a year when very few people had that kind of money. The company went broke or folded in 1935. Parts are scarce. Very scarce."

"What if it needs parts that you can't find?"

"Then we have them made to the original specifications—and that can get expensive."

Cooper nodded again, not so happily this time, and drank the last of his martini. "How much? I mean for everything."

"I wouldn't even guess. As I told you over the phone, we charge by the hour for actual work performed. Our rates are high, but we guarantee authenticity. We had one car—a 1934 Hispano-Suiza that we kept for eighteen months. The final bill was almost twelve thousand dollars, but it was in sorry shape when we got it."

Cooper flinched at that, but not too much, and then nodded quickly. He seemed to like to nod a lot. "They say you guys do the best work on the coast. Maybe after you look at the car you can give me an estimate."

"We'll be able to give you a minimum price. The maximum will depend upon a number of things."

"It was a hell of a car," Cooper said.

"Not many people remember it," I said. "They get it confused with the Stutz Bearcats of the twenties."

"I remember it all right," Cooper said and signaled for another drink. "My old man used to drive one. I got to ride in it sometimes."

"Your father had good taste."

"My old man was a chauffeur for $17.50 a week in 1933," Cooper said in a low, flat voice. "The only time I got to ride in it was when he drove it down to get gas or something. He took care of six cars. And then he got fired."

There was more to the story, but I didn't encourage it. I didn't have to.

"Six months ago I read in the papers that the last of this family had died."

"The one with the six cars in 1933," I said.

"Right. So I took a wild-assed chance and called my lawyer in San Francisco and told him to find out if this guy who died still had the Stutz. He was that kind of a nut, or recluse as the papers called him. My lawyer checked into it and found that the car was still sitting

46

in the garage. I told him to buy it. Well, it's taken them this long to settle the estate, but I got it."

"It must mean a lot to you," I said.

"You're right, Mr. Cauthorne, it does," he said and gazed over my left shoulder at some distant spot where for all I knew he kept a private vision of his slightly more than two tons of nostalgia.

After I told Trippet about Callese's call he returned to the back of the shop and I spent the rest of the afternoon in the office cubicle. I used the dictaphone for half an hour to answer some correspondence; successfully tried out my sales resistance on a man who wanted us to adopt a simplified bookkeeping system that I didn't quite understand; talked to three sixteen-year-olds about the Cadillac; reminisced with a seventy-two-year-old pensioner about some cars he had once owned, and spent a half hour with a prosperous plumber in mapping out a campaign to convince his wife that the Cadillac would be a sound investment. I also answered the phone six times.

At five o'clock I pushed the button under the desk twice to inform Trippet and our three employees that it was time to quit. I waited for Trippet to get rid of his siren suit, wash up, and wander out front to join me in our usual drink at one of the neighborhood bars.

"The wife and I are dining out tonight," he said as we settled into a booth in one of the taverns. "Afterwards I thought I might drop by to see whether we're still in business."

"If we're not, give me a ring."

"I'll do that."

Over the drinks we talked about the hamburger king and his Stutz and then I asked Trippet if he would like a ride home.

"No thanks," he said, "I think I'll walk."

It was a little over four and a half miles to his Beverly Hills home and every night I asked him if he would like a ride, and every night he said he thought he would walk. Sometimes his route carried him a mile or so out of his way through the Farmers Market, but he walked it religiously, a solitary stroller in a town that rolled on wheels.

After leaving Trippet I drove up to Hollywood Boulevard, turned left and followed it to Laurel Canyon. I lived in my father's house on a dead-end street off Laurel about halfway up to Mulholland Drive. It had been built on the side of a hill just before World War II and it still boasted something of a view. I lived there because it was paid for, the taxes were cheaper than rent, and because it was too much trouble to move. I parked the Volkswagen, checked the mail, and let myself in. The house somehow seemed emptier than usual and I ran down a mental list of young ladies who wouldn't mind sharing a steak and a bottle of wine. I tried a couple of numbers and when I got no answer I said to hell with it and went into the kitchen where I took a small T-bone steak from the refrigerator and put it on the drainboard to age for an hour or so. Next I turned on the oven, smeared some butter on a large Idaho potato, wrapped it in a sheet of foil, and put it in to bake. By the time the potato was done, the steak would be somewhere near room temperature. It took another three or four minutes to make a salad of lettuce, tomato, spring onions, oil, vinegar and garlic. On days that the salad proved too much trouble I settled for cottage cheese. Highly nourishing, I understand.

I opened the refrigerator again, took out a bottle of Mexican beer, and brought it into the living room where I turned on the television set to watch the continuing story of Vietnam. It was another grim episode. Company at dinner that night was the first half hour of a ninety-minute western with pretensions of serious overtones. Four persons were killed in the first thirty minutes, not counting some Indians and the odd Mexican. I took critical note of a fight in the barroom and thought it might have been a bit more effective if the hero's fist just once had come closer to the villain's jaw than six inches.

After the dishes were safely in the dishwasher and the garbage was tamped down the disposal I sat in a chair by the window that offered the view and stared out at the lights of Los Angeles. It came back then as it had done every evening for nearly two years. Once again I was on the stern of the Chinese junk in Singapore harbor and Angelo Sacchetti hung out over the water with a line in his left hand and a cutlass in his right. I made the thrust we had rehearsed, but Sacchetti didn't parry and I could still feel my cutlass slicing through the rope as if it were a piece of string. And then Sacchetti fell again and I just glimpsed his upturned face and the left eye that closed in a grotesque, knowing wink.

The hallucination, or whatever it was, came along every night around dusk and it was accompanied by a severe case of the shakes and a cold sweat that drenched my clothing. It never happened while I was driving or walking; only when I was someplace where nothing would happen except, often enough, acute embarrassment. It usually lasted for forty-five seconds to a minute.

This was about the seven-hundredth time that I had gone through it. The first time happened after I came back to the States and went out on a stunt job. I froze at the crucial moment and then there was the vision of Angelo Sacchetti, falling and falling in slow motion, and winking that big, broad, almost lecherous wink. I tried two more stunt jobs, but the same thing happened, and after that I didn't try any more, but it didn't really matter because the word about my freezing got around and the phone quit ringing and my agent was in conference the four times that I called him. I didn't call him any more after that and he didn't seem to mind.

I had seen the film of the accident some forty times. I had gone over it frame by frame, just like the Zapruder film, but it hadn't helped any, nor did the nine months that I spent going to an analyst. Sacchetti still fell and winked every night.

I had tried to get rid of it through the analysis and Dr. Melvin Fisher seemed mildly interested in what he called my repetitive hallucinations. "They're a little rare," he said, "but not extremely so. They disappear

49

when the patient no longer needs them as an adaptive tool for getting well."

"You mean it's no worse than a bad cold?" I said.

"Well, not exactly. A person who hallucinates as you do has regressed to the most primitive mode of perception. Freud said somewhere that hallucination is the result of the cathexis passing over entirely from the memory system to the perception system. That's what you're doing. When you decide to get over it, you will."

"I'm ready now," I said.

The doctor looked at me with his sad dark eyes and smiled. "Are you really?"

"I'm ready," I said again.

He shook his head slightly. "Come back and see me when you are."

I never went back and the hallucination continued. It grew no better or worse and that night when I was through shaking and sweating I poured a brandy and opened a novel about a thirty-eight-year-old advertising executive in Des Moines who suddenly decided to leave his wife and three children and find the real him in Mexico. In Cuernavaca, I think. By midnight he was still looking and I no longer cared. It had been another evening of taut adventure in the glamorous life of a Hollywood used-car dealer and I was ready for sleep.

The clock by the side of my bed said it was three in the morning when the phone rang. It was Trippet and his tone was more clipped than usual, a sure sign that he wasn't happy.

"Sorry to awaken you, but I'm at Mount Sinai."

"Are you hurt?" I asked.

"No. It's Sydney, I'm afraid. The doctor is with him now."

"What happened?"

"Your friends. Your friends did something to him. To his hands."

"What?"

"They slammed a car door on them."

"Jesus."

"They slammed it twice."

"I'll be right there. How is he?"

"If they're lucky," Trippet said, "they'll save them both."

CHAPTER VI

Sydney Durant was barely twenty years old when a car full of UCLA students found him wandering down the middle of Sunset Boulevard at two-thirty in the morning, his mangled hands held out before him, almost chest high, the palms turned inward. The students thought he was either drunk or high until they saw the hands. Then they put him gently into their car and rushed him to Mount Sinai hospital. The only thing that Sydney said to the students was: "They had to do it twice. The bastards had to do it twice." At the hospital he told them his name and also managed to mention Trippet's. Then he collapsed.

Trippet told me all this as we waited for someone to come out of the operating room and tell us about Sydney and whether he would have one hand or two or none.

"I was able to reach Doctor Knofer," Trippet told me.

"Good," I said.

"He's a specialist in this sort of thing, you know."

" 'Messy cases,' he called them."

"He knows Sydney," Trippet said. "When we were doing that old Aston Martin for him he used to drop by at odd times and just watch Sydney work. He came to know him rather well."

"What's he predict?"

"He doesn't. The bones aren't just broken, some of

them are crushed, and there's also extensive nerve damage. Then there are the veins to worry about. He didn't sound optimistic."

Nobody was waiting for Sydney Durant to come home; there was no one that we should call. He had wandered in off the street eighteen months before, looking for a job, and equipped only with the totally unsupported claim that he was, in his own profane estimate, "the best goddamned body man in town, especially aluminum." He offered no references or information about his past other than that he came from "back east" which, in our town, could have meant Syracuse or Salt Lake City. Because Trippet prided himself on being an extraordinary judge of character, Sydney was hired on the spot.

He proved to be as good as he said he was, perhaps even better, and when the business expanded it was Sydney who recommended Ramón Suarez as "the best goddamned cloth man in town." Ramón, who at nineteen spoke a vague brand of English, turned out to be superb with canvas and leather. Our third employee, Jack Daugherty, a Negro who was older than the other two by a couple of years, was another Sydney Durant find. All that Sydney had said to Trippet about Daugherty was: "He knows engines—almost as good as you." He did.

Dr. Benjamin Knofer looked exhausted when he finally came into the waiting room at five-thirty that morning and slumped into a chair. He bummed a cigarette from Trippet, puffed on it moodily, and then held his hands out in front of him. He stared at them for long moments.

"Goddamn, you're good, Knofer," he said softly. "You're really good."

In his late thirties, the doctor was a rake of a man with extraordinarily small bones and a face that wore a look of what seemed to be perpetual exasperation. He also found it difficult to communicate without cursing.

"It was a bitch," he said to us finally, and ground out his cigarette on the floor. "A real bitch. I saved the kid's hands, but he won't even be able to blow his nose

52

or wipe his ass by himself for a long time to come. What was it, a gang fight?"

"We don't know really," Trippet said. "All we know is that he said that someone slammed a car door on his hands. Twice."

"Somebody sure had a hard-on for him," Doctor Knofer said. "Have you talked to the police?"

"Not yet," I said.

"The hospital's been in touch. They'll probably be around to see you tomorrow." He yawned and looked at his watch. "Jesus, it's five-thirty and I've got another one at ten. Who gets the goddamned bill?"

"We do," I said.

"For everything?"

"Yes," I said.

"I'll fix it with that broad in admittance," he said. "She was getting ants up her fanny about who was going to pay." He held out his hands before him and stared at them again. "A real bitch," he said, "but goddamn, Knofer, you're good."

"When can we see him?" Trippet asked.

"Tomorrow," the doctor said. "Around two. Cheer him up, will you? Tell him his hands will be okay. He's a goddamned good kid."

When the doctor had gone, I turned to Trippet. "I've decided to see the man in Washington."

He nodded, as if he hadn't expected me to say anything else. "Your new friends are most persuasive."

"It's not that," I said. "It's not that at all. Angelo Sacchetti has been on my back for two years. You know all about it. You've seen me freeze a couple of times. Now they say he's alive. I think I've got to find him unless I want to carry him around with me for the rest of my life."

Trippet was silent for almost a full minute. "I think," he said slowly, "that it's out of our hands now. I think it's time to let the police handle it."

"All right."

"You agree?" Trippet asked. He sounded surprised.

"Why not?" I said. "I don't want to go to Washing-

53

ton, not now, not even in cherry blossom time. But the police have nothing to do with my going. If they can find the goons who smashed Sydney's hands, I'm all for it. But I already know who's ultimately responsible, and he's in Washington, and there's no way in God's world that they can ever pin it on him. But I have something that Charles Cole wants, or thinks he wants, and he also has something that I want and that something's Angelo Sacchetti. And perhaps eventually they'll all pay for Sydney's hands."

"Which, if not victory, is yet revenge," Trippet murmured.

"Yours?"

He shook his head. "Milton's."

"Then you're both wrong," I said. "It's not revenge I'm after. They just owe me something. They owe me for Sydney—that's first—and they also owe me for two years of the sweats and the shakes. I'd like to collect."

"How?" he asked.

"I don't know. I won't know until I see Cole in Washington and maybe I won't even know then."

Trippet chewed on his lower lip for a while and then said: "They must want you most desperately."

"Enough to do what they did to Sydney. If I say no once more, they won't hesitate to repeat the performance. I don't like hospitals. I don't want to have to come around asking how the cast feels and when are they going to take it off and whether you'll be able to walk again without a cane."

A nurse entered the waiting room, gave us a curious glance, and disappeared through another door, moving with that no-nonsense stride that most nurses seem to have. Trippet stirred on his chair, as if to relieve a cramped muscle.

"Do you really think you can take on this man Cole in Washington—and all the brethren—by yourself? I don't mean to be rude, Edward, but the fact that you dealt in violence for a number of years doesn't exactly qualify you—" He let the sentence fade away and even seemed a bit embarrassed that he'd made it. As I've said, he was polite.

54

"What do you think I have in mind? A showdown in the lobby of the Washington Hilton?"

"I'm afraid of something like that, but then I'm an incurable romantic."

"I didn't deal in violence," I said. "I dealt in action, or at least that's what they liked to call it. It was spurious violence—faked—no more real than the death scenes. This country has a taste for violence, both real and faked, but I think it's having a hard time separating the two. You can switch on a news program and watch a South Vietnamese police chief put a pistol to a VC's head and pull the trigger. Thirty minutes later you can watch a western marshal gun down the visiting bully. Which is more real to the viewer? The police chief or the marshal? I'll put my money on the marshal."

"But your new friends are real," Trippet said.

"Very real."

"And you think I might be their next target if you refused again—or would it be Ramón or Jack?"

"There's somebody else," I said.

"Who?"

"Your wife."

For the first time since I had known him, Trippet almost lost his poise. He ran a hand nervously through his long, grey hair. "Yes," he said, "I suppose they are capable of that. I hadn't thought of it." He paused for a moment, then rose, turned to me, and made a small, almost apologetic gesture. "I say, would it be terribly inconvenient for you to give me a lift home?"

CHAPTER VII

There was a reception committee for me that late afternoon or early evening when I landed at Dulles International Airport and rode the doodlebug contraption from the plane to the lobby of the soaring terminal building that somehow seems a little lonely sitting out there all by itself on the edge of the Virginia hunt country. It was a committee of one who introduced himself as John Ruffo and nobody could fault him on his manners. He insisted on collecting my bag and carrying it out to the longest, blackest six-door Cadillac that I've ever seen except for one that's owned by a certain Los Angeles funeral parlor. At the car the bag was almost snatched from Ruffo by a uniformed chauffeur who opened one of the two rear doors for us, saw to it that we were tucked safely inside, and then stowed the bag away in what must have been a cavern of a trunk.

"Mr. Cole is delighted that you could come," Ruffo said. "Did you have a pleasant flight?"

"I'd already seen the picture," I said, "but the Scotch was excellent."

"Yes," Ruffo said, drawling the word as if my remark had been particularly profound. "We've taken the liberty of booking you into the Sheraton-Carlton. It's not the Century Plaza, but it's quite comfortable, I assure you."

"I like older hotels," I said. "Their employees are usually older, too, and that makes for better service."

The envelope had been waiting for me at the United desk at Los Angeles International, just as Salvatore Callese had promised it would be. It contained a

56

round-trip, first-class ticket to Washington, ten one-hun-
dred-dollar bills, fairly new, and a typed, unsigned
note which read:

"Mr. Charles Cole's car will meet you at Dulles International Airport."

The car that met me was now gliding down a four-
lane highway that seemed almost deserted and my escort, the well-mannered Mr. Ruffo, explained that it
was a direct access route to the airport which no other
traffic was allowed to use. "Unfortunately," he added,
as if he really cared, "Dulles didn't draw all the air
traffic that its planners thought it would, but it has
been picking up lately, I understand."

"That's most interesting," I said, determined to
match Ruffo's politeness. "When do I get together with
Mr. Cole? That's Mr. Charles Cole, isn't it?"

"Yes," he said again, as if still convinced that I was
the wise man from the West. "Mr. Cole thought it
might be nice if you could join him at his home for
dinner this evening."

"That might be nice," I said, "but it might be even
nicer if I knew what the agenda was going to be."

Ruffo laughed in what I suppose was meant to be a
well-bred, yet deprecatory way. "I'm afraid that is
something that Mr. Cole will have to discuss with
you."

"You just run the pickup and delivery service."

"Something like that, Mr. Cauthorne," Ruffo said
and laughed another laugh that matched his J. Press
suit and his Eastern seaboard accent. "I suppose you
could say that I do something like that."

Thirty-five minutes after we left Dulles Airport the
chauffeur steered the oversized Cadillac into the semi-
circular driveway before the Sheraton-Carlton at 16th
and K Streets and the doorman hopped to it when he
saw the car. "Good evening, Mr. Ruffo," he said as he
opened the door and I noticed that Ruffo didn't tip
him. The doorman probably got one of those fairly
new hundred-dollar bills every Christmas just to remind him to say, "Good evening, Mr. Ruffo" a half-
dozen or so times a year.

The chauffeur transferred the bag to the doorman who transferred it to a bellhop who seemed to think it was a privilege. Ruffo, slightly preceding me, demanded the key to my room from an alert clerk who handed it to the bellhop with the admonition to see to Mr. Cauthorne's comforts.

Then Ruffo turned to give me the benefit of an exceedingly white, exceedingly deferential smile. "I thought I'd give you an hour or so to get settled and relax," he said. "I'll call for you around—" He looked at his watch. "Say around seven-thirty. Will that be satisfactory?"

"Perfectly."

"I had some Scotch and soda sent up to your rooms," he said. "If there's anything else you need, just ring for it."

"That was very thoughtful of you," I said.

"Not at all. Just part of the pickup and delivery service." He smiled again, that nice white smile, but he neglected to put any grin into it and I noticed that the olive skin, the neatly trimmed black hair, the dimpled chin, and the six feet or so of what appeared to be supple muscle failed for the first time to disguise the contempt that his dark brown eyes flicked over me for only a second. In the polite Mr. Ruffo's social book I was nothing. Perhaps a little less than nothing.

The bellhop followed me into the elevator with my bag where another septuagenarian fiddled with the controls and we wheezed up to the sixth floor.

"Six-nineteen," the bellhop said. He was a kindly looking little man who probably was fond of his grandchildren. "This way, sir." I followed him down the corridor and he unlocked the door and ushered me into a two-room suite.

"John L. Lewis always liked this suite," the bellhop said as he put the suitcase on a rack and pulled back the curtains. "He liked it because of the view." Obediently I walked over to the window and looked out. By craning a bit I could see Lafayette Park and beyond that the White House.

"He probably wanted to keep a check on what was

58

going on," I said and handed him a dollar. The bellhop liked that and said so. After he left, I inspected the bathroom whose fixtures were newer than the hotel and then unlatched my bag and hung a suit in the closet. When you've done all that there's not much else to do in a hotel room except have a drink or call somebody. Convinced that nobody in the White House cared whether I was in town or not, I decided to have a drink and went in search of the Scotch that Mr. Ruffo had promised.

It was in the sitting or living room which contained some club chairs, a couple of divans, a writing desk and a coffee table which held a bucket of ice, six glasses in case I had company, a bottle of soda and a fifth of Chivas Regal which proved to me that Mr. Ruffo was indeed thoughtful even if he didn't like my manners.

I put three cubes in a glass, poured in some Scotch, and then journeyed to the bathroom to fill it up with water. On the way back to the sitting room I started to sweat and I managed to get the glass back down on the coffee table before the shakes came. It lasted for no longer or shorter a time than usual. Angelo Sacchetti fell in slow motion again, still clutching his cutlass, and his face turned up to me and he winked again, that grotesque Sacchetti wink that screwed up the entire left side of his face. Then it was over and I downed the drink and took some small comfort in the knowledge that I wouldn't see Sacchetti's face again for at least twenty-four hours. After the drink I showered, decided to hell with shaving, and did Mr. Charles Cole the honor of brushing my teeth and putting on a fresh shirt. I was halfway through my second drink when the telephone rang and the ever-polite Mr. Ruffo said that he would await me in the lobby.

The ride to Mr. Charles Cole's residence on Foxhall Road took about twenty minutes and along the way Mr. Ruffo pointed out some of the Washington sights that he thought might prove of interest. They didn't really, but he seemed to think it was part of his job and for all I knew it may well have been.

Foxhall Road in northwest Washington is where the rich live. They live other places, too, I understand. In Georgetown and Virginia and Maryland. A Vice-President once lived in an $89,000 cooperative apartment in southwest Washington because it was convenient and he sometimes liked to walk to work. He moved into the apartment after the President decided that a separate mansion for a Vice-President would cost the country too much money. The Vice-President wasn't rich and I doubt that he could have afforded Foxhall Road. I know he couldn't have afforded the house that belonged to Charles Cole.

It looked as if it were located on at least ten acres of wooded ground, but then I'm city oriented and an acre remains a dimly defined area. But in Los Angeles the grounds would have composed a good-sized city block. There was a bluegrass lawn that grew right up to the trunks of the pines, the oaks, and the maples and I knew just enough about horticulture to realize that all that required a full-time crew of skilled gardeners. There were a few magnolias and some dogwood. They lined the crushed oyster-shell drive that wound leisurely up to what at first glance looked like Tara. There were eight white columns that went three stories high to support a Federal arch. Each side of the main house boasted a two-story wing that seemed large enough to house the full staff of the Portuguese Embassy. The windows were flanked with white wooden shutters that apparently really worked and the entire structure was built of soft, red used brick which was supposed to make it look old and almost succeeded. There was no garage that I could see and I assumed that it was discreetly out of sight in back along with the swimming pool and the servants' quarters.

The Cadillac crunched up the drive and stopped in front of the entrance to the house which was dominated by a huge wrought-iron lantern that hung on a thick metal chain. The chauffeur was out and had the door open on my side of the car almost before it came to a full stop. I climbed out and paused when I noticed that Ruffo made no move.

"Aren't you invited?" I said.

"This is as far as I go, Mr. Cauthorne," he said and let me have another look at his winning smile. "As you say, I just run the pickup and delivery service."

I didn't have to ring the bell at the wide double doors that served as the entrance to the white-columned mansion. One of them opened as soon as I mounted the thirteen steps and started to cross the bricked veranda. And if I expected a silver-haired, Negro butler in a white coat, I was in for a disappointment. The man who opened the door was young, tanned, and dressed in a black suit, white shirt and black tie. He looked at me carefully, taking his time, and when he was through he said: "Mr. Cauthorne."

"Yes."

He nodded and stepped back, opening both of the double doors wide as he did so. "Mr. Cole is expecting you in the library." In back of me I could hear the Cadillac move off, bearing the polite Mr. Ruffo to wherever he went that time of evening.

I followed the young man in the black suit into a formal entrance hall that was paved with large squares of black and white marble. There was an immense crystal chandelier about halfway down the hall and its lights played upon some pieces of cherrywood and walnut furniture that looked old and well cared for and terribly expensive. To the right of the chandelier was a gracefully curving staircase that floated up to the second floor, but we didn't get that far. Instead, the young man stopped at a paneled sliding door, knocked once, and then pressed a button that caused the door to move silently into its recess in the wall. The young man entered first and I followed. Then he stopped, stepped to one side, and in a flat voice, without inflection, said: "Mr. Cole, Mr. Cauthorne is here."

It was a big room, oblong in shape, and it smelled of leather and the burning apple wood that flamed and crackled in the fieldstone fireplace which, at first glance, looked large enough to roast a medium-sized ox. A man rose from one of the dark leather chairs that were placed on either side of the fireplace, dropped a newspaper to the floor, and moved towards me, his right hand outstretched. I stood where I was and it took him a while to walk the thirty or so feet from the fireplace across the thick, dark brown carpet to where I waited.

"Mr. Cauthorne," he called, "I'm delighted you could come."

"Everybody is delighted but me," I said and took the proffered hand and shook it politely. There didn't seem to be anything else to do.

Charles Cole turned to the young man in the black suit. "We'll dine in here, I think, Joe." Not Jonathan, or James, or even Malcolm. Just Joe. "But first," Cole added, "I suggest that we have a drink."

"Yes, Mr. Cole," Joe said. He turned and disappeared through the sliding paneled door which closed behind him. For the first time, I noticed that the door had no handles.

"There's a bit of a chill in the air for so late in the spring," Cole said as he took my arm and steered me towards the fireplace. "I thought a fire would be pleasant."

He indicated that I should take one of the leather chairs and he lowered himself into the other one. Then he rested his elbows on the arms of the chair, formed a steeple of his fingers, and looked at me pleasantly enough, almost as if he were the friendly family counselor who had helped many a young man out of similar difficulty. Charles Cole, I noticed as I returned his friendly gaze, was not a tall man, but neither was he short. He had an oval face and wore his hair long at the sides, perhaps to compensate for his ears which stuck out a trifle, and perhaps to compensate also for the top of his head whose pink skin glistened in the light from the fire and from the two reading lamps that stood by each of the leather chairs. His eyebrows were grey as was his hair, but the carefully trimmed military mustache that he wore beneath a straight thin nose was pure white. The mouth, now forming a slight smile, gave way to a firm chin which was just threatening to grow another one beneath it. His eyes were brown and

62

large, or perhaps magnified by the thick black-framed glasses that he wore, and they either twinkled or sparkled behind the lenses. I was never sure.

"They say," I said, just to be saying something, "that they call you Charlie the Fix."

He laughed at that as if it were genuinely funny. "Do they indeed?" he said. "And who, may I ask, is they—my old friend Christopher Small? I thought he might mention me in passing."

"He said you went to school together—a long time ago."

"That's right, we did," Cole said. "And it was a long time ago. I've made it a point to see most of his films. Some of them were quite ghastly, but he's done fairly well for himself."

I glanced around the room. There were some more chairs and a couple of comfortable-looking sofas, all leather. Books lined two of the walls and from where I sat it looked as if someone might have read them all at one time or another. There was a pair of refectory tables, nicely carved, and at the far end of the library, placed so that it would catch the light from the French windows, was a large partners' desk that would have dominated any lesser room. In Cole's library it fitted perfectly.

"Both of you seem to have done fairly well," I said.

"Expensive trappings are sometimes useful to impress the impressionable," Cole said. "I would be disappointed in you, Mr. Cauthorne, if you were overly impressed."

"Then why the treatment?"

One of his eyebrows cocked itself into a questioning arc. "Treatment?"

"Sure," I said. "The block-long Cadillac, the Ivy League messenger boy, the suite in the old, but quite comfortable hotel, the bodyguard at the front door, and dinner in the library in front of the crackling fire. I'd call it the treatment."

Cole chuckled. "How could you tell that Joe was a bodyguard? You're right about Ruffo, of course. Yale law school is something that one can scarcely disguise, but I thought Joe's camouflage rather good."

"You forget one thing," I said. "As a one-time stuntman I studied movement. I'd say that Joe would be very handy to have around in a neighborhood brawl, providing this neighborhood ever has a brawl."

Cole chuckled again. "And you're observant, too. I like that, Mr. Cauthorne, I really do."

The sliding door disappeared silently into the wall again and Joe wheeled in a well-stocked bar. He pushed it over to near where we sat and looked at Cole expectantly. "The usual, Mr. Cole?" he asked.

"The usual is a very dry martini which Joe does quite well, Mr. Cauthorne. Would you care to join me?"

"A martini would be fine."

"Any particular kind of gin, Mr. Cauthorne?" Joe asked.

"Any kind," I said.

"On the rocks or straight up?"

"It doesn't matter."

Joe nodded and quickly mixed the drinks with the deft, economical movements of an experienced bartender. He served me first and then handed Cole his drink. "Dinner in twenty minutes, Joe," Cole said.

"Yes, Mr. Cole," Joe said and trundled the movable bar across the thick carpet and through the sliding door which again closed silently behind him.

"Well, Mr. Cauthorne," Cole said, "shall we drink to something?"

"How about to crime?"

Cole chuckled again. I decided that it was a fairly pleasant sound. "Very well, sir, to crime."

We drank and I lit a cigarette and then waited for Cole to get to the point, providing that there was one. I didn't have to wait long.

"You know, Mr. Cauthorne, I debated with myself for almost six weeks about whether to invite you to Washington."

"If your other guests receive invitations like the one I got, you must be rather lonely."

Cole frowned and shook his head. "Yes, I heard about that—your young employees and the vandalism. I've already taken measures to compensate you for everything. It was most unfortunate."

"It would have been even more unfortunate if the kid had lost a hand. How much is a hand worth in your book?"

Cole brushed his mustache with the knuckles of his left hand and then sighed. "The old methods are slow in dying, especially among the older generation. But progress is being made, I assure you, and once again I must apologize for the totally unnecessary methods of persuasion that were employed."

"I don't know if they're as outdated as you claim," I said. "They got me here."

Cole took another sip of his drink. "Did they really, Mr. Cauthorne? Was it the violence, and the threat of further violence, that convinced you to come, or was it the news that Angelo Sacchetti is still alive?"

"I wondered when you would get around to him," I said. "I was betting on after dinner—over the brandy."

"I've had considerable research done on you, Mr. Cauthorne." He made a vague gesture towards the draped windows. "Over there, in my desk, is a rather thick file—or dossier, if you prefer. It's all about you. I've been given to understand that you suffer from a mild psychological disturbance which stems from the time that Angelo disappeared in Singapore."

"A lot of people know that," I said.

"True. But also in that file—or dossier—are copies of the notes made by the analyst that you consulted for —I believe it was nine months. A Dr. Fisher."

"Fisher didn't give them to you."

"No," Cole said, smiling slightly. "He didn't. He doesn't even know that I have them. As I said, they are copies."

"Then you do know a lot about me."

"More, perhaps, than you know about yourself."

"I see."

"I must say, Mr. Cauthorne, you are taking all this extremely well."

"You want something from me, Mr. Cole. I'm just waiting to find out what it is so I can say no."

"Well, now, let's not get ahead of ourselves. Let's just go a step at a time. From your analyst's notes, I gather that you suffer from mild, periodic seizures during which you experience trembling, excessive perspiration, and a recurring hallucinatory experience which has Angelo falling into the sea and winking at you as he falls. That's not exactly Dr. Fisher's description, but rather more of a layman's translation of his notes."

"As lay translations go," I said, "it's not bad."

"Dr. Fisher's notes imply that you blame yourself for Angelo's alleged death and that this created a certain amount of deep-seated guilt which triggered the recurring hallucinatory experiences (again, I must say I'm paraphrasing the good doctor). I've taken the liberty, Mr. Cauthorne, to have two other qualified medical persons go over Dr. Fisher's notes. Your name, of course, was carefully obliterated. It's their opinion that if you personally were to find Angelo Sacchetti alive, your psychological discomforts would disappear. Otherwise, they may grow worse."

I finished my drink and put the glass on a table. "So the deal is that in exchange for finding Angelo for you, I cure myself. That's the surface deal, but there's more to it than that, isn't there?"

"A great deal more," Cole said.

"Why don't you use your own people to find Angelo?"

"I don't think that would do."

"Why not?"

"Because my dear godson is blackmailing me."

"Some of the boys could take care of that, couldn't they?"

Cole put his glass down, made a steeple of his fingers again, and stared up at the ceiling. "I'm afraid not, Mr. Cauthorne. You see, if the persons I would ordinarily call on in such a situation were to find out what Angelo is blackmailing me with, I'm afraid that I would remain alive—at the most—for only twenty-four hours."

66

CHAPTER VIII

Before Cole could continue, the sliding door opened again and Joe, the bodyguard, wheeled in the dinner which he served on a small table with the same efficient movements that he had used to mix the drinks. I decided that he must be handy to have around. Dinner was a thick filet, a superb salad, and a baked potato. A bottle of burgundy was equally excellent.

"It's what you usually have at home, isn't it, Mr. Cauthorne?" Cole said after Joe had gone.

"Your chef is better than mine."

"Well, let's enjoy our dinner and then we can continue our discussion afterwards—over the brandy, as you suggested earlier."

"It was growing interesting," I said.

"It will get even more so," Cole said and started to carve up his steak.

We ate almost in silence and when we were through Joe promptly appeared and cleared away the dishes and served the brandy and coffee. When he had gone once more, Cole offered me a cigar which I refused, carefully lighted one for himself, took a sip of his brandy, and said, "Now, where were we?"

"Angelo Sacchetti was blackmailing you."

"Yes."

"I assume that you've been paying."

"I have indeed, Mr. Cauthorne. In the past eighteen months I have paid only slightly less than a million dollars."

I smiled for what must have been the first time that evening. "Then you're in real trouble."

"You seem inordinately pleased."

"Wouldn't you be in my position?"

"Yes, as a matter of fact, I suppose I would. My enemy's troubles are my good fortune and all that sort of thing. You do consider me your enemy?"

"Let's just say I doubt that we'll ever be close friends."

Cole drew on his cigar and then slowly blew the smoke out. I noticed that he inhaled it. "You've heard," he said, "that they call me Charlie the Fix. Do you have any idea of what the nickname implies?"

"Some," I said. "The corruption of public officials and civil servants probably. A few bribes here and there. A little subornation of perjury, I suppose, plus the discreet use of a sizable political slush fund."

Cole smiled slightly. "I see," he said. He paused for a moment, as if deciding about how much he could safely tell. "I came to Washington in 1936—the year you were born, I believe. And despite my rather excellent education, I was, as they say, grass green. I needed a mentor, someone to guide me through the bureaucratic and political maze. I told them that I needed this and they quickly found just the man."

"You've been using 'they' and 'them,'" I said. "I've asked who they are before, but I've never got a satisfactory answer. Who are 'they,' the outfit, the organization, the mob, the Mafia, the Cosa Nostra? Is there a name for them and they?"

Cole smiled again, even more slightly than before. "It's a peculiarly American trait, I suppose, this insistence upon a descriptive noun. It was poor old Joe Valachi who called it the Cosa Nostra because the Government was pressing him to give them a title. So one Narcotics Bureau Agent said 'cosa' and Valachi came back with 'nostra,' and they ran with it from there. Of course, if two persons of Italian descent were speaking about a mutual project, they might say, *'Questa è una cosa nostra,'* but they would really be saying, 'This is an affair of ours.' They certainly wouldn't be saying 'I am a member of "our thing" or "our affair." ' "

68

"What about the Mafia?" I said. "Or is that old hat?"

"It implies a Sicilian organization, and although there are certain ties with it in Sicily—Luciano during World War II, for example—there is no Mafia as such in the United States."

"What is there then?"

"A group of totally amoral businessmen of Italian and Sicilian descent who control the vast majority of organized illegal activities that go on in this nation. They don't call themselves anything."

"And they are the ones you turned to in 1936 when you needed your mentor or guide?"

Cole tapped his cigar ash into a tray. "Yes. They were the ones who sent me through college and law school. When I told them that I needed a guide, they promptly secured me a full partnership in a most respectable Washington law firm, the same one in which I'm now senior partner, Harrington, Mecklin, and Cole."

"Mecklin I've heard of," I said.

"He almost became a Supreme Court judge."

"What happened?"

"Harrington had died by the time I came along in 1936. Mecklin, unfortunately for him, was a compulsive gambler. Everything. Horses, poker and bridge, but especially poker. So one evening at a most respectable club here in Washington my sponsors, shall we call them, slipped a mechanic into the game and he took Mr. Mecklin for around fifty thousand dollars that night. Another game was arranged later in the same week, and Mecklin dropped seventy-five thousand dollars. The mechanic, who was also a consummate confidence man, as most of them are, agreed to yet another game to give Mecklin a chance to win. This time he dropped ninety thousand dollars and, of course, he couldn't pay. The confidence man grew impatient, threatened exposure, and my sponsors hurriedly came to the rescue with a loan which enabled Mecklin to pay off the debt in full. However, my sponsors grew just as impatient for full repayment and when Mecklin was unable to meet their, shall we say, rather importunate demands, they suggested that the firm take me in as a full partner."

"Then it cost them around $215,000 to get you a partnership," I said.

Cole chuckled his pleasant sound. "Not at all. It cost them only a thousand or so for the con man's services. The money that they lent Mecklin to pay off his debts was promptly returned to them by the con man."

"Then what happened?"

"Word got around, as it always does, and Roosevelt changed his mind about Mecklin. The man grew absolutely bitter. He began to take an almost perverse delight in plunging into legal tangles whose outcome could only embarrass the administration. More often than not, he was successful, and he took me along with him. He taught me the art of accommodation and compromise and believe me, Mr. Cauthorne, they are most valuable skills."

"I don't quite follow you," I said.

"Every so often, a crusader dons his sword and buckler and journeys forth against the infidel who goes by the name of organized crime. In the early 1950's, it was the good Senator Kefauver. Then Senator McClelland tilted his lance against the same foe in the 1960's and later in the decade along came the Task Force on Organized Crime, appointed by the President."

"I remember," I said. "I also remember that nothing much happened."

"After the rather tawdry findings of each of these investigations were released, there was a brief public outcry, a kind of 'My, isn't that awful and why don't they do something about it' type of outcry, if you will."

"But not much else," I said.

"Very little, and for very good reason, too. You see the law enforcement agencies, state and local as well as federal, are perfectly aware of what's going on and who's profiting from it. They have, over the years, worked out a degree of accommodation with those responsible, a tacit understanding concerning territories and scope of operation. In exchange for the discipline which my sponsors, as I've referred to them, are capable of exercising, the law enforcement authorities are content to compromise on some minor but essential points—so long as they know where the ultimate responsibility lies. One of my principal tasks is to maintain this *détente*."

"And a few hundred thousand dollars can work miracles," I said.

"A few million, you should say."

"And you have it to offer?" I asked.

"Yes, I have it to offer, but not quite in the way or to the persons whom you might suspect. Suppose I wanted to influence a Senator in behalf of a client so that the Senator would influence someone else. There would never be a direct approach. It would come instead from the Senator's bank or a chief political supporter or even from another Senator whose own bank might be exerting similar pressure on him. It's all quite indirect."

"But eventually somebody, somewhere gets bribed."

"For every corruptor there must be a corruptee and in the thirty-three years that I've spent in Washington I have seen money accepted greedily by some most respectable persons up to and including those of cabinet rank."

"You do a nice lecture on morality," I said, "but none of it explains how Angelo Sacchetti is blackmailing you, does it? And why tell me all the secrets? I'm no confession booth."

Cole was silent for a moment. He closed his eyes briefly as if again debating with himself about how much more he could safely say. "I'm telling you the details, Mr. Cauthorne, because it is one way, perhaps the only way, that you will be impressed with the importance and gravity of what I'm going to ask you to do. I promise to be as brief as possible, but when I'm through I think you'll realize the utter seriousness of the present situation. Only my complete frankness can convince you of that."

"All right," I said. "I'll listen."

"Good," he said and paused again as if trying to remember the thread of his tale. "My former partner, the late Mr. Mecklin, realized quickly what had happened to him. He was not a fool, but his bitterness towards the administration caused him to plunge into the affairs of my sponsors in an almost gleeful manner. He became obsessed with their potential ability to exercise power, and power was all that really ever interested Mecklin other than gambling. So he advised them to diversify."

"And they did?"

"Not at first. They were reluctant to take advice from one whom they considered to be an outsider. After Mecklin died I advised them to do the same thing, and they did. They went into the stock market, into banking, into manufacturing, and a number of other legitimate enterprises."

Cole paused. I waited for him to continue. When he did, his voice was low and thoughtful, almost as if he were speaking to himself.

"During our years together, Mecklin grew quite fond of me and he once said, quite early in our association, in fact, 'Protect your flanks, son. Records. Keep records of everything. Tangible evidence, Charlie, will be your only protection when they finally turn on you and, by God, they will.' "

"You followed his advice, I take it."

"Yes, Mr. Cauthorne, I did. I have been counselor or, if you prefer the more romantic title, *consigliere,* to my sponsors for nearly thirty years. It has not always been a harmonious relationship, of course. There were some who opposed me."

"What happened to them?"

Cole smiled and when he did, I could almost feel sorry for whomever he was thinking of. "Several of them were deported when the authorities suddenly discovered that they were not really born in the United States as they had claimed. Others were arrested, convicted, and sentenced to rather lengthy prison terms on the basis of new evidence that mysteriously came into

72

the hands of the appropriate law enforcement agencies."

"The evidence was carefully documented, of course."

"Most carefully. It was always sufficient to provide an airtight case."

"It's nice to know that sometimes you cooperate with our national guardians," I said.

"They have learned to live with me—and I with them. Actually, we both seek the same ultimate goal —a rational structure for illegal activities."

"And this is where Angelo Sacchetti comes into the picture?"

"Indeed he does, Mr. Cauthorne. You may not know that Angelo and I were never close despite my being his godfather, which has an unusually deep significance among my sponsors. I tried to educate him, but that failed miserably. He was expelled from three colleges and whenever that happened, he turned up in New York where my sponsors promptly spoiled him with too much money and too many women. They thought he was wonderful while I couldn't abide him —even when he was a child. I was more than happy when he decided to enter the motion picture industry. He wanted to be an actor. God knows he had the looks, but unfortunately he couldn't act."

"So I've heard," I said. "I've also heard that he was a complete ham. That's probably the real reason he winked when he went over; he couldn't bear to keep the act to himself."

"You are quite probably right," Cole said. "At any rate after he moved to Los Angeles he sometimes flew into Washington, usually to borrow money which, for foolish, sentimental reasons, I quite readily lent him. At least I did until a little over two years ago."

"Why did you stop?"

Cole shrugged. "I didn't really. I merely asked him when he intended to repay the sums that he had already borrowed. He went into a total rage and stormed out of the room. This very room, in fact."

"Then what?"

"He left that same night, quite suddenly, but not empty-handed."

"He took something of yours with him?"

"Yes."

"Something you'd like back?"

"Yes again."

"What?" I said.

"There is a safe in this room—or there was. Angelo simply opened it, probably in search of cash. He found something better. Microfilmed records. As I've said, I keep meticulous records."

"How did he open the safe, with a nail file?"

Cole sighed and shook his head. "Angelo is not stupid. When he wanted to learn, he could, and my sponsors and their associates in New York were willing teachers when he visited them. He learned a great many things from them and one of the things that he learned was how to open a safe. I had suddenly been called out of town; the servants were asleep, and Angelo simply blew it open."

I rose and walked over to the cut-glass brandy bottle and poured myself another drink without asking. Then I moved over to the fireplace and watched the apple logs burn for a while. After a time, I turned to Cole who was watching me carefully.

"I can understand most of it," I said. "Angelo found out that you were providing evidence on a more or less regular basis to the police or the FBI or God knows who. If your associates or sponsors or whatever you call them found out about it, you'd live another day, possibly two. So Angelo blackmails you out of nearly a million dollars which you paid and probably didn't miss too much. But what I don't understand is why Angelo pretended to die, nor do I understand why you've suddenly decided that I can do something to get you off the hook."

"I'm afraid it's a little complicated, Mr. Cauthorne."

"Most things involving a million dollars are."

"Yes, they are, aren't they? But let's take you first. What I want you to do is fairly simple. I want you to find Angelo Sacchetti, retrieve the missing records, and

74

return them to me. For this I am willing to pay you fifty thousand dollars."

"In Los Angeles, it was only twenty-five thousand dollars."

"The matter has become more urgent since then."

"Urgent enough to double the price?"

"Yes. Plus expenses, of course."

"All right, let's say I accept."

"I hope that you will."

"I haven't yet, but let's say that I do. Where do I find Angelo?"

"In Singapore."

I stared at Cole. "You mean he was always in Singapore?"

Cole shook his head. "No, after he disappeared and pretended to be dead, he went to Cebu City in the Philippines. From there I understand that he went to Hong Kong and then established his present operation some eighteen months ago in Singapore."

"What operation?"

Cole sighed and stared into the fire. "With the help of my reluctant financing and with the knowledge of tactics and procedure that he learned from my sponsors in New York, Angelo Sacchetti now runs a rather smooth operation in Singapore."

"What kind?"

"Name it. He's introduced numbers; he is most prominent in the loansharking business, and he has branched out lately into business insurance, or so I understand."

"You mean the protection racket."

"If you prefer."

"You understand from whom?"

Cole rose and joined me at the fireplace. He gazed into it while I warmed my back. "In my dealings with the government, Mr. Cauthorne, there is as I mentioned earlier a certain amount of mutual accommodation. Quid pro quo, if you like. The government knows that Angelo is not dead and that he was in Cebu and Hong Kong and they also know what he's doing in Singapore."

"And that's where you got the pictures of him," I said. "From the government."

"From the government," he said.

"All right," I said. "It's clear so far. But why did he have to pretend to be dead?"

"Because he didn't want to get married."

Someone sighed deeply and I was almost surprised when I realized that it had been me. "You said it was a little complicated."

"Yes, I did, didn't I?" Cole said.

"Shall we try it again?"

"It's not really all that complicated; it just takes a while."

"I've made it this far; I may even go the distance."

Cole nodded. "I'm sure that you will, Mr. Cauthorne."

He moved back to his leather chair and sank into it. For the first time the strain that he was under seemed apparent. His hands twitched slightly and he kept crossing and uncrossing his legs.

"Marriage among my sponsors and their associates is a most serious matter. Virtually all of them are Catholic, at least in name, and divorce is uncommon, if not rare. They marry for life and because of the rather unusual nature of their businesses, if you will allow the term, the children of one group of my sponsors tend to marry the children of another group."

"I've heard that they are called families, not groups."

"All right. We'll use that term, if you prefer."

"Angelo was quite popular among the members of a certain New York family which is headed by Joe Lozupone. No doubt you've heard of him?"

I nodded.

"In fact, Lozupone was so taken with Angelo that he flew down to Washington to see me. His proposal was that Angelo marry his daughter, Carla."

"Why didn't he ask Angelo?"

"Because this is the way that things are arranged. There would be a substantial dowry, of course, and Angelo would be welcomed into the family firm, if he so desired."

"What happened?"

"I approached Angelo who was in Washington on one of his periodic visits. He agreed and promptly hit me up for a loan of fifteen thousand dollars. I think he was gambling heavily. I informed Lozupone and he informed his daughter who was then a sophomore, I believe, at Wellesley. Lozupone himself never got past the eighth grade."

"Then what?"

"Lozupone held an engagement party in New York. The girl, whom Angelo hadn't seen in years, came down from Massachusetts and Angelo flew in from Los Angeles or Las Vegas or wherever he was. They literally despised each other on sight. Angelo told me the engagement was off and flew back to Los Angeles that same night. I immediately assumed my role as counselor and tactfully suggested to Lozupone that the engagement be a long one—long enough to allow the girl to get her degree and perhaps even take a tour of Europe. Lozupone readily agreed. I telephoned Angelo, and for once he was amenable. He even called Lozupone and borrowed five thousand dollars from him on the strength of his new status as future son-in-law. Well, two years ago Carla was nearing graduation and the Lozupone family was making plans for a rather sizeable wedding."

"And it was then that Angelo decided to play dead," I said.

"Yes. But he needed money and that's when he came to Washington and blew the safe. Then he disappeared in Singapore and began to blackmail me a few months later. Lozupone, of course, has his own sources and he's found out that Angelo isn't dead. He's now furious and has directed his anger at me. Our relations cooled, then grew strained, and finally disintegrated. Lozupone announced to his family, and to the four other families in New York, that he considered me his enemy and Joe Lozupone, I needn't add, is a most dangerous enemy to have."

I shrugged. "Why don't you get rid of him like you got rid of the others?"

"I'll answer that in a moment. When Angelo's death was reported, Carla went into mourning. When it was discovered that he was alive, Lozupone swore that Angelo would marry her. It was an affair of honor to him and he takes such things seriously. In an effort to heal the breach between Lozupone and myself, a representative of another New York family approached me and suggested that I provide Carla with an appropriate escort to Singapore where she intends to find Angelo and to marry him. I agreed. I agreed to provide you, Mr. Cauthorne."

"Then you made a mistake," I said. "But you still haven't told me why you just don't take Lozupone out of circulation by dropping some of that mysterious evidence in the mail to the FBI or somebody."

"Because, Mr. Cauthorne, I don't have it. Angelo has the only copies that exist. And I need that information. I need it very much and this charade with the girl Carla will give me breathing time."

"He'll still keep on blackmailing you; he's smart enough to have had other copies made."

"I'm not worried about the blackmail, Mr. Cauthorne. I'm worried about Lozupone. Angelo can be bought; Lozupone cannot. The only thing that concerns me about Angelo is that nothing must happen to him, or the blackmail material will be promptly forwarded to New York by a third party. The arrangement wheezes with age, but it works."

"You're in trouble, Mr. Cole," I said. "It's almost a pity that I can't help you."

Cole gripped the arms of his chair and leaned towards me. His eyes no longer twinkled or flashed behind the thick glasses. They seemed to grow still and flat. His tone lost its warmth when he spoke and his voice had the accents of someone who had grown up in East Harlem, the hard way.

"Don't give me that shit, Cauthorne. There's a phone on my desk. All I have to do is pick it up and by tomorrow morning your partner's wife will be in the hospital with acid burns and they aren't easy to fix."

"Don't try it," I said.

"I have nothing to lose," he said and I hoped that his threat was as empty as his voice.

I looked at him for what seemed to be minutes, but it could have been only five seconds or so. "You never really got all the way out of it, did you?"

"Out of what?"

"The gutter."

"This is no game, no make-believe, sonny boy. For the sake of your physical as well as mental health you've got two things to do. You'll take the girl Carla to Singapore and you'll also retrieve the documents from Angelo."

"How?"

"I don't know how. That's your job. Use the girl. Charm her. Tell Angelo you'll get her—and the family, especially the family—off his back in exchange for the documents. Figure it out yourself. That's what you're being paid fifty thousand dollars to do."

I made the decision then, the decision that I had known I would make all along. I rose and started towards the door.

"Acid, Cauthorne," Cole called after me. "You're forgetting the acid."

I stopped and turned. "I'm not forgetting anything. I'll go, but not because of anything you've said. I'm going for myself and I'm not taking any jilted female with me."

"That's part of it," he said. "I need the time."

"Not my part."

"She goes."

"Why doesn't she go by herself? She can talk Angelo into getting married and they can spend their honeymoon in Pago Pago."

"I don't think so," Cole said.

"Why not?"

"Because Angelo married a Chinese girl in Singapore a year and a half ago."

CHAPTER IX

After that there was some more conversation, but nothing important, and Joe, the ubiquitous bodyguard, escorted me to the elongated Cadillac where I was faintly surprised to find that the polite Mr. Ruffo was absent, but I decided that even Yale law school graduates needed their rest.

At the hotel I undressed and sat in a chair by a window and stared out at the quiet Washington scene. I thought about Charles Cole in his huge white-columned house and wondered why there wasn't a family and a wife in a pleasant room in one of the wings, playing Monopoly perhaps, while the head of the household plotted in the library to keep himself from getting killed. I thought about Cole for a while and what he wanted me to do, and then I thought about Angelo Sacchetti and speculated about how he was spending all of his money. Unwisely, I hoped. Then I quit speculating and went to sleep and I was doing quite well at it until eight o'clock the next morning when somebody started to bang on the sitting room door. I got up, struggled into a robe, and stumbled towards the noise.

"Who is it?" I yelled through the door.

"The FBI. Open up."

"Christ," I said and opened the door.

He needed a shave for one thing, and for another his blue suit, stained and unpressed, had a hard time buttoning itself over his belly. He shoved past me into the room, asking: "How's it going, Cauthorne?" as he moved.

I slammed the door shut. "You're not the FBI. You're not even the house dick."

"Don't kid yourself, buster," he said and tossed a shapeless felt hat on one of the chairs.

A few thick strands of black hair were matted across a wide, white dome and the rest of the hair was going grey above the ears. He had a big round face and a double chin with a Major Hoople nose that glowed merrily. Some capillaries had exploded in his cheeks and his eyes, despite the redness of the whites, offered deep blue pupils that were steady and calculating.

"I'm Sam Dangerfield."

"Not Dangerfield of the FBI?"

"You got it right."

"Never heard of you. Is there anything to prove it?"

Dangerfield looked up at the ceiling. "Every goddamn one of them has seen that lousy TV series." Then he looked at me and his eyes seemed not only calculating, but curiously alive and intelligent. "I've got something to prove it. You want to see?"

"Even then I wouldn't believe it."

Dangerfield started to search his pockets, finally produced a folding, black case from his hip pocket, and handed it to me, but even it was a little dogeared. It said that he was Samuel C. Dangerfield, special agent for the Federal Bureau of Investigation. I handed it back to him.

"So what can I do for you?"

"You can offer me a drink, for one thing," Dangerfield said and headed for the Scotch that still sat on the coffee table. "I got a bad one." He poured three fingers of Scotch into a glass, emptied some of the melted ice from the bucket into another, and downed the drink, chasing it with the water. Then he poured another one, moved over to the chair where his hat rested, tossed it on the floor, and sat down with a sigh. "That's better," he said. "Much better."

I went over to the phone. "I'm going to have some breakfast sent up. Do you want some or will you just drink it?"

"You buying?"

"I'll buy."

"Four fried eggs, a double order of bacon, home fried potatoes, lots of toast and some coffee. And see if you can get another bottle."

"At eight in the morning?"

"I'll try when the bellhop gets here." He gave the bottle on the table a judicious glance. "There's enough left to coast on."

"How about some ice?"

"Never use it."

While I phoned the order in Dangerfield searched his pockets again and finally found a crumpled package of cigarettes in one of them, but it turned out to be empty. "You got a cigarette?" he asked after I had hung up.

I found a pack on the coffee table and tossed it to him. "Anything else?"

"If you got an electric razor, I'll borrow it after breakfast," he said, running a thick-fingered hand over his stubble.

"Did you really want to see me, or is it just that your check was late this month?"

"I want something," he said.

"What?"

"I'll tell you later. Go take a shower, get dressed. You look like a goddamned ponce in that silly looking robe."

"Go to hell," I said and started towards the bedroom. I paused at the door. "If the breakfast comes, forge my name. You ought to be pretty good at that. And add a twenty percent tip."

Dangerfield waved his drink at me and grinned. "Fifteen percent's plenty."

Mr. Hoover's finest was attacking his breakfast when I came out of the bedroom. I pulled a chair up to the room-service table and took the metal cover off my plate and regarded my poached egg without enthusiasm. Dangerfield poured a shot of Scotch into his coffee and sipped it noisily.

"Eat up, but if you can't, I'll take care of it for you."

"I need the strength," I said and started on the egg.

Dangerfield finished the four eggs, the bacon, the potatoes, the toast and a third cup of Scotch-laced coffee before I finished my egg and one cup of coffee. He leaned back in his chair, patted his belly, and said: "By God, I might live."

I put my fork down and looked at him. "What do you want?"

"Information, Brother Cauthorne, information. It's how I make my living, such as it is. You know what I am after twenty-seven lousy years in the bureau? I'm a lousy GS-13, that's what. And you want to know why? Because I haven't got what they call managerial potential. You know what a GS-13 makes? With a five-step increase like I've got he makes a lousy $16,809 a year. Christ, punks right out of law school make that much. And you know what else I've got to show for it? I got a Levittown house out in Bowie with a twenty-year mortgage, two kids in college, four suits, a five-year-old car, and a fat wife."

"And a thirst," I said.

"You got it right. A thirst."

"But for more than booze."

Dangerfield grinned at me. "You're not as stupid as I thought, Brother Cauthorne."

"I studied hard at night school. But one thing I don't get. Why the fake lush act? You're no lush; not even a good fake one. You eat too much and the last thing a lush thinks about is food."

"I thought it was a pretty good show," Dangerfield said, grinning once more. "It's supposed to disarm people—make them think that maybe I'm not really listening or don't understand what they're saying. It usually works."

"Not with me," I said.

"Okay," Dangerfield said, unlodged a morsel of bacon from between his teeth with his little finger, and inspected it carefully before flicking it to the carpet. "You've got trouble, Cauthorne."

"Everyone has trouble."

"Not your kind."

"It's got a name?"

"Sure," Dangerfield said. "It's called bad."

"Thank God you're here to help, Special Agent."

He looked at me sourly. "You don't like it much, do you?"

"What?"

"The fat man in the forty-nine fifty suit who busts in and drinks your booze at eight in the morning."

"You can drop the lush act," I said. "They wouldn't keep you on the payroll five minutes if you were a real drunk."

Dangerfield grinned at that. "I think I'll have another small one just to settle the nerves," he said. He poured one, rose, and walked over to a chair, taking the bottle with him. "Care to join me? The hop's bringing up a refill at ten."

"I've got a plane to catch at ten."

"There's another plane at twelve. You'll catch that one. We've got some talking to do."

"About what?"

"Don't start being dumb again, just when I got my hopes up," Dangerfield said as he raised his glass and smiled at it contentedly. "I don't get much Chivas Regal. Can't afford it."

"Neither can I."

"But Charlie Cole can, huh?"

"So they say." I got up from the table and moved over to one of the couches.

Dangerfield watched me over the rim of his glass. When he finished his drink he wiped his mouth with the back of his hand and put the glass down on the coffee table. "That'll do for a while. Now we'll talk a little."

"What about?"

"About you and Charlie Cole and Angelo Sacchetti. How's that for a start?"

"That's all it is."

Dangerfield leaned back in his chair and looked at the ceiling some more. "You flew in yesterday on

84

United and were met at Dulles by Johnny Ruffo in that hearse that Cole spins around town in. Ruffo dropped you here at the hotel at six-thirty and picked you up an hour later. You got to Cole's at ten to eight and stayed till eleven when the hearse brought you back here. You didn't make any phone calls and I didn't get to bed until two and got up with a hangover at six to get here by eight. I live in Bowie."

"You told me."

"But there's something I didn't tell you."

"What?"

"I don't want anything to happen to Charlie Cole."

"Neither does he."

Dangerfield snorted. "You can bet your sweet ass he doesn't. Outside of you I don't know of anybody who's in more trouble than Charlie Cole. Not only has he got Angelo putting the blocks to him somehow or other, but he's got Joe Lozupone down on him and that's about as bad as news can get. He tell you about that?"

"A little," I said.

"You know something," he said. "I knew a guy that Joe Lozupone got down on back in the early fifties. So you know what Joe did? He invited this guy out to his house for a big party. And when the party was going good down in the rec room all of Joe's friends took out their knives and carved this guy up into little pieces and then the wives got down on their hands and knees in their party dresses and scrubbed up the mess."

"So what did you do about it?"

"Me? I didn't do anything about it. In the first place I couldn't prove it and in the second place Joe didn't break any federal law."

I got up and walked over to the coffee table. "I think I will have a drink."

"You can fix me another one, too."

I picked up two of the clean glasses and made another journey to the bathroom for water. When I came back I asked Dangerfield if he wanted his mixed and he said no. I poured him another three fingers and a smaller amount for myself and then added water to mine.

"You don't look like the type that drinks in the morning, kid," he said as I handed him his drink.

"Don't tell the coach."

"You are healthy looking," Dangerfield said. "I just wonder how long you're going to keep that way."

"I thought you were worried about Cole, not me."

"I'm not *worried* about old Charlie. I just don't want anything to happen to him until he comes through."

"With what?"

"With some information that he's been promising for two years."

"About who?"

"Joe Lozupone, that's who."

"He hasn't got it anymore," I said and sat back to enjoy Dangerfield's reaction.

It wasn't what I expected. He grew very still and then he put his drink down carefully on the table beside his chair. He looked around the room slowly, leaned forward, rested his arms on his thick knees, stared at the carpet, and then asked in a very quiet voice: "What do you mean he hasn't got it anymore?"

"Angelo's got it. In Singapore."

"Cole's got copies," Dangerfield insisted to the carpet.

"Not this time."

"He told you about it, didn't he?"

"How else would I be telling you?"

"You're not lying," he said to the carpet. "No, you're not lying. You're not smart enough to lie."

He looked up then and for a moment I thought that there was anguish in his eyes and on his face, but it passed too quickly for me to be certain. "I've never been in that house, you know," Dangerfield said.

"What house?"

"Cole's. I've been dealing with him for twenty-three years and I've never been in *his* house. I've listened to his fuzzy crap about *accommodation* and *compromise* in half the crummy bars in half the jerkwater towns in Maryland, and I listened to it because he always came

86

through. I sat there in those lousy bars and drank cheap whiskey and listened to his crap about 'shared goals' and about how 'appeasement is not bad in itself if it works' because I knew at the end of the crap he'd hand over what I was after and then ask some two-bit favor in return. And all the time I was buttering him up for just one thing. Just one goddamned thing."

"Joe Lozupone," I said.

Dangerfield stared at me with reproach. "You think it's funny, don't you? You think it's really funny that I should get shook just because something I've been after for twenty-five years has been snatched away. You got a real sense of humor, Cauthorne."

"Twenty-five years is a long time, and I didn't say it was funny."

Dangerfield started talking to the carpet again, holding his big domed head in his hands. "It started during World War II. Blackmarket gasoline stamps, B stamps, but you're too young to remember about that."

"I remember," I said. "My old man had a C sticker on his car."

"I got on to Lozupone then. He had more than a hundred million gallons worth of B stamps that he was peddling, but he dumped them wholesale on small timers before we could get him. We busted it up all right, but we never got close to Lozupone."

"Have another drink," I said. "It'll cheer you up."

Dangerfield went on talking to the carpet. "Then after the war he started branching out. The bureau kept me on him—on all of them. I made the contact with Cole and with what I had and with what he gave me I knocked a lot of them off, but I never got close to Lozupone and he kept on getting bigger and bigger. He's in everything now. Trucking firms, clothing manufacturing, banks, unions, even investment houses, and all the time it's still rolling in from the gambling and the loansharking and the garbage collecting and God knows what else. Millions he's got. And you know something, we're just about the same age, me and Lozupone. He sent his daughter to Wellesley and I'm lucky to get mine into the University of Maryland. He's got an eighth grade education and I got a law degree. He's got at least thirty-five million stashed away and I've got $473.89 in my checking account and maybe two grand in savings bonds which I haven't had to cash yet."

"You're on the wrong side," I said.

He looked at me then and shook his head sadly. "Maybe you're right, Cauthorne, but it's too late to switch now. Take a good look at me. Twenty-five years of it, screwing around with punks and chiselers and half-witted hoods. It's rubbed off on me. I talk like them. I even think like them. Christ, don't kid yourself that I didn't know what you were expecting when I said 'FBI' through the door. You were expecting something young and neat with lots of hair in a nice suit with manners to match. And what do you get? You got a fifty-one-year-old fat man in a Robert Hall outfit with a pig's manners, that's what you got."

"Have another drink," I said.

"You know why I look like I do?" Dangerfield asked.

"Why?"

"Because they don't like it."

"Who doesn't like it?"

"The waspwaists down at the bureau. To hell with them. I got twenty-seven years in with three years to go and I know more about it than anybody else so they're not going to say anything. And I got Charlie Cole for them and because of that they damn sure won't say anything."

I walked over and picked up Dangerfield's glass and poured some more Scotch into it. "Here. Drink this and then you can cry on my shoulder."

Dangerfield accepted the glass. "I hear you're a little nuts, Cauthorne. A little screwy in the head."

"Really?"

"The boys out on the coast say that you went a little crackers because you thought you'd killed old Angelo."

88

"What else do the boys say?"

"They say that Callese and Palmisano have been leaning on you."

"I sat back down on the divan and crossed my legs. "You can tell the boys that they're right."

"What's Charlie Cole want with you?"

"He wants Angelo off his back for one thing."

"Angelo's in Singapore. Doing real well, I understand."

"You got the pictures of him for Cole, didn't you?"

Dangerfield nodded. "I got them. I hear that Charlie's been moving big money through Switzerland to Singapore. I figured it was to Angelo. Am I right?"

"You're right," I said.

"What's Angelo got on him?"

"Everything. Everything he ever gave you and unless Cole keeps paying, Angelo's going to give it to your friends in New York."

Dangerfield thought about that for a moment. He rubbed his big red nose and frowned. "And Angelo's got the stuff on Lozupone?"

"The only copy—or copies by now."

"And where do you fit in?"

"Unless I get it back, Cole is thinking about having some acid thrown in the face of my partner's wife."

"What did you tell him?" Dangerfield said.

"I told him I'd go to Singapore. But I was going anyway when I found out about Sacchetti. I was going wherever Sacchetti was."

Dangerfield nodded his big head slowly as if confirming something to himself. "They said you were a little crazy. They were right."

"Why?"

"Because you don't know how much trouble you're in."

I got up and poured the last of the Scotch into my glass. "You mentioned that before, I think."

"I didn't go into details."

"But you will."

"Later," Dangerfield said. "Right now we've got some planning to do."

"Planning what?"

Dangerfield smiled. He looked cheerful and relaxed, even happy. "About how you're going to get that stuff on Joe Lozupone away from Angelo Sacchetti and back to me."

CHAPTER X

After the plane landed at Los Angeles International I took a cab to Santa Monica and La Brea and got there too late for lunch with Trippet, but in plenty of time to learn that I had an appointment at the Beverly Wilshire at six that evening with Miss Carla Lozupone.

"Someone called about an hour ago," Trippet said. "He didn't sound very friendly."

"I haven't met any of them who are."

Trippet wanted to know what had happened so I told him, leaving out only Cole's threat concerning the acid. I also told Trippet about the plan that Dangerfield dreamed up to retrieve the evidence from Sacchetti. I had spent four and a half hours on the plane thinking about Dangerfield's plan, trying to improve on it, and the only conclusion I had come to was that it would probably land me in either of two places, the hospital or the cemetery.

"Surely, you're not going through with it?" Trippet said and brushed his long grey hair from his eyes.

"There's only one thing I know that I'm going to do. That's fly to Singapore and find Angelo Sacchetti."

"And the evidence?"

"I don't know. If he hands it over to me, fine. But I don't think I'll wrestle him for it."

Trippet rummaged through the office desk. "Where do we keep the stationery?"

90

"Bottom left-hand drawer," I said.

He found a sheet, took out his broad-nibbed fountain pen, and began to write. "You don't know anyone in Singapore, do you?"

"Just Angelo Sacchetti."

"This is a letter of introduction to Sammy Lim. He's an awfully nice chap. We were at school together, you know."

"I didn't."

"Yes," Trippet said and kept on writing. "His grandfather and mine founded one of the first Chinese-British export-import firms in Singapore. Trippet and Lim, Ltd. It caused a terrible stir. Sammy's full name is Lim Pang Sam. He's now managing director and also principal stockholder, although I still hold some interest. Haven't seen him in years, but we correspond quite regularly."

Trippet signed the letter with a bit of flourish, asked me if there was a blotter, and I told him no, that I hadn't used a blotter in years, probably because I hadn't owned a fountain pen in years. He said he couldn't stand ball-point pens and I told him he was against progress. By this time he had waved the letter around enough for the ink to dry, so he handed it to me. Trippet wrote a nice hand and it read:

DEAR SAMMY:

This is to introduce Edward Cauthorne, my good friend and business associate. He is in Singapore on a rather confidential matter and if you could lend him any and all assistance, I would be forever grateful.

You owe me a letter, you know, and when are you making that long postponed trip to the States? Barbara is dying to see you again.

As ever,
DICKIE

"Dickie?" I said and handed the letter back to him.

Trippet rummaged around in the desk until he found an envelope. "Well, after all, we were at school together," he said as he folded the letter and placed it in the envelope and handed it to me.

"Thanks very much," I said and put the envelope in an inside jacket pocket.

"Not at all. When do you think you'll leave?"

"I don't know. I'll have to get a smallpox shot first and I guess it'll depend on the fair Carla and her wishes."

Trippet shook his head. "I fail to see, Edward, why you agreed to serve as her escort or chaperone or whatever you are."

"Because it was easier to acquiesce than to argue, I suppose. Or maybe I just like to have people walking over me."

Trippet frowned. "That sounds suspiciously like self-pity."

"Whatever it is, I plan to get rid of it in Singapore."

"You're banking an awfully lot on this trip, aren't you?"

"Yes," I said. "I suppose I am. Wouldn't you?"

"I don't know," he said. "In my rather haphazard life I have, upon occasion, attempted the geographical cure, I suppose you might call it. But I always found that it had one distinct drawback."

"What?"

"I had to go along with me."

We walked around the corner to one of the bars and had a drink while Trippet brought me up to date on Sydney Durant. He had visited Sydney at the hospital earlier that day and all our principal body repair man could tell him was that there had been four of them. They had picked him up in front of his rooming house at one-thirty in the morning and had driven him to a quiet residential street, just off Sunset. Two of them had held him while another had clamped a gag over his mouth. The fourth member of the party had slammed the door. Then they hopped into their car and sped off, leaving Sydney to wander down to Sunset holding his shattered hands in front of him. It had

92

been dark and he couldn't give a good description of the men to either Trippet or the police.

"I assured him that his hands would be all right," Trippet said. "When he gets well enough to leave the hospital I plan to take him home with me so that Barbara can look after him."

"I may not get the chance to see Sydney," I said. "But tell him that when he gets well enough we need him to help out in front until his hands are healed. Tell him we want him to learn the management side."

"Sometimes, Edward, the humanitarian side of your nature absolutely surprises me."

"Sometimes, Dickie, it surprises me, too."

Trippet began his usual leisurely stroll homewards and I stood on the corner for fifteen minutes until I hailed a cab which dropped me in front of the Beverly Wilshire at five minutes after six. I asked the room clerk for Miss Lozupone's room number and he informed me that the hotel policy was not to give out such information and that if I wished to speak to Miss Lozupone, I should use the house phone. I told him I thought that the hotel policy was sound and asked where the house phones were located. He pointed them out and I picked one up and asked for Miss Carla Lozupone. A male voice answered.

"Miss Lozupone, please," I said.

"This Cauthorne?"

"Yes."

"Come on up. She's waiting for you."

I asked the voice what the room number was. He told me and I rode the elevator up to the seventh floor, walked down the hall, and knocked on a door. A tall man of about thirty with long, wavy black hair and acne-scarred cheeks opened the door.

"You Cauthorne?"

"I'm Cauthorne," I said.

"Come on in," he said and opened the door wide enough to let me enter, provided I turned sideways.

Inside I found myself in what must have been the Beverly Wilshire's Spanish Fandango suite. The furniture was all black mahogany with red velvet upholstery that was held in place by brass nailheads. There were some tables with beaten brass tops that looked a little Moorish and Mexico got in its innings with some pictures of peasants in wide sombreros leaning against white adobe walls in what looked to be an impossibly yellow sunshine.

She was sitting on a low, long divan that matched the rest of the furniture in the room. Her dress was navy blue and had three large white buttons down the front and ended far enough above her knees for the view to be fascinating. She wore her black hair long and straight and it framed a pair of dark eyes, an almost perfect nose whose nostrils flared just a little, and a full, lipsticked mouth that seemed to have pouted its way through life. Except for the pout, and a chin that some might have thought too small, she could have been called striking, or even beautiful, if you were feeling generous that day. But with or without the pout she was undeniably sexy and I had the notion that she spent a lot of time working at it.

"So you're Uncle Charlie's idea of a babysitter," she said as if she didn't care much for Uncle Charlie's ideas.

"Uncle Charlie is Charles Cole?" I said.

"That's right."

"Then I'm Uncle Charlie's idea of a babysitter."

She bent forward to reach for a tall drink that rested on a long, low table in front of the divan and the navy blue dress gaped open enough to show that she didn't like to bother with a brassiere. She took a swallow of her drink and looked at me some more.

"Sit down someplace," she said. "Do you want a drink? If you do, Tony will mix you one. That's Tony over there."

I sat down in a highbacked chair that was pulled up to the table in front of the divan and started to say hello to Tony, but the shakes hit, and then the sweating started, and Angelo Sacchetti fell into the ocean again and winked his Singapore wink at me as he fell

94

Then it was over and Carla Lozupone stared curiously as Tony bent over me.

"I'll take that drink now," I said, took out a handkerchief and wiped the sweat off my face.

"Give him a drink," Carla said.

Tony looked at me dubiously. "What the hell's the matter with you?"

"Nothing that a drink won't cure," I said.

Tony moved over to a table that was stocked with bottles and mixed me a drink. "Bourbon okay?" he said as he handed it to me.

"Fine."

"What have you got, some form of epilepsy?" the girl asked.

"No. It's not epilepsy."

"Christ," she said, "it might as well be. You were gone for five minutes."

"No," I said. "Not five minutes. Maybe forty seconds or a minute at the most. I've timed it before."

"Does this happen often?" she asked.

"Every day," I said and took a swallow of the drink. "Except today it was a little early."

Carla Lozupone pushed her lower lip out a little farther. "What am I supposed to do with a babysitter who throws a fit at six o'clock every evening?"

"The best you can, I suppose."

"What? Stick a wooden depressor in your mouth so that you won't bite through your tongue? You're supposed to look after me, Mr. Cauthorne, or whatever your name is."

"It's still Cauthorne," I said. "Edward Cauthorne."

"You want I should throw him out?" Tony inquired pleasantly enough and moved over to my chair.

"Tell him not to try," I said.

Carla Lozupone looked at me and then at Tony. The pout disappeared and she licked a pink tongue over her lower lip. "Throw him out, Tony."

The tall man with the wavy black hair fastened his hand on my left arm. "You heard the lady," he said.

I sighed and threw the rest of my drink in his face. Then I was up. His hands went to his face and I hit him twice, a little above the belt. He doubled over just enough for my knee to catch his chin, and as he went down I chopped him, not too hard, on the back of the neck. Tony sprawled on the floor, breathing heavily but steadily through his mouth. I picked up the glass I had dropped and walked over to the table and mixed another drink. There was some Scotch, so I poured that instead of the bourbon. Then I went back to the chair, stepped over Tony, and sat down.

Carla Lozupone stared at me, her mouth slightly parted. At least she wasn't pouting.

I raised my glass to her and then took a swallow. "I am getting a little sick of being leaned on," I said. "I am also getting a little sick of the Lozupones and the Coles and the Calleses. But I'm especially sick of Angelo Sacchetti and that's why I'm going to Singapore. So I can stop being sick of Sacchetti. If you want to tag along, you can. If you don't, you can always take Tony with you. He should be good at keeping track of the passports and the luggage."

Carla Lozupone looked at me thoughtfully. "Why do you think I'm going to Singapore?" she said.

"To patch up a busted romance, I understand."

She laughed and she put a certain amount of bitterness into it. "With Angelo? Don't be stupid. I can't stand him and he can't stand me. We never could, even when we were kids."

"You weren't kids together," I said. "Angelo's at least ten years older than you are."

"Nine," she said. "But he was around when I was twelve and he was twenty-one. I spent a very unpleasant Saturday afternoon with Angelo when I was twelve."

"I can imagine."

"I doubt that you can," she said.

"Then why did you go through with the engagement and the rest of the act?"

She drained her glass. "Mix me another one."

When I made no move, she added: "Please."

I rose and picked up her glass. "I thought they must

96

have taught you something at Wellesley. What are you drinking?"

"Vodka and tonic."

I mixed her drink and handed it to her. "You didn't answer my question," I said.

"Do you get *The New York Times* out here?" she said.

"Not any more. We have to make do with the local product."

"Than you don't get a chance to read much about my father."

"I know who he is."

"I get to read about him all the time," she said. "The nicest thing that they call him is a criminal. He's supposed to be the nation's number-one gangster. How would you like to read that about your old man?"

"I don't know," I said. "He's dead."

She paused and lighted a cigarette. Then she blew some smoke at her glass. "I suppose he is," she said in a low voice.

"What?"

"America's number-one gangster. But he's still my father and I like him. You know why?"

"Why?"

"Because he likes me and he's been good to me. He's been very good to me."

"That's a reason."

"And now he's in trouble."

"Your father?" I said.

"He's in the middle of it and it's all about Charles Cole."

"From what I've heard," I said, "your father started it."

"Then you heard it wrong. They forced him to and now Angelo's just providing the excuse."

"Do you always talk like this?" I said.

"Like what?"

"In fragments. You know, bits and pieces. Why don't you just spell it all out? Start with the beginning. That's a good place; then go through the middle, and wind up at the end. With luck, I can follow you."

She took a deep breath and pushed the top of her dress out in an interesting manner. "Okay," she said. "From the beginning. It all started several years ago. I was a sophomore at Wellesley and I'd come home for a weekend. It was a Saturday afternoon and they were in my father's den."

"Who?"

"My father and his friends. Or associates or whatever you want to call them. There were four or five of them."

"All right," I said.

"I eavesdropped. I was curious, so I eavesdropped."

"All right," I said again.

"The door to the den was open. It opens into the living room and they didn't know I was there. Sometimes they talked in Italian and sometimes in English."

"About what?"

"About Charles Cole or Uncle Charlie. They were telling my father that he should be eliminated. Killed or murdered is more accurate."

She paused and took a long swallow of her drink. "I'd read about it. I had read everything I could find about it and about my father, but I'd never heard them talk like that. I couldn't help but listen."

"To what?"

She took another deep breath. "Those who wanted Cole out of the way said that he had too much power, that he'd become too expensive, and that he was producing too little. My father argued against them and it got rough. I mean really rough. I didn't know my father could talk like that. They didn't reach any decision that night, but I could tell my old man was worried. He had argued that Charles Cole knew too much; that there were too many documents in his possession. If he were to die, those documents might get in the wrong hands. His associates didn't want to listen to him."

"But they had to?" I said.

She nodded. "He's number one, I guess you could call it. They had to listen to him, at least for a while.

98

But then, about six months later, my old man drove up to Wellesley for parents' day." She paused and stared into her drink. "That was funny."

"What?"

"My father in his Mercedes 600 driving up to Wellesley with Tony here. They all knew who he was, of course."

"Who?"

"My friends at school."

"How'd they react?"

"How do you expect?"

"You were snubbed?"

She smiled and shook her head. "Just the opposite. I was made. All they had for fathers were stockbrokers and lawyers and corporation presidents. I was the only one who had a real live gangster with a certified hood for a chauffeur. There was my father, a little round man without too much hair, an eighth grade education, and a noticeable accent. And there were all the young girls making over him as if he were their favorite poet-politician. He liked it. He liked it very much."

"But he didn't drive up just for parents' day," I said.

"No. He came up to ask me to become engaged to Angelo. He had never asked me to do anything before. Nothing for him anyway. So I asked him why and he told me. It was the first time that he'd ever really talked to me. You know, as if I were an adult."

"What were his reasons?"

She looked at me then. "How much do you know about all this?"

"More than I should probably, but it seems to be a different version."

She nodded at that and said, "You may as well have the right one."

The right one, it seemed, was that Joe Lozupone asked his daughter to become engaged to the godson of Charles Cole for one reason only, and it wasn't because he was overly fond of Angelo Sacchetti, as Charles Cole had claimed. The five New York families were divided, three to two against Cole. Lozupone felt that if his daughter became engaged to Sacchetti it would provide him with the excuse that he needed to side with Cole. There would be a blood tie, or at least something that was close to a blood tie. Carla Lozupone agreed. The engagement was announced, the party was held, and the rest was much as Charles Cole had told me, except for one thing. Lozupone could now hold out no longer against the three families after it was learned that Angelo Sacchetti was still alive, but had not returned to marry the daughter. He was forced to announce his opposition to Cole.

"I kept up with it all," Carla said. "I even went into mourning when Angelo was reported dead. And then when they discovered that he was alive, I told people I was going to Singapore to marry him. I did all this without consulting my old man. It's given him time. Now he and the rest of them have run out of time. But as long as they think there's a chance of my marrying Angelo, my old man can stall, and Charles Cole will stay alive."

"And if you don't marry him?"

She shrugged and it was a fatalistic, resigned expression. "My father will have to vote yes on Charles Cole's death and when he does, he'll also be voting for his own death because he's certain that enough evidence will turn up in Cole's files to convict him. He has a bad heart; a prison sentence would kill him."

She was silent for a while as she fiddled with the ice in her glass. "He has an alternative, of course."

"What?" I said.

"He could start a war. It would be easy and while it lasted, they'd forget about Cole. If he won, Cole would still be safe. If my father lost, it wouldn't matter. He might as well be dead."

"So by going to Singapore, you're buying him time."

"That's about all, isn't it?" she said. "Two weeks, three weeks at the most. Maybe he can work something out in the meantime. He's very good at that."

"You must care about him a great deal," I said.

She shrugged. "He's my father and as I said he's

been good to me. The only thing I wouldn't do for him is marry Angelo Sacchetti. I just can't do that."

"I wouldn't worry about it," I said, as Tony began to stir on the floor beside me. "I don't think you'll have to."

CHAPTER XI

It is about 9,500 miles from Los Angeles to Singapore and Pan American Airways doesn't seem to be in much of a hurry to get there. I understand that other flights are offered from Los Angeles, but the only one for which Carla Lozupone and I could get first class reservations was number 811 which left at 9:45 P.M.

I had spent most of that Saturday getting the tickets and a smallpox shot so that my International Certificate of Vaccination could be brought up to date. A call at a travel agency had given me vague assurance of two rooms at the Raffles Hotel providing that the wire got to Singapore before we did and providing that two rooms were available.

Carla Lozupone, with Tony bringing up the rear as well as the luggage, met me in the lobby of the Beverly Wilshire. She was dressed for travel in a lightweight black and white checked pants suit and her pout was back in place. "What do we do," she said instead of hello, "fly all night?"

"All night and part of the day after tomorrow," I said.

"San Francisco's better. There's a direct flight out of San Francisco."

"We'll try that next time," I said.

Tony joined us after he paid Carla Lozupone's bill, entrusted her luggage to a bellhop, and ordered his rented car to be brought up from the hotel's garage. "Had your fit yet?" he asked.

I looked at my watch. "About two hours ago, thanks."

"That drink in the face crap," he said. "I seen that on television lots of times."

"That's where I learned it."

He nodded pleasantly enough. "You didn't hurt me bad though. I been hurt worse than that."

"I pulled them," I said. "If I hadn't, you'd have been in the hospital with your jaws wired together and your neck in a cast."

He thought about that for a moment. "Thanks for pulling them then."

"You're welcome."

"But my stomach still hurts some."

"I didn't pull those," I said.

"No," he said, "I didn't think you did."

The car that Tony had rented was a new Chrysler and he drove it well. There wasn't much conversation until we reached the airport and he pulled up in front of the Pan American entrance. Then he turned around in the seat. "Not much use in me coming in, is there, Carla?"

"None," she said and started gathering up her purse and cosmetic kit.

"What'll I tell the boss? I'm flying back tomorrow."

"Tell him whatever you want to."

"I mean do you want I should tell him you're okay and everything?"

"Yes," she said. "Tell him that."

Tony looked at me. "I wouldn't want you to make me out a liar, friend. Take good care of her."

"You sure you wouldn't like to come along?" I said. "You could look after both of us."

"I'm not kidding, friend," he said.

"I didn't think you were."

We touched down at Honolulu International a little after midnight, some fifteen minutes late, switched to Flight 841 which took off at 1:45 A.M., another fifteen
102

minutes late, and then flew forever until we reached Guam. After they picked up the milk there we flew for what seemed to be another couple of weeks until we landed at Manila International. From Manila we flew to Tan-Soh-Nhut, which is four and a half miles outside of Saigon where all the fun goes on, and then, finally, a month or so later, we landed at Paya Lebar International Airport at 1:10 P.M. Monday. We were seven and one half miles from the center of Singapore and only forty minutes late.

Carla Lozupone, I discovered, didn't care much for airplanes. She had three martinis in quick succession after we left Honolulu, tossed down a couple of red capsules, and fell asleep. She awakened in Manila, asked where we were, ordered a double martini, and promptly went back to sleep. Vietnam failed to interest her and thirty minutes out of Singapore she departed for the ladies' room with her cosmetics kit and the comment: "I'm a mess."

It was a long, long flight and it gave me time to think, more time than I really needed. I thought about Charles Cole for a while and decided that his summoning me to Washington had been the desperate, or even frantic, act of a thoroughly frightened man who would do anything if it would let him live a little longer, a year, a month or even a day. He apparently was convinced that his only hope was for me to recover the blackmail kit from Angelo Sacchetti. The only way that I could do that was to use the scheme advanced by the rumpled and unlikely FBI agent, Sam Dangerfield. I thought about what I had come to regard as the Dangerfield Plan for a few moments, but not many, because it was too much like wondering if I had six friends who would serve as pallbearers only to discover that I didn't. Essentially, Dangerfield and Cole wanted the same thing and that was the information now in Angelo Sacchetti's hands or his safe-deposit box or under his pillow—information that could put Joe Lozupone away in Leavenworth or Atlanta to either run a sewing machine or grow vegetables in the greenhouse for years to come. But if the girl with the pout, who slept next to me on the plane that flew over the Pacific, were telling the truth, Joe Lozupone was the only thing that stood between Charles Cole and a bullet, a knife, a one-way excursion on Chesapeake Bay, or whatever was in style that year.

There seemed to be only one constant and that was Angelo Sacchetti, and while I was wondering about him, somewhere past Guam, I fell asleep and dreamed a dream that I couldn't recall, but which had me sweating when I awakened as we landed in Manila, the town that they once called the Pearl of the Orient.

At Singapore airport they sent a bus to transport us from the plane to the Arrivals Building. It was hot, but then it's always hot in Singapore. We breezed through the health and immigration authorities, recovered our baggage from customs, and found a smiling Malay porter who located us a cab while I changed some American Express checks into Singapore dollars.

The cab was an old yellow-topped Mercedes whose Chinese driver wove it in and out of the traffic on Serangoon Road, turned left with a certain amount of flair on Lavender Street, then right on Beach Road, and dropped us off before the white colonial facade of the Raffles Hotel that fairly glistened in the hot sun. I paid him his three Singapore dollars, tipped him another fifty cents to show that I was a sport, and followed Carla Lozupone into the dim, cool interior of the hotel where a beaming Chinese clerk happily informed us that our reservations were in order. Carla Lozupone's only comment during the ride from the airport had been: "It's hot."

In the lobby she looked around at the century-old building. "I've heard about this place ever since I was a kid," she said.

"I like old hotels," I said.

She gave the lobby another appraising glance. "You'll be happy here."

Our rooms were on the second floor, across the hall from each other. Just outside her door, Carla Lozupone turned to me as the Malay bellhop inserted a key in the lock. "I'm going to take a bath," she said.

"Then I'm going to get dressed and then you're going to buy me a drink. A special drink."

"What?"

"I didn't fly nine thousand odd miles for nothing. I'm going to have a Singapore Sling in the bar of the Raffles Hotel. After that, we'll do whatever we're going to do. But we'll do that first."

"It's as good a way to start as any," I said. "Maybe even better."

I followed the bellhop into my room which was high-ceilinged, large, and furnished in what I suppose could be called British Empire modern. At least the bed looked comfortable. I gave him a Singapore dollar, felt like a miser, and was relieved when he grinned and thanked me effusively. After I had unpacked, and shaved and showered in the enormous bathroom, I put on a lightweight suit, found the telephone book, looked up a number, and made a call to Mr. Lim Pang Sam, the only person whose name I knew in Singapore other than Angelo Sacchetti's. I didn't think that Angelo's name would be in the book, but nevertheless I looked. It wasn't. I had to go through two secretaries to reach Lim, but when I identified myself as Richard Trippet's associate, he was exceedingly cordial and wanted to know how Dickie was. I told him that Dickie was fine and we agreed to meet at Lim's office at ten the following morning. After I hung up I began to feel that asking a respectable Singapore businessman about an American blackmailer might not prove to be an auspicious beginning. Yet it seemed better than asking the Sikh doorman in front of the hotel. Better, perhaps, but not much.

Singapore, which has some aspirations of becoming the New York of Southeast Asia, is fairly new as cities go, having been founded by Sir Thomas Stamford Bingley Raffles in 1819. That, if you don't count what was there before the Javanese leveled it during a raid in 1377, makes Singapore younger than both New York and Washington, but older than either Dallas or Denver. It likes to think that it offers "instant Asia" to the touring Garden Club from Rapid City, South Dakota.

A more apt description might be "Asia without tears," because the water can be drunk from the tap, the city is fairly clean, there are no beggars, but numerous millionaires, and almost everybody that a tourist encounters either speaks or at least understands English.

I was telling all this to Carla Lozupone as we sipped our Singapore Slings in the Elizabethan Room's small, comfortable bar.

"What else has it got?" she asked.

"The world's fifth largest port—or perhaps busiest, I'm not sure. A hell of a naval base which the British are giving up soon because they can't afford it now, any more than they could afford it when they built it in the twenties and thirties—"

"That's the one where the guns were all pointed the wrong way during World War II, isn't it?" she asked.

"Towards the sea," I said. "The Japanese walked and pushed their bicycles down through Malaya which was supposedly impenetrable and there wasn't much that the British could do about it."

"So what is it now?"

"What?"

"Singapore."

"It's a republic now. Eight or nine years ago it was a crown colony, then a self-governing state under British protection, then a member of the Malaysian Federation until it was kicked out in 1965. Now it's a republic."

"It's a little small, isn't it?"

"A little."

Carla tried her drink again, lit a cigarette, and looked around the bar which, at three o'clock in the afternoon, was almost empty. "Do you think he ever comes in here?"

"Sacchetti?"

"Yes."

"I don't know. I didn't even know he was alive until four days ago. But if he can show his face, I suppose that he'd come here. It's popular and stylish and Angelo, as I recall, always liked places like that."

"I knew he was alive six weeks ago, perhaps even seven," she said.

"How did you find out?"

"One of my old man's associates heard about it. You can substitute anything you want for associates."

"You didn't choose your parents," I said.

"No, but one of them tried to choose my husband."

"He seemed to have had his reasons."

"Reasons," she said. "All the wrong ones."

She was wearing a simple, yellow sleeveless cotton dress which was probably more expensive than it looked. When she turned in her chair to look at me the dress tightened across her breasts and I could tell that she still didn't have much use for brassieres.

"Tell me something," she said. "What happens when you find Angelo? Are you going to beat up on him, as the boys down on the corner used to say?"

"What good would that do?"

"I don't know," she said. "Therapy maybe. It might cure your St. Vitus dance or whatever it is that you've got."

"I have to find him first."

"When do you start looking?"

"Tomorrow," I said.

"Fine," she said and drained her glass. "That gives me plenty of time to have another one of these."

I ordered two more of the drinks that I didn't much care for but which seemed to be the thing to do the first day in Singapore. When they came, Carla took a swallow of hers and lit another cigarette. There were six of them in her ashtray and we had been there less than forty-five minutes.

"You smoke a lot," I said, keeping up my end of the conversation.

"I'm nervous."

"About what?" I said.

"About Angelo."

"Why should you be? The way you tell it, you're just along for the ride."

"Angelo may not think so," she said.

"So?"

"How well do you know him?"

"That's what everybody asks me," I said.

"All right. Now I'm asking. How well do you know him?"

"Not well. Not well at all. We worked together a few times. I think he once bought me a drink or I bought him one. I'm not sure which."

She found a flake of tobacco on her tongue, picked it off, and flicked it into the ashtray. She did it as well as or better than any woman I had ever seen.

"So you don't know him?"

"No."

"I do."

"Okay. You know him."

"He has something going for him here in Singapore, doesn't he? I mean he has a Sacchetti-type thing going."

"So I understand."

"And it's making money," she said. "Otherwise he wouldn't stay."

"I've heard that, too."

"I know this about Angelo. If he's making money, he's not doing it legitimately. That's number one."

"What's number two?"

"If anyone gets in his way, he'll walk on them."

"Don't tell me you're planning to get in his way?"

She didn't answer for a moment. Then she looked at me and her face was no longer pretty. It was as if she had slipped on a pale mask that had been designed to portray only one emotion and that was an intense dislike that bordered on hatred. When she finally spoke, her voice was cold and somehow remote.

"I don't know if I'll get in his way or not," she said. "It depends."

"On what?"

"On what he says after I talk to him."

"When do you plan to do that?"

"As soon as possible."

"What do you plan to talk about, old times in New Jersey?"

She shook her head. "I have a few questions."

108

"Only a few?"

"Three. Maybe even four."

"And if his answers are correct?"

She stared at me again, this time as if I were some stranger who had made her a particularly indecent proposal.

"You don't understand, Cauthorne."

"Understand what?"

"There aren't any right answers to my questions. There aren't any right answers at all."

CHAPTER XII

Just like a couple of well-heeled American tourists determined to discover the real Singapore, we had dinner that night in Bugis Street which runs through one of the Chinese sections. The two- and three-story buildings that line the street are about the size of a low-cost American row house, except that as many as fifty persons might be living inside, or at least sleeping there. This forces the cooking to be done outside, virtually on the sidewalk. The specialties are displayed in stalls and served at small tables covered with fairly clean white cloths.

It was the dinner hour. Later, the street would become a market center where the stalls would sell sport shirts and razor blades instead of eight-inch prawns and steamed cockles. We found a table, sat down, and almost immediately a young Chinese appeared, carrying two hot scented towels in wooden tongs.

"What's this for?" Carla said.

"You're supposed to be hot and sweaty," I said. "You can dry yourself off with it."

I asked the man who had brought the towels what

his specialty was and he claimed that he served a most remarkable roast duck. We decided to try the duck as well as some *pau,* which are riceballs that contain meat and prawns heavily spiced with chilis and sweetened with something that tastes like plum sauce. We began with a soup that I couldn't identify but which turned out to be almost as good as our duck specialist promised it would be. The man who sold ducks dispatched a youngster for the *pau* and the soup which were the specialties of a couple of stalls farther down the street. The service was good, the price was wonderful, the duck was excellent, and if you didn't mind a motorcycle or two going off in your ear, the blast of what seemed to be a hundred transistor radios, all tuned to different stations, and an occasional elbow in your neck from the passing crowd that thronged the street, it was all very nice, friendly and, I suppose, quite Chinese in a touristy sort of way.

When we were finished I asked Carla if she would like to take a trishaw back to the hotel.

"You mean one of those things where the man rides a bicycle in front?"

"Yes."

She shook her head. "That's where I draw the line, Cauthorne. I'll do a lot of things, but I'm not going to cause another human being to have a heart attack because he has to pull me around."

"You're thinking of rickshaws," I said. "They don't have them in Singapore any more. I think the rickshaw men used to last a maximum of five years before they died of tuberculosis."

"How long do they last pumping away on their bicycles?"

"I don't know," I said.

"Really? What a pleasant surprise."

Before I could say something clever to that a cab appeared and I hailed it. The driver just missed a very old woman who hobbled along on tiny feet that must have been bound when she was a child, cut smartly in front of a long-haired Chinese youth on a big Honda,

110

and came to a stop before us as if he were surprised that his brakes still worked.

I have a theory, largely unsubstantiated, that countries whose traffic moves on the left have a higher accident rate than those where it keeps to the right. It may be an entirely provincial notion, but it was lent additional support by the driver who cowboyed us the short distance back to the Raffles, never keeping more than four inches between his bumper and the car in front, and passing a couple of times when there wasn't any space to pass. Despite my former trade, I kept closing my eyes at crucial moments which seemed to occur every fifty feet or so. It apparently didn't bother Carla Lozupone at all.

At the hotel, I paid the driver, tipped him handsomely because I was glad to be alive, and suggested a brandy in the courtyard to Carla. She agreed and we sat there, sipping Courvoisier under the palm trees, and admiring the golf-green-like grass.

"What's on for tomorrow," she said. "More local color?"

"I have to see a man."

"What about?"

"He may have some suggestions about where I can find Angelo Sacchetti."

"And if he doesn't?"

"I don't know," I said. "I may run an ad in the personal column."

"When do you see the man?"

"At ten."

She looked at her watch. "I think I'll go on up," she said. "I'm a little tired." I started to rise, but she added: "You may as well finish your drink. Knock on my door when you get back from your appointment."

"All right."

I watched her walk across the courtyard and enter the hotel. For no good reason at all, I left some bills on the table and followed. Carla Lozupone entered the lobby, turned towards the entrance, and spoke briefly to the turbaned Sikh doorman under the canopy. He whistled up a cab and Carla got in. I looked at my watch. It was ten-thirty and I wondered where a girl who didn't know anyone in Singapore might be going at that time of night. I was still wondering when I fell asleep a little after midnight.

Lim Pang Sam's office was on the ninth floor of the Asia Building on Raffles Quay not too far from Telok Ayer Basin. It was a corner office with a fine view of the harbor. A secretary ushered me in and Lim rose from behind a teak desk, walked around it, shook hands with me, said he was delighted that I was in Singapore, and managed to sound as if he really meant it.

"I have a letter for you from Trippet," I said and handed the envelope to him. He read it, standing up, and smiled.

"I never could understand what Dickie is doing in the car business," Lim said.

"His wife says that he likes to get out of the house."

Lim read the letter again and smiled once more. "We were at school together, you know."

"So I understand."

"Please," Lim said, motioning to one of the teak and fabric chairs that was drawn up to his desk. "I was about to have some tea. Would you care to join me, or do you prefer coffee?"

"Tea would be nice."

He picked up his telephone, pushed a button, and said something in what I took to be Mandarin Chinese. He was a smooth-faced man of middle height, with just the trace of a pot. He must have been Trippet's age or even older, but his hair was full and black and his eyes were steady and clear behind gold-rimmed Ben Franklin glasses that he wore half-way down a broad nose. His dress was that of the typical Singapore businessman: white shirt, tie, and slacks. His voice and accent were very much like Trippet's and when he smiled, which he did often, I couldn't help but feel that he enjoyed doing whatever he did.

The secretary served the tea and Lim kept the ceremony to a minimum. After his first or second sip, he leaned forward in his chair, offered me a Lucky Strike which I accepted, and lit it for me with a silver desk lighter.

"American cigarettes are one of my vices," he said. "It always make me feel rather relieved when I find someone else who still smokes. So many of my friends and acquaintances have quit."

"They are probably wise."

"No doubt," he said and smiled again. "But one of the keenest pleasures in life is to succumb to one's vices."

I smiled at that and sipped my tea. "Dickie's letter says that you are here on a confidential matter," he said.

"Yes," I said. "I'm looking for someone. An American."

"May I inquire whom he might be?"

"A man named Angelo Sacchetti."

"Yes," Lim said in noncommittal voice, drummed his fingers on the desk, and peered at me over his spectacles.

"By that I take it that you may know him," I said.

"No, I don't know him. Let us just say that I've heard of him. He——" Lim broke off and turned around in his chair to take a look at the harbor. He enjoyed the view for a few moments before he spun around and spoke. "Mr. Cauthorne, please excuse what you may consider to be my rudeness, but you are not with the CIA or one of those other intelligence organizations that the Americans and the British seem to be so fond of creating?"

"No," I said. "I'm not with the CIA."

There was a pause and Lim swung his chair around so that he could count the ships in the harbor. "I'm sure that Dickie would not have provided a letter of introduction if you were, but still I had to make sure."

"Maybe the letter's a fake."

Lim swung back again and gave me another smile. "No," he said, "after you telephoned yesterday, I called Dickie in Los Angeles. You are who you say you are. More tea?"

"Please. It seems strange that a businessman would

go to all that trouble, but then I'd say that you are more than just a businessman."

"Yes, it does seem that way doesn't it?" Lim said as he poured my tea.

I decided that if Lim had something that he wanted to tell me, he would, so we sipped our tea and looked at each other over the rims of our cups until Lim made up his mind about what he wanted to talk about next.

"We are a small nation, Mr. Cauthorne. A tiny one of only two million persons and seventy-five percent of us are Chinese. We have great wealth here and also great poverty, although it is not nearly as severe as it is in other Asian countries. Next to Japan, I suppose, Singapore is better off than any other country. Asian, that is. We are southeast Asia's major entrepôt, or at least we like to think so and our economy rests primarily on this international trade, although we are making some progress in industrialization. Still, we have neither the time nor the money to engage in the full-time business of espionage. But we are curious about persons who come to Singapore and take up residence here. Not that we don't welcome foreign capital—from virtually anyplace—but still we are, shall we say, rather curious."

Lim paused and smiled again. "I suppose one could say that I am Singapore's secret service."

"Then it doesn't seem to be much of a secret."

"Oh, it isn't. It isn't at all. Everyone knows it and sometimes we all joke about it. But someone had to do it and the Prime Minister decided that I was the one."

"Why you?"

"Because, I would say, I can afford it."

I took a deep breath. "I beg your pardon, Mr. Lim, but does this bring us any closer to Angelo Sacchetti?"

He nodded. "Indeed it does. I became interested in Mr. Sacchetti when he turned up here a year and a half ago after he had drowned in our harbor." Lim reached into his desk and brought out a manila folder and flipped through it. "I believe you were involved in that so-called accident, Mr. Cauthorne?"

"You know I was."

"Yes. There's a report on it here and then Dickie refreshed my memory when I spoke to him last night. Refreshed my memory! My word, I'm beginning to sound like a policeman or a spy or something equally sinister."

"What about Sacchetti?" I said.

"He turned up here, back from the dead, as it were, a year and a half ago. He arrived on a flight from Hong Kong and his perfectly valid passport indicated that he had spent some time in the Philippines. Cebu City, I believe. Yes, here it is in the file." Lim moved his finger down the page of the file he held before him. "He opened a rather large account with a draft from a Swiss bank, rented a luxurious apartment, and proceeded to become quite social."

"Then what?"

"Then a most curious thing happened. It seems that almost everyone in Singapore began to select a combination of three numbers and wager small sums that this number would turn up the following day as the last three digits on the totalizators either at the Singapore Turf Club or the race courses in Malaya or even in Hong Kong."

"Totalizators?" I said.

"Yes," Lim said. "I believe you call them pari-mutuel machines in the U.S."

"I believe we do."

"Well, up until then our gambling (and we Chinese are incurable gamblers) had been dominated by our so-called secret societies. At last count, I think there were about three hundred fifty of them. They not only ran the gambling, but also prostitution, what's left of the opium trade, most of the smuggling, and just about everything else that might be described as illegal—even a bit of piracy."

"You said up until then."

"Yes, I did," Lim said. "It seems that these small bets on the combination of race course digits are now being collected by hitherto unemployed youngsters, juvenile delinquents, I think one could call them, who have banded together in packs and describe themselves

115

as the Billy the Kid Gang or the Yankee Boys or even Hell's Angels."

"We try to spread our culture around."

Lim smiled. "The films do it: that and television. At any rate, our Criminal Investigation Department has got onto it and they've found that an extraordinary amount of money is being collected daily by these youngsters."

"How much?" I asked.

"Around one hundred thousand dollars a day."

"That's about thirty-three thousand, American."

"Yes."

"Are there payoffs?"

"I beg your pardon," Lim said.

"Does anyone ever win?"

"Oh, to be sure. People win every day."

"What are the odds?"

Lim turned to his file again. "I'll have to look it up. Yes, here it is. The payoff, as you call it, is four hundred to one."

"That's low," I said.

"How?"

"The real odds are about six hundred to one. Whoever's running it is skimming about two hundred dollars off the top of each hit."

"Interesting," Lim murmured. "I'll make a note of that." And he did.

"Let me guess," I said. "You found that the numbers racket was set up by Angelo Sacchetti."

Lim nodded. "Yes, and he has it quite well organized. Not only that, but he's gone into several other activities. For instance, if a merchant doesn't pay a certain weekly sum, he finds his establishment vandalized."

"What about your secret societies? Don't they resent an outsider moving in?"

The Lucky Strikes were offered again by Lim and once again I accepted one because it made him feel better. "At first," he said. "Then there were a couple of mysterious deaths and the societies' opposition

116

seemed to diminish. Considerably. The deaths were, I believe, most painful."

"Why don't you just throw him out?" I said.

"Sacchetti?"

"Yes."

Lim inhaled his cigarette and blew out a thin stream of smoke. "I'm afraid, Mr. Cauthorne, that it's not as simple as that."

"Why? He's a foreigner. Just don't renew his visa."

"Yes, he is a foreigner, but Mr. Sacchetti married just after he arrived here."

"So I heard."

"Did you hear whom he married?"

"No."

"It was the daughter of one of our leading citizens who is quite active in politics. He has used his considerable influence to prevent any move being made against his new son-in-law."

"What was it, love at first sight?"

Lim shook his head slowly. "No, I don't believe so. I understand that Mr. Sacchetti paid a little over three hundred thousand American dollars for the hand of his bride."

CHAPTER XIII

Lim told me the rest of it. After Angelo Sacchetti came back from the dead, via Cebu City and Hong Kong, he gave what amounted to a marathon party that lasted for almost a month. It went on night and day in his fashionable apartment, an open house for friends who brought friends who, in turn, brought their friends and eventually Sacchetti met the persons that he wanted to meet, the minor politicians who might be bought and the hard cases who were not at all averse to expanding their activities if there were prospect of a tidy profit. Sacchetti simply showed them how to make it faster.

He also made a few enemies along the way, but opposition melted after two of his more intransigent opponents were found, floating face-down in the Singapore River. The secret societies, badly fragmented, backed Sacchetti as long as he didn't interfere with their normal graft and as long as they received a cut from the proceeds. The only real opposition was the Singapore government and Sacchetti fixed that by marrying the youngest daughter of Toh Kin Pui, a politician who had a large and extremely left-wing following, and who just happened to be down on his luck at the time.

"Mr. Toh now espouses his rather China-oriented political philosophy from the back seat of a handsome Rolls-Royce which his son-in-law gave him for his birthday," Lim said. "Although we can't prove it, we strongly suspect that a percentage of Mr. Sacchetti's profits are being channeled into his father-in-law's political war chest. By now, I rather think that the chest is almost full."

"What will he do with it—buy votes?"

Lim shook his head. "No, there's no election for another four years and the Prime Minister's party now controls every seat in Parliament—fifty-one out of fifty-one, a most regrettable situation."

"Why?"

"You need some opposition, you know. Otherwise your own politicians will have nothing to rail against. Suppose, for example, that your Democrats suddenly won every seat in your Congress."

"They'd fight with each other," I said.

"Exactly. That's why Toh is useful to the government. He provides a target, a whipping boy, and Lord knows one is needed."

"But he has no real power?" I said.

"Yes, Mr. Cauthorne, he has power. With the money he now controls he can launch a full-scale race riot whenever he chooses. That's the threat that Angelo Sacchetti's father-in-law holds over our government, and it's a gravely serious one. We simply cannot afford another riot at this time."

"You had one some time ago, as I recall."

"Two. Back in 1964." Lim shook his head and turned to stare at the ships in the harbor again. "We in Singapore like to pride ourselves on our multi-racial harmony. We like to think that despite the preponderance of Chinese we are Singaporeans first, and that all of us—Chinese, Malay, Indian, Pakistani, Eurasian and what have you—can live in harmony and peace. This is what we like to think, but in 1964 we had race riots—bad ones. The first started in July and another in September and thirty-five persons were killed, hundreds injured, and the property damage was enormous. The first riot began over a small incident: there was a Malay religious parade and a Malay spectator got into a fight with a Chinese policeman. In September, a Chinese trishaw operator was murdered. But I suppose I don't have to tell you how race riots start, Mr. Cauthorne. Your country has had its share."

"More than our share."

Lim spun around from his study of the harbor. "Then you realize what a powerful weapon the threat of a riot can be."

"A form of blackmail, isn't it?"

"One could call it that, I think. But the price we pay is far cheaper than a riot."

"Couldn't you get the U.S. Embassy to revoke his passport?"

"Sacchettti's?"

"Yes."

Lim shook his head again and closed the file on his desk. "Passports or citizenship don't mean very much to men like Angelo Sacchetti. If your government were to revoke it, he would acquire a new one the next day from another government that is in the business of selling them. I can name you four or five who would be most eager to supply him with any credentials that he might need. You see, Mr. Cauthorne, for a person without money, citizenship is most important. But for a person with virtually unlimited funds, and who is inclined to live outside or above the law, one country is very much like another. Although again I have no proof, I seriously doubt that Mr. Sacchetti ever intends to return to the United States. But I've talked enough. Now tell me, what is your interest in him? Your real interest, I mean."

"I thought I had killed him," I said. "It bothered me. It still does."

Lim looked at me searchingly and then smiled. It was a tight, thin smile, not his usual happy grin. "It's really a pity that you didn't. It would have saved everyone a great deal of bother."

"Everyone but me," I said.

"When did you learn that he was still alive?"

"Only a few days ago."

"Really?" Lim sounded surprised. "It's strange that your State Department didn't notify you."

"Not so strange, considering our State Department."

This time Lim smiled happily. "I hesitate to confess that I agree with you. But apparently you wish to find Sacchetti and see for yourself that he is alive and well."

"Just that he's alive," I said. "Do you have an idea where I can find him?"

Lim reached into his desk and brought out a pair of powerful-looking binoculars. "I can do better than that; I can show you where he lives—at least most of the time."

He rose and moved to the window where he gazed down at the harbor through the binoculars. I joined him and he pointed with his forefinger. "The rather large, white one with the raked stack."

He handed me the binoculars and I looked. It was a white yacht, not more than 150 feet long, that probably cost no more than a million or so. But then I hadn't priced 150-foot yachts lately. It rode nicely at anchor in the basin, and I could see some figures moving around its main deck, but the binoculars weren't strong enough for me to tell whether they were crew or passengers. I handed the glasses back to Lim.

"Nice," I said.

"Yes, isn't it? It formerly belonged to the Sultan of Brunei. Sacchetti bought it for a song, I understand."

"How much does a song bring in North Borneo?" I said.

"Around two million Singapore dollars. I believe it cost four originally."

"The Sultan hard up?"

"His oil reserves are playing out and I understand that he needed some ready cash."

"Mr. Lim," I said, extending my hand, "you have been most helpful. Thank you."

"Not at all, Mr. Cauthorne," he said as we shook hands. "Just one thing. As head of Singapore's Secret Service—" This time he did giggle. "I really should ask you what your plans are as far as Mr. Sacchetti is concerned. Just a matter of form, you understand."

I looked out at the yacht again. "I suppose I'll go calling."

"Would you like one of my staff to accompany you? When I say staff, please don't misunderstand. I have three good men and when they are not busy with their counter-espionage duties—if you'll pardon the term— and that's most of the time, they work here in the office. One is office manager, and the other two are accountants."

"I don't think so," I said. "But I appreciate the offer."

"The reason I made it is that Sacchetti's open house has long been over. He's not at all as social as he once was and I understand that unexpected callers are turned away, often in the most abrupt manner. On the other hand, a more or less official visit . . ." Lim made a slight gesture as his sentence trailed off.

"I understand what you're saying. But I'm sure Angelo will see an old friend—especially an old friend who once helped him die for a while."

I was looking for a cab in Raffles Place, not too far

from Change Alley, a kind of a joyous Thieves Market, when a four- or five-year-old Chevelle sedan that looked like a cab pulled over towards me. The driver slowed to three or four miles an hour and the passenger in the back seat rolled down a window. The closed car indicated air conditioning and I was just getting ready to say how happy I would be to share it with him when I saw the revolver pointing at me. A voice behind me said, "Watch it, buddy!" but he needn't have bothered. I was already dropping and the shove that I got may have helped. I hit on my right shoulder with my hands breaking the fall and my chin tucked down into my chest. I landed hard, but that was all right. I had landed hard lots of times before when the star was too hungover to try it. The revolver went off and something seemed to smack into the pavement beside me, but it may have been my imagination. I continued the roll and came up on my feet. There weren't any more shots and the cab, with the window rolled back up, was busy losing itself in the thick traffic. I brushed myself off while the pedestrians flowed around me on the sidewalk with only an occasional curious glance. No one said anything; no one yelled for the police; no one wanted to know whether I'd torn my slacks. But then they may have thought that the shot was a firecracker. Firecrackers go off night and day in Singapore and the citizens there, like every place else in the world, put a very high premium on personal involvement.

"You did that real nice," a voice said behind me. It was the same voice that had told me to watch it. I turned and saw a compact, deeply sunburned man who could have been either thirty-five or fifty-five. He wore a faded khaki shirt with officer epaulets, white duck trousers that were held up by a wide leather belt with a brass buckle, and grimy white tennis shoes, the kind that come up to the ankles.

"You give me the shove?" I said.

"You didn't really need it."

"I'm not so sure. An inch or two either way could have made a difference."

The man jammed his hands in his trouser pockets and squinted his green eyes up at the sun. "I was just heading across the square for a beer. You look as if you could use one."

"You're probably right."

We settled ourselves at a table in a bar that was air-conditioned, not too brightly lighted, and almost empty. The waiter brought us a couple of beers and then went back to his newspaper. The man in the khaki shirt ignored the glass and drank his out of the bottle, a long, gulping drink. When he finished he put the bottle back on the table and took out a flat tin of tobacco, some papers, and rolled himself a cigarette. He rolled it quickly, not concentrating on it, just doing it as automatically as I would if I were to shake one out of a pack. When he had the cigarette going, he squinted at me through the smoke and I noticed that the wrinkles at the corners of his eyes didn't disappear when he stopped squinting. I put his age at closer to fifty-five than thirty-five.

"I'm Colonel Nash," he said.

"Colonel in what?" I said and told him my name.

"The Philippine Guerrilla Army."

"That goes back a few years."

He shrugged. "If you don't like Colonel, you can call me Captain Nash."

"Of the Philippine Guerrilla Navy?"

"Of the *Wilfreda Maria.*"

"What's that?"

"A *kumpit.*"

"And a *kumpit* is a what?"

"It's an eight-ton ship. I bought it from a Moro pirate. I'm a smuggler."

"We all have to make a living," I said, "but I don't know if we have to be so explicit about how we do it."

Colonel or Captain Nash took another drink of beer from the bottle. "What the hell," he said, wiping his mouth with the back of his hand, "we're both Americans, aren't we?"

"You have me there."

"Anyhow, I don't smuggle anything into Singapore. I just sell stuff here."

"What?"

"Timber, mostly from Borneo, out of Tawau. I load up a cargo of copra in the Philippines, sell it in Tawau where I get a good price for it in U.S. dollars, take on a cargo of timber, and sell it here. They use it for plywood."

"When do you find time to do your smuggling?" I said.

"When I get back to the Philippines. I load up here with watches, cameras, sewing machines, English bikes, cigarettes, and whisky and then run it into either Leyte or Cebu."

"You ever get caught?" I said.

"Not any more. I've got four engines in the *Wilfreda Maria* now and she'll do thirty knots easy. I can always duck around in the Sulu Islands if things get too hot."

"Where do you live in the Philippines?" I said.

"Cebu City."

"For how long?"

"Twenty-five years. I was with the guerrillas from forty-two on and then I was liaison between the Americans and the guerrillas towards the end of the war."

"I knew a guy who was in Cebu City about two years ago," I said. "An American."

"What's his name?"

"Angelo Sacchetti."

Nash had his beer bottle halfway up to his mouth when I mentioned the name. He stopped, looked at me with green eyes that suddenly seemed wary, and said: "Friend of yours?"

"An acquaintance."

Nash took his interrupted drink of beer, a long, gurgling draught that emptied the bottle. "You looking for him?"

"In a way."

"Either you're looking for him or you're not."

"All right. I'm looking for him."

"Why?"

124

"A personal matter."

"I don't think he wants to see you," Nash said, and signaled for another beer.

"What makes you think so?"

Nash was silent until the waiter served the beer and returned to his newspaper. "Sacchetti dropped into Cebu City about two years ago and he didn't have a dime. Well, he may have had a couple of bucks, but he wasn't eating filets and his name wasn't Angelo Sacchetti then either."

"What was it?"

"Jerry Caldwell."

"How long was he there?"

"About three or four months. He looked me up with a proposition. Loan sharking. You know, borrow five pesos and pay back six. I told him I wasn't interested so he put the touch on me for a couple of thousand."

"Why you?"

"Hell, I was an American like him."

"Sorry. I forgot."

"So I loaned it to him and he loaned it out to a couple of gamblers. For one week. They were supposed to pay him back twenty-five hundred, but they didn't get around to it. Caldwell or Sacchetti didn't push them too hard, at least not for a couple of weeks. Then he went downtown and bought himself a baseball bat. You know what he did with that bat?"

"No, but I can guess."

"He got those two gamblers and broke their legs with it, that's what. They paid up real quick after that and I don't know of anybody else who borrowed from him who was late."

"Why did he leave?"

"Cebu? I don't know. He hung around the race track mostly. Gamblers were his best customers. Then one day he comes by my place. I wasn't home, but my old lady was and she told me he took out a roll the size of a cabbage and paid off the two thousand he owed me. Then he left town. Just like that. Disappeared. The next time I see him is about two or three months later. He's in the Hilton here with this good-

125

looking Chinese doll. I was supposed to meet a guy there but he hadn't showed up, so I go up to Caldwell and say: 'Hello, Jerry.' He just looks at me like this." Nash made his face go cold and blank. "Then he says, 'Sorry, mister, you've got the wrong party. The name is Sacchetti. Angelo Sacchetti.' So I said, 'Okay, Jerry, any way you want it.' Then he turned around and walked off. So later I checked him out with this guy I'm supposed to meet in the Hilton and this guy tells me that Sacchetti is the latest local power. He's in everything, even numbers. So I keep track of him."

"Why?" I said.

"Hell, why not? I gave him his start, didn't I? I knew him when and all that crap. So now he's married into society or whatever they call it here and he lives out in that yacht of his that he named *The Chicago Belle* and ain't that a hell of a name for a yacht?"

"He's probably just sentimental."

"I thought he was from L.A. At least that's what he told me. He also told me that he used to be in pictures, but I sure never saw him in any."

"He was in pictures," I said.

"Is that where you knew him, in L.A.?"

"That's right."

"And you're a friend of his?"

"Let's just say I know him."

Nash took another giant swallow of beer. "Well, it's like I said, I don't think he's too anxious to see you."

"What makes you think so?"

"The guy in the back of the taxi, the one that took a shot at you."

"What about him?"

"He works for Sacchetti."

I suppose I didn't have to say anything. It was all there in my face and I found that it took a conscious effort to close my mouth. Nash grinned at me.

"Not used to getting shot at, huh?"

"Not for real."

"Well, if you think it over and still want to find him, I'll run you out in my launch. You can get me at this number." He wrote something on a scrap of paper with a ballpoint pen and handed it to me.

"Why stick your neck out?" I said.

Nash waved his hand in a deprecatory gesture. "Hell, we're both Americans, aren't we?"

"Sorry," I said. "I almost forgot again."

CHAPTER XIV

I had just stripped off my clothes and was fiddling with the handles on the shower in the immense bath-cum-dressing-room that the Raffles provides its guests when I heard the knock. I wrapped a towel around my middle, went to the door, and asked who it was.

"Carla."

I opened the door. "Come on in. I was just about to take a shower. You can join me if you like."

She came into the room wearing another dress that I hadn't seen, a tan silk sheath that emphasized her figure through indirection. She sank into a chair, crossed her legs so that I couldn't miss anything interesting, and ran her eyes over me slowly as if reappraising a painting that had turned out to be more interesting than she had thought at first glance.

"You have good shoulders," she said. "And your stomach's nice and flat. I like flat stomachs. Most of the men I know have pots, even the young ones. They have that little roll that hangs over their belts and turns their pants tops down."

"They just need a new tailor to move the belt loops up."

"I thought you were going to knock on my door when you got back," she said.

"I wanted to smell nice for you."

"How sweet. Have you got anything to drink?"

"No, but you can order a bottle. Just ring that bell over there and the houseboy will bring it." I turned and headed for the bathroom again.

"Take your time," she said.

I was taking my time by letting the hot water beat down on the shoulder that had landed on the cement sidewalk when a hand reached in and tapped me on that same shoulder. Carla Lozupone pulled the heavy shower curtains aside and stepped into the bath. "I decided to take you up on the invitation," she said. I couldn't see any reason to scream so I put my arms around her and found her mouth hungry and her hands curious, then demanding. We left the shower running and made it to the bed where she looked up at me, ran her pink tongue over her lips, and said, "Say them to me."

"What?"

"The words."

So I said the words that I thought she wanted to hear, most of them with four letters, invented a few more, and her eyes glistened and her hands became more frantic and her mouth demanded everything. Afterwards she lay staring up at the ceiling as her hands ran over breasts and down to her thighs.

"You're as good as you look," she said. "Even better. I like it that way."

"What way?"

"In a hotel when it's casual and exciting and sensual. Like when it's with a stranger almost. But don't get any ideas, Cauthorne."

"About what?"

"About me."

"I was just going to comment that you're a pretty good lay. One of the best, in fact."

"We didn't do everything."

"No, I suppose we didn't."

She propped herself up on her left elbow and her right hand went exploring again. I noticed that the pout was gone and that her tongue was once more playing

128

around her lower lip. "Would you like to try everything?" she said.

"I don't see any reason why we shouldn't." And we did. At least there wasn't anything else that either of us could think of, and she had a rather fertile imagination.

After we were dressed and the houseboy had brought a bottle of Ballantine's, and some sandwiches and Carla was on her second drink, she looked at me and said, "Well?"

"Well, what?"

"Well, what happened?"

"You mean now that sex time's over let's get down to business."

"I take it when and where I want it, Eddie."

"Just like a hot bath, huh?"

"Did it mean any more to you than that?"

"No, I guess it didn't."

"Well, what did you find out?"

"Oh, that. I found out where Angelo lives. It wasn't hard. I could have asked the room clerk and saved a lot of time. Angelo's a rather prominent citizen now. He's also married, but you already knew that, didn't you, even before you left the states, so the excuse about stalling for your father was just another lie in what I feel must be a long series of them."

"All right," she said. "So I knew he was married. I still have to see him."

"Come off it, Carla. You've already seen him. You saw him last night after you left me. You told him that I was here and that I was looking for him and that I was going to see a man at ten o'clock this morning. You set me up, sweetheart, and when I came out of the building where I had my appointment, Angelo had somebody there to take a shot at me. It was more or less a friendly shot, just a warning. Nobody could have missed at that distance unless he was trying."

None of what I said caused her to spill her drink. Instead, she gave the fingernails on her left hand a careful study. Then she looked up at me and smiled as if I had just complimented her on the new way that she wore her hair.

"You know what Angelo did when I told him you were in Singapore?" she said. "He laughed. He thinks you're some kind of a joke. A none-too-funny one that he's heard before. I don't think he wants you around."

"I'm sure of it," I said.

"Then why stay?"

"Because I want to see him."

"Is that all?"

"That's enough."

She shook her head. "You're keeping it all very nice and cozy, aren't you? Angelo laughed until I told him that you were hooked up with his godfather. Then he quit laughing. Why did Uncle Charlie pick you as my babysitter, Cauthorne? Not just because he likes the dimple in your smile, although I've heard that he swings that way sometimes."

"I was available and I was anxious to see Angelo."

"No," she said. "There's something else. My Uncle Charlie wouldn't have gone outside if there weren't something else."

"Outside of what?"

"What do you think?" she said.

"I think you're clannish."

"I'm doing what I have to do."

"And getting me shot at is part of it."

"That's your hard times."

"You seem to have some of your own," I said.

"All right," she said. "I'll spell it out for you. Angelo has something that belongs to my father. I'm here to buy it back."

It all fell into place then. I could almost hear the click. Angelo was not only blackmailing Charles Cole for having furnished incriminating information about old friends and acquaintances to the proper authorities, he was also blackmailing Joe Lozupone with the letters or records or whatever it was that he had stolen from his godfather's safe. Angelo Sacchetti, I decided, must be making a great deal of money.

"Why you?" I said.

130

"Because there wasn't anyone else."

"You mean that there was no one else that your father could trust to make the payoff and not keep whatever it is that you're trying to buy back."

"That's right."

"How much?" I said.

"A million."

"Where do you keep it, in your cosmetic kit?"

"You're not funny, Cauthorne. It's in a Panama bank. They're better than the Swiss ones; they ask fewer questions. All I have to do is give Angelo a letter and he'll be a million dollars richer."

"Then it sounds simple. You could have done that last night, picked up whatever it is that he has, and caught the first plane out this morning."

"That was the plan."

"But something came up?"

"That's right," she said.

"Angelo wanted something else. More money, I'd say."

"No. He'll settle for a million."

"He will this time, but what about next time?"

"There won't be a next time," she said.

"If it's blackmail, there will be. Your father seems like an easy touch."

"My father," she said in a thin, hard voice, "is not easy about anything. And that's something that Angelo knows. He'll risk it this time; never again."

"Blackmailers are strange," I said. "Their victims make it simple for them and their greed is almost pathological, otherwise they wouldn't be blackmailers."

Carla stared at me. "My father gave me a message for Angelo. He made me memorize it. That wasn't hard to do because it was a simple message. I gave it to him last night."

"What was it?"

"It was, 'Once, I pay; twice, you're dead.' "

"As you say, it's simple."

"Angelo understood it."

"So everybody's happy."

"Everybody but Angelo. As I said, he wants something else."

"What?"

"He wants you out of Singapore."

"Why? I'm harmless."

"Angelo doesn't think so."

"What does he think?"

"He thinks you're in Charles Cole's pocket."

"And that bothers him?"

"It makes him nervous."

"Angelo was never nervous in his life."

Carla made an impatient gesture with her left hand. "All right, Cauthorne, we can sit here and have some more of this bright and brittle conversation, but it's beginning to drag. Angelo won't give me what I want until you're gone. I don't know the real reason why you want to see Angelo and I don't really care. I suspect that it's as he says, you're Charles Cole's heavy, either for money or because you have to. I don't care about that either. But if you are after Angelo, I mean really after him, either for your own reasons or because dear Uncle Charlie has you in some kind of a box, I strongly advise you to forget it. You see, if anything happens to Angelo, if he were to get shot or drowned or run over, then a copy of the information he has goes to Washington and my father goes to jail which really means that he goes to his grave because prison would kill him." She paused and stared at me again. "But not," she said, "before somebody killed you."

"You know, Carla, you're really rather good."

"At what?"

"At passing along secondhand threats. What's more, you seem to enjoy it. But I'm not at all interested in what you say that somebody else says that they're going to do to me because, first of all, you're a liar—a good one—but still a liar. And second, I'm in Singapore for one reason and that's to find Angelo Sacchetti."

"Why?"

"Because I owe him something."

132

"What?"

"I won't know until I've paid him."

"Angelo doesn't want to see you."

"I won't interfere with his plans for the weekend."

She rose and headed for the door, but turned just before she got there.

"You say you don't like secondhand messages, but I have one more for you. From Angelo."

"All right."

"He said you have three days. He said to tell you that. He said you would understand."

"What happens after three days?" I said.

She looked at me thoughtfully for several moments. "He didn't say. I asked him, but he didn't say. Not in so many words at least."

"What did he do?"

"He winked," she said. "That's all. He just winked."

CHAPTER XV

Despite its pretensions of multi-racial hegemony, Singapore remains essentially a Chinese city. Many of its citizens have realized only recently, as history goes, that they won't, after all, retire on their savings to a comfortable old age in Shanghai or Canton or Fukien Province or northern Kwangtung.

But these are the older Chinese and more than half of the population of what Somerset Maugham once called "the laughing city" is under twenty-one and has forgotten, or never knew, the old ties with the mainland whether it was China, Malaya or India.

However, old and young alike remember when their prime minister, the ebulient Mr. Lee, who sometimes talks of a third China, wept when he was forced to announce that Singapore was, almost overnight, because of racial and political conflict, no longer a part of the Malaysian Federation. It was then that the new republic emerged, untried and shaky, to find itself balancing alone on a political tightrope that stretched from east to west.

From what Lim Pang Sam had told me, the father-in-law of Angelo Sacchetti could make that tightrope vibrate dangerously because of his tight control over Singapore's militant far left elements who apparently were quite willing to start a race riot at a nod from the father-in-law, Toh Kin Pui. A prolonged riot among Chinese, Malays, and Indians could wreck Singapore's economy and crush its government. So, in essence, Angelo Sacchetti, who got his name from a box of noodles and whose father died young, with only Sonny from Chicago engraved on his tombstone if, indeed, there were one, now had the fix in at Singapore. And I had to agree with Lim Pang Sam. It seemed unlikely that Angelo Sacchetti would be heading back to the United States anytime soon.

Still there was hope for Singapore. A Lochinvar from the hills of Hollywood had arrived in town, equipped with a bad case of the shakes and the horrors. In addition, Lochinvar had the Republic's four-man secret service on his side, providing they weren't too busy totting up the books, and there was also a friendly smuggler standing by to lend assistance because, after all, he and Lochinvar were both Americans.

But it was an even richer scene than that, I thought. There was the nervous counselor for the mob, or whatever it was called, roaming through the empty rooms of his mansion on Foxhall Road and wondering if his years of playing the informer had finally caught up with him. There was Joe Lozupone, so alone and friendless and frightened that the only person he could trust to pay off his blackmailer was his daughter, the comely Carla, whose attitude towards sex might be described as comfortably casual, and finally, there was Sam Dangerfield of the FBI who after twenty-seven

134

years in the bureau, still seemed astonished that crime actually paid. I wondered what Dangerfield was doing that evening and I decided that he was probably drinking somebody else's whisky.

Perhaps richest of all was the deadline—the three days that I had to get out of town. I wondered why it was three days and not four or two, or even twenty-four hours. There seemed to be only one way to find out so I took a scrap of paper out of my pocket and called the telephone number that was on it.

A woman answered the phone and she had to shout over a Stones record that was blasting away in the background. She shouted "hallo" and I asked for Captain Nash.

"Who?"

"Nash. Captain Nash."

"Oh, you mean Snooky. Here, honey, it for you."

"Hello, Snooky," I said. "This is Cauthorne."

"I thought you might call."

"You mentioned that you had a launch."

"Well, it's not really a launch, it's more of a runabout."

"Will it get us out to *The Chicago Belle?*"

"Sure. You want to go tonight?"

"I thought I might."

"You got an invitation?"

"No."

"Uh-huh."

"What does that mean?" I said.

"Nothing. Just uh-huh. You on the expense account?"

"Isn't everybody?"

"Well, we're both Americans and all, but if you're on the expense account—"

"How about a hundred dollars?" I said.

"U.S.?"

"U.S."

"Tell you what," Nash said. "I'm in Chinatown. You take a cab to the corner of Southbridge Road and Gross Street. Then get a trishaw and tell him you want to go to Fat Annie's. He'll know where it is."

"All right. When?"

"Be here around eight o'clock and we'll eat something first."

"What's Fat Annie's, a restaurant?"

Nash chuckled. "It's a whorehouse, pal, what'd you expect?"

"A whorehouse," I said and hung up.

Singapore is never quiet really, and Chinatown, a square mile jammed with tiled-roofed buildings, seems to scream all night and all day. Packed into the mile are 100,000 persons and an old sweat who had been born in Shanghai in 1898 once told me that it reminded him more than anyplace else in the world of the China that he had known before the fall of the Chings in 1912. I suppose you can find anything you want in Singapore's Chinatown, from an opium den to what may be the last of the wandering minstrels who will sing you a plaintive love song from the Tang for a dime. There is not much privacy there; every square foot is constantly in use and sometimes it is rented by the hour to those in need of a nap. The colors can almost blind you, and foot-high Chinese characters in searing red and gold and violet tout the merits of fresh young puppy and year-old eggs.

My pedicab driver pumped me down Chin Chew Street, yelling at the pedestrians who cheerfully yelled back. The family wash, impaled on long bamboo poles, almost formed a canopy across the street and the hawkers poked whatever they were selling into my face. Four Samusis walked by, dressed in their blue blouses and pantaloons, tough, broad-shouldered women who belong to a sisterhood that shuns men and embraces hard, manual labor instead.

It was all there: the stalls selling red and white cakes and squid and rice and monkey; the key makers and the goldsmiths pounding away on their metal, sometimes in rhythm to the music, Chinese, American and English, that growled out of the never silent transistors; the stench of dirt and sweat mingled with the more subtle odors of crushed frangipani, sandalwood,

136

and charcoal fires, and always the sound of human voices endlessly calling to each other from balcony to street, and from street to unshuttered window.

Fat Annie's didn't look like much and I asked my human engine, a medium-sized Chinese who seemed to have lost most of his teeth, whether he was sure that he had the right place. He rolled his eyes as if to describe the thousand and one delights that awaited me inside so I paid a dollar for the quarter-hour ride, which was three or four times what I owed him, and pushed through an open red door into a small cubicle where an old woman sat on a low bench smoking a long-stemmed pipe.

"Captain Nash," I said.

She nodded and pointed her pipe at another door. I went through that into a larger room where there were some tables and chairs, no customers, a rattan bar in one corner with some bottles behind it, and what seemed to be a brand new National cash register on top of its left end. Next to the cash register was an abacus and a woman who sat quietly on a low, sturdy stool. The woman weighed at least three hundred pounds.

She watched me walk towards her with black eyes that had almost disappeared into the fat folds of her round face. "I'm looking for Captain Nash," I said.

"He's in the parlor through that door," she said and moved her head a half an inch towards a door to the left of the bar. It took her a while to move her head and even longer to get it back into place. Her voice was surprising, not just because of its American accent, but also because of its soft, even melodious tone.

"You from the States?" she asked.

"Los Angeles."

She nodded. "I thought so. That's why Snooky comes here, because I'm from the States."

"San Francisco?"

She laughed and her whole body jiggled like a three-hundred-pound bowl of vanilla pudding. "Not even close. I was born in Honolulu. You want a girl?

137

They're not all up yet, but I can promise you a nice young one."

"You must be Annie," I said.

"Not Annie, *Fat* Annie!" she said and roared out another laugh as she clapped her hands to her stomach and jiggled it mightily. When she was through laughing and jiggling she wiped her eyes with the back of her hand. "What about a girl? Make you a hell of a good price with a young tricky one seeing it's so early."

"Later maybe. Right now I have to see Nash."

"Like I said, through that door."

I went through the door and into what Fat Annie had called the parlor and found that her description was accurate. It was a medium-sized room filled with dark Victorian furniture and lighted with softly glowing lamps that sat on marble-topped tables whose legs were carved into whorls and clefts and curlicues. The floor was covered with a dark oriental rug and the pale green walls held gilt-framed nostalgic paintings of rural England. In the center of the room was a small table of dark wood that held a chess set. Bent over the pieces were Nash and a very young, very pretty Chinese girl dressed in a miniskirt. It apparently was Nash's move and he didn't seem too sure about what it should be.

"Hello, Cauthorne," Nash said without looking up. "Be with you in a moment."

He studied the chessboard and then moved a bishop. The girl shot her queen down the board and said: "Check and mate in two move."

Nash studied the board a few moments and then sighed and leaned back in his chair.

"That's three in a row," he said.

The girl held up four fingers. "Four in row. You owe me four dollah."

"All right, four," Nash said and took the money out of his shirt pocket and paid her. "You run along now, Betty Lou."

The girl rose gracefully, smiled at me, and left through the door that I had entered.

"Betty Lou?"

"It's close enough," Nash said.

"When can we leave?" I said.

"Let's eat first." He shouted something in Chinese and an old man dressed in a black blouse and black trousers shuffled in. Nash spoke again in Chinese and then handed over some money. The old man asked a question, Nash replied, and the man, who looked eighty, but may well have been forty-five, shuffled out.

"He'll pick it up along the street," Nash said.

"Where did you learn Chinese?" I said.

"I got a Chinese wife. Nothing's better, unless maybe a Japanese one, but I still don't like the Japs on account of I got to know them too well during the war. Mean bastards. But let's have a drink." He rose and crossed the room to a table where a bottle of whisky and some glasses stood. I started to say "fine," but I never got it out because the shakes hit, and Sacchetti started falling into the harbor again, and when I came out of it Nash stood in front of me, holding two drinks, and staring at me the way everyone stared at me, as if they were afraid they might miss something really interesting when I swallowed my tongue.

"Malaria?" he said. "If it is, its the goddamndest case I ever saw."

I found my handkerchief and dried my face and hands. My shirt was soaked. "It's not malaria," I said.

"Happen often?"

"Often enough."

He shook his head in what I assumed was sympathy and handed me a drink. "You feel up to going?"

"It won't happen again. At least not today."

We had the drink and some ten minutes later the old man was back with a tray full of food that he served on the small table. I could identify the rice, the noodles drenched with thick brown gravy, the strips of pork, and giant prawns. A couple of dishes were unfamiliar. We ate with chopsticks and considering my lack of practice, I got along well enough.

"What's this," I said as I picked up a morsel from a common bowl and chewed it thoughtfully. "Veal?"

Nash sampled a piece of the meat, frowned, shook

his head, and then tried another. "Puppy," he announced. "Good, isn't it?"

"Delicious," I said.

Nash's boat was a fairly new fiber glass speedster that was about fifteen feet long and powered by a large outboard engine. It was tied up at a crowded quay on Singapore River between two broadbeamed *tonkangs* with eyes the size of automobile tires painted on their bows to ward off evil spirits. At least, that's what Nash said. We went down the ten steps to the water's edge where Nash used his foot to wake a sleeping Indian who had a line to the runabout tied to a big toe.

"My watchman," he said.

"Where do you keep your *kumpit?*" I said.

"Out in the roads. One of these tonkangs will lighten my cargo tomorrow or the next day."

The watchman held the runabout while we climbed in. He then sprawled out on the bottom step and went to sleep again. Nash started the motor, backed us out into the river, and headed for the harbor and *The Chicago Belle.*

"What are you going to do when we get there?" he shouted above the engine.

"Ask to see Sacchetti."

He shook his head and then shrugged as if he had dealt with fools before. *The Chicago Belle* was riding at anchor about one hundred yards out into the basin and the closer we came, the larger she looked.

"She's a beauty, isn't she?" Nash yelled.

"I don't know that much about yachts."

"Built in Hong Kong, 1959," he yelled.

All I could tell about it, or her, was that she looked large, fast, and expensive. We came alongside where an accommodation ladder led down from the deck to a foot or so above the water. Nash tossed me a line and I made the runabout fast to the lowest step of the ladder. I stood up in the runabout and started to step onto the ladder when a blinding light from the deck hit me in the face and a voice asked: "What do you want, please?"

"My name's Cauthorne. I want to see Mr. Sacchetti."

"I knew it wasn't going to be simple," Nash said as I ducked my head and used a hand to shield my eyes from the glare of the searchlight.

"Mr. Sacchetti is not here," the voice said. "Please go."

"I'm coming aboard," I said and started up the steps.

The blinding light went out and I looked up. A tall, lean Chinese in a white shirt and dark slacks stood at the top of the steps, illuminated by the lights from the yacht. He looked familiar and I suppose he should have because the last time I had seen him he had been pointing a gun at me through the window of a taxicab on Raffles Place. He still had a gun, it was still pointed at me and it looked very much like the one that I had seen before.

CHAPTER XVI

There seemed to be only one thing to do so I did it. I moved up another step.

"You're crazy," Nash said.

"I know," I said.

"No more," the man at the head of the steps said.

"Tell Sacchetti that I want to see him," I said and stepped on to the next riser.

The man at the top of the steps called something in Chinese but he didn't turn his head to do it. A male voice answered in Chinese and the man at the top of the steps nodded slightly. "You wait there," he said to me and the revolver in his hand moved a little as if to underscore the suggestion.

"What did he say?" I asked Nash.

"He sent for somebody."

"Sacchetti?"

"I don't know," Nash said. "He didn't say, but I wouldn't take that next step if I was you."

It was a two-minute wait. I stood on the third step of the accommodation ladder, gripping its rail and staring at the Chinese at the top of the ladder who stared back as he aimed the revolver at what seemed to be the fourth button on my shirt. He didn't seem to feel that it would be a difficult shot.

The male voice that I'd heard before spoke again in Chinese and the man at the head of the steps replied. Then he waved his gun at me. "You come up," he said. "The other one, too."

"I'll just stay here and mind the boat," Nash said.

"You come," the man said and shifted the aim of his revolver so that it pointed down at Nash.

"All right," Nash said.

"He's convincing, isn't he?" I said as I started up the steps.

"For a hundred dollars I don't get shot at," Nash said.

At the top of the steps the man with the revolver stepped back. "Follow him," he said and gestured with the revolver at another man, a stocky Chinese with a crescent-shaped scar on his left cheek and a small automatic in his right hand. We followed the man with the automatic down a flight of stairs and along a corridor that was carpeted in dark grey. The walls looked as if they were paneled in teak and if the yacht had cost as much as I had been told, they probably were.

The man with the scar and the automatic stopped at a door and knocked. Then he opened it, waved at me with the automatic, and said: "Go in."

I went in, followed by Nash and the two Chinese. The cabin or saloon was larger than I had expected. There was a thick, dark red carpet on the floor or deck and the color was repeated in the silk drapes that covered the oblong portholes. The furniture was of a dark, almost purplish wood that was intricately carved and all of its arms and legs seemed to end in dragons' mouths and claws. At the far end of the room was a low table that held a silver tea service. She sat behind the table in one of two matched chairs that were large enough to serve as thrones in some minor kingdom. She sat, leaning slightly forward, her hands resting comfortably on the arms of the chair which were carved into the heads of two dragons who seemed to be snarling at each other about something. She wore a dark blue dress whose collar mounted high on a slim white throat and whose hem ended several inches above her knees. Two strands of pearls hung halfway to her waist. She wore her black hair piled high, perhaps to give her more height and to lengthen her delicate face which may have been a trifle round. But there was nothing delicate about her gaze which flicked over me, made a bleak assessment, rested briefly on Nash, seemed to discover some more shoddy goods, and then settled again on me.

"Who is your friend, Mr. Cauthorne?" she said.

"He speaks English," I said.

"I'm Captain Jack Nash."

"Captain of what?"

"The *Wilfreda Maria*," Nash said.

"I remember now," she said as if she wished that she hadn't. "My husband once spoke of you. I believe you're a smuggler of sorts."

"You're Mrs. Sacchetti?" I said.

"Yes, Mr. Cauthorne, I am."

"Where's your husband?"

"My husband is not here."

"Where is he?"

She was small, delicate, and almost perfectly proportioned. The voice that came out of her full, slightly lipsticked mouth was clear, musical, with no trace of sing-song, and sounded as if she either had been educated in England or had spent a lot of time there. "My husband," she said, "sent you a message today. He very much hoped that you would understand and accept its content."

143

"I got the message," I said, "but I still have to see Angelo."

"You really don't seem to understand, Mr. Cauthorne. My husband is not going to see you and I'm afraid that's quite final."

"That's it, pal. Let's go," Nash said.

"You should heed your friend's advice, Mr. Cauthorne."

"I'm here for two reasons. One is personal and the other is to give Angelo a message from his godfather."

"You can give me the message," she said. "I shall see that my husband gets it."

"All right," I said. "Angelo gave me three days to leave Singapore. You can tell him that his godfather has given him exactly the same time in which to return it."

"Return what?"

"What Angelo stole from him."

She laughed then. It was a light laugh that tinkled up and down the scale. "You are a ridiculous man, Mr. Cauthorne, and even a little pathetic. You try to force yourself aboard and then you make such melodramatic threats. I hope that there's more to your performance."

"There is," I said. "The rest of it is all about what happens to Angelo if he doesn't return what he stole."

"And what is supposed to happen?"

"There are three men sitting in a hotel room in Los Angeles waiting for a telegram. If your husband doesn't return his godfather's property to me in three days, then they won't receive the telegram and they'll catch the next plane to Singapore."

"These men are friends of yours?" she said.

"No. They've been hired by the godfather."

"To do what?"

"To kill Angelo Sacchetti."

It was step number one in the Dangerfield Plan and she laughed at it. I couldn't blame her. With two guns aimed at me, it didn't seem to amount to much of a threat. In fact, it didn't seem to amount to anything at all.

144

"My only regret," she said, "is that my husband is not here to watch your performance. He would be highly amused."

"It was no performance," I said. "I was just delivering a message."

"And now you've done it," she said.

"Yes."

She tapped a finger against the arm of the chair. "My husband thought that you might not heed his earlier message."

"You mean the one that came with the bullet?"

"If you like. In such an event, he gave me certain instructions. So it would seem, Mr. Cauthorne, that we both have our assignments."

"Let's go," I said to Nash.

She said something in Chinese and the two men with guns moved a step or two towards me. I backed up.

"My husband said that you might need to be convinced of the sincerity of his earlier messages. You will find these two gentlemen most persuasive."

"You're kidding," I said.

She rose and moved to the door. "No, I'm not kidding, Mr. Cauthorne. Nor am I quite sure how they will go about convincing you. I really don't care. Good night." She opened the door, turned to say something in Chinese to the two men, and then left.

"What was all that?" I said to Nash.

"You mean the Chinese?"

"Yes."

"She told them to mind the furniture," he said and backed toward a corner.

The tall, lean Chinese turned to Nash. "You," he said, "sit over there." Nash quickly sat in one of the heavy carved chairs.

"What are you going to do, just watch?" I said.

"Friend, I don't have much choice."

The stocky Chinese with the crescent-shaped scar tucked his automatic into the waistband of his slacks. The tall, lean one slipped his revolver into his hip pocket. I found that I had backed as far as I could. I stepped away from the wall and turned my left side to

145

the two men who moved in slowly, their arms low and extended before them.

The stocky one was first. He came in fast, his left hand extended with the knuckle of his middle finger sticking out in the proscribed method. He aimed at my throat and I caught his hand, found the nerve that I wanted between his thumb and forefinger, turned, pulled down, and let the weight of his body snap his arm. He yelled once and I kicked at his head but missed and caught him in the neck. The tall, lean Chinese was better. Much better. The edge of his right hand slammed into my jaw just below my right ear. I tried for the base of his nose with my left palm, but he ducked and I caught him on the forehead instead. He stumbled back and stepped on the broken left arm of the stocky man who lay on the floor. The stocky man screamed once and then seemed to faint. The tall, lean Chinese fumbled for his revolver and got it out of his hip pocket as I jabbed at his throat. He brought the gun down hard on my right shoulder and my arm went numb. I tried once more to jab his throat with my left hand, but the revolver came down again, this time on my neck. It may have come down several more times, but by then I was long past caring.

The Indian in the dirty white turban squatted on the fifth step that led down from the quay to the water and grinned at me with yellow teeth. He said: "Aaaah!" when he saw that my eyes were open.

I tried to sit up and the nausea hit. I vomited the puppy and the rest of the dinner I had eaten at Fat Annie's over the side of Nash's runabout. When I was through, I sank back on the bench-like seat. Somebody groaned and if I hadn't hurt so much, I would have felt sorry for him. Then I realized that it had been my groan and I was glad that I could feel sorry for myself.

Someone wiped my face with a wet cloth. I opened my eyes again and saw Nash bending over me, a fairly clean towel in his hand.

"How do you feel?" he said.

"God awful."

146

"You've been out for a half hour or more."

"What happened?"

"You got beat up."

"How bad?"

"He knew what he was doing. After he slugged you with the gun, you went down and he kicked you a few times. Twice in the stomach. Does it hurt?"

"It hurts."

"You damned near killed that other one."

"The short one?"

"You broke his arm."

"Good."

"Well, that made the tall one mad and he kicked you a couple of extra times on account of that."

"Then what?"

"Then he and I carried you up the stairs. He wouldn't help me get you down into the boat so I sort of had to bump you down the ladder."

"Nothing broken?"

"I don't think so. I checked you over and I don't think there's anything broken. He didn't kick you in the head so you probably don't have a concussion unless you got one when I bumped you down the ladder."

I sat up slowly and ran my hands over my face. My right arm ached, but I could move it. My stomach was a sharp separate pain that almost doubled me up when I tried to take a deep breath. He must have kicked me in the legs, too, because they felt as if someone had been jumping on them.

"I feel rotten," I said.

"You want a drink?" Nash asked.

"Have you got one?"

"Got some Scotch. Nothing to mix it with."

"Just hand me the bottle." I took a long drink of the Scotch. It went down and promptly came back up.

"That wasn't such a good idea," I said after I wiped off my face again with the towel.

"Maybe you'd better see a doctor," Nash said.

"I'll get one at the hotel."

Nash sent his watchman to find a trishaw. He was

back in ten minutes and both of them helped me up the steps of the quay. The watchman grinned at me again, skipped down the steps, tied the line from the boat to his toe, curled up and went back to sleep. I climbed into the trishaw with Nash's help.

"You can drop me off at Fat Annie's," he said. "Unless you want me to go with you to the hotel."

"No, I can make it okay. You've done enough." I reached into my pocket and found my wallet. I took out five twenties, thought about it, and added another one. "Here," I said. "I think you earned it."

Nash took the bills, folded them, and stuck them into his shirt pocket. "What was all that talk about Sacchetti and the stolen stuff and the three guys coming in from Los Angeles?"

"You really want to know?" I said.

He turned to look at me. "Come to think of it," he said. "I don't guess I do. But you want to know something? You were lucky."

"How?"

"Well, nothing's broken."

"That's why I'm lucky?"

"You're lucky about that," Nash said, "but you're even luckier that Sacchetti wasn't there."

"And if he had been?"

"Then there damn well sure would have been something broken."

CHAPTER XVII

I was awake when someone knocked on my door around eight o'clock the following morning. I was awake because my head ached, my stomach throbbed with each breath, there was a tightening vise on my right shoulder, and a large dump truck seemed to have rolled over my legs during the night.

The young Chinese doctor who clucked over me as he wound some tape around my ribs the night before had said: "You have a very low pain threshold, Mr. Cauthorne. What do you do for a living?"

"I'm a poet."

"Ah, then that explains it."

The knocking continued at the door and I yelled "all right" and started to get out of bed. I found that it wasn't something one did without careful pre-planning. Consultants should have been brought in. A committee should have been appointed to determine how to ease the sheet back. A seminar on how to place one's feet on the floor would have proved useful. Highly skilled technicians would have been invaluable in solving the problem of how to walk across the room and open the door.

He had on a different suit this time, a bottle green one that was turning slightly purple at the knees. He wore a cream straw hat with a faded blue band and a brim that rippled up and down as if it had been shoved too far back on the closet shelf when it was stored away at the end of last summer or the summer before. His shoes were an off white and the perforations in their toes attempted to resemble fleurs-de-lis without much success. He also wore a big smile on his face which still needed a shave. The face belonged to Dangerfield.

"Don't you ever sleep?" I said.

"You still hanging in there, Cauthorne?" he said as he brushed by me and into the room.

"By my thumbs."

"Where's the booze?"

I started the long journey back to the bed. "Over there," I said.

Dangerfield crossed to the bureau where the Scotch bottle rested, picked up a glass and poured his usual three fingers. He drank it down and for a moment I thought I was going to be sick.

149

"Hell of a long trip," he said and poured himself another drink.

"Aren't you a little off your usual route?" I said and eased myself back into the bed.

Dangerfield took off his hat and sailed it at the couch. The hat landed on the floor but he didn't seem to notice. "Got a cigarette?" he said and I motioned towards the bureau again. He found the pack, lit one, and settled into an armchair.

"You got a nice room," he said.

"Are you staying here?"

"I'm paying my own way, Cauthorne. I'm at the Strand up on Bencoolen Street. Six bucks a night, U.S."

"Why won't the Bureau pick up your tab?"

Dangerfield snorted. "I didn't even ask. I just put in for a couple of weeks annual leave, cashed in my savings bonds, and took off. I got a little worried about you."

"Why?"

"You don't look too good."

"I feel the same way."

"What happened?"

"The Dangerfield Plan happened," I said. "It's a wonderfully brilliant scheme, special agent."

"Okay; you're funny. What happened?"

"Sacchetti had someone take a shot at me yesterday morning. Last night he had someone beat me up when I dropped by to see him on his yacht."

"His what?"

"His yacht. *The Chicago Belle.* Only he wasn't there."

"Who was?"

"His wife and two of her friends. But don't worry; I got the message across. I told her about the three guys in Los Angeles."

"What else?" Dangerfield said.

"Well, there's Carla Lozupone."

"Where's she?"

"Across the hall, I guess."

"What about her?"

"She saw Angelo, she said. But she lies a lot."

"When?"

"Yesterday. She wanted to pay him a million dollars."

"Goddamn it, Cauthorne, tell it straight."

"Okay. Sacchetti is not only blackmailing Charles Cole, he's also blackmailing Joe Lozupone. The Lozupone girl flew here for one reason only. To pay off Sacchetti and to warn him that if he asks for another payment, he'll be dead. She said that Sacchetti went along except for one provision and that provision is that I get out of Singapore in seventy-two hours—forty-eight hours now, I guess. Then she gave me some more advice. She said that if I caused anything to happen to Sacchetti, her father would take a very dim view of it."

"What else did you find out?"

"Sacchetti's got the fix in here."

"How?"

"He married well."

"And his father-in-law's got the clout?"

"He has it."

I told him the rest of it then in chronological order from the time I left Los Angeles until he knocked at the door. I talked for almost half an hour and when I was through Dangerfield rose and started to pace the room. He paced silently for almost five minutes. Then he stopped and stood by the bed.

"Don't you ever get dressed?"

"Look, Dangerfield, we've only gone through phase one of your plan and it got me shot at and knocked silly. I'm just resting up for phase two. If my guess is right, that'll call for the water torture and the bamboo shoot that grows right up the ass."

"When are we going to eat?"

"Always to the point at hand; that's what I like about you. Just ring the bell over there and give your order to the man when he comes."

"You want something?" Dangerfield said.

"Coffee," I said. "Lots of coffee. But right now I'm going to get dressed. That's after I get out of bed.

Then I'm going to take a shower and if it still seems like a good idea, I'll brush my teeth, and after that, if I'm still conscious, I might even shave. So you see I haven't been idle. I have the entire morning planned."

Dangerfield went over to ring the bell for room service. "You sure they didn't hit you on the head?"

"The only thing I'm sure of," I said, "is my wild anticipation of events yet to come."

"What's that supposed to mean?"

"Such as phase two of the Dangerfield Plan and how we put it into operation."

"Simple," Dangerfield said and borrowed another cigarette from my pack. "We tell Angelo what I told you we'd tell him."

"We?"

"You get in trouble, Cauthorne. You need a chaperone."

"I won't argue that. But where do we find Sacchetti if he doesn't want to be found?"

"He lives on that yacht, doesn't he?"

"So I understand."

"Then we go out to the yacht."

I was sitting on the edge of the bed by then. Another hour or so and I'd make it into the bathroom. "All right," I said. "We go out to the yacht. They don't like visitors out there, but we go anyway. What makes you think they'll let us aboard?"

Dangerfield sighed and then yawned. "Sometimes, Cauthorne, I think you've got shit for brains. He knows about the three guys and the telegram. You told his wife about that, right?"

"Right."

"He won't believe it. But he'll want to know *why* we *want* him to believe it."

"So he'll see us?"

Dangerfield cast an exasperated glance at the ceiling. "I swear to God they must have hit you on the head last night."

It took me a while in the bathroom. The shower drove needles into my back and the razor seemed to weigh ten pounds. When I finally came out Dangerfield looked up from the remains of what seemed to have been an immense breakfast.

"You look real pretty," he said. "Clean, too. I signed your name to the bill."

"With a little more practice, you can sign my checks. Any coffee left?"

"Plenty."

The telephone rang and I crossed over to answer it. When the voice said "Mr. Cauthorne?" I recognized it immediately. It belonged to Mrs. Angelo Sacchetti, and she didn't bother to identify herself.

"I gave my husband your message," she said.

"I got his after you left last night. It was just as you promised: most sincere."

That didn't seem to require any comment from her. "My husband has changed his mind, Mr. Cauthorne. He would like to see you as quickly as possible."

"This morning?"

"If possible."

"It is," I said. "Where?"

"At my father's house; it's more convenient than the yacht."

"All right. What's the address?"

She told me and we set the time for eleven o'clock. After I hung up the phone, I turned to Dangerfield who was pouring himself another drink.

"That was Sacchetti's wife," I said.

"He wants to see us, right?"

"Right."

"The Dangerfield Plan," he said with a contented smile. "It seems to be working out just fine."

After Dangerfield borrowed my razor and poured himself another drink we caught a cab at the hotel and headed out Orchard Road past the Instana Negara Singapura.

"Who the Christ lives there?" Dangerfield said.

"It used to be the residence of the British governors, but now it's home to Singapore's president."

"That's not this guy Lee, is it?"

"No. He's the prime minister. The president is Inche Yusof bin Ishak."

"How do you remember all that?"

"I like foreign names."

"That's some lawn," he said.

Another mile or so and the driver turned around and said, "This is Tiger Balm King's house. Over there."

It was a huge, white, two-story house that featured round Moorish turrets on either end and some Corinthian pillars to hold up the roof. It perhaps was the most flamboyant mish-mash of architecture that one could hope to see. On top of the roof were two-foot-high letters that read: "Tiger Balm House of Jade."

"What's Tiger Balm?" Dangerfield asked.

"It was very powerful medicine that was manufactured by Aw Boon Haw," the driver said as he nipped past a Honda. "He made many millions of dollars. Then he bought newspapers and when he died they turn his house into a museum."

"Why is it called 'House of Jade'?" I said.

"Over one thousand pieces of jade inside. Very, very valuable. Very ancient, too."

The house of Angelo Sacchetti's father-in-law, Toh Kin Pui, was about a mile and a half past the patent medicine king's mansion and located in the Tanglin residential section which, the driver informed us, featured more millionaires per square mile than anyplace else in the world. He may have exaggerated, but the neighborhood looked as if it were trying to live up to the reputation. Toh's house, set well back from the road, was a rambling white two-story stucco structure with a red tile roof and a five-sided cupola that stuck up an extra story for no apparent reason at all except that the architect may have thought that it would lend a nice touch. The lawn was smooth and green and well-tended, and flowers bloomed everywhere. The asphalt drive curved up to a covered verandah across from which a fountain played lazily into a rocked-in pool. A Rolls-Royce Phantom V limousine was parked in the driveway and a chauffeur was running a dust cloth over its antelope brown finish. I don't know why he bothered because it looked as if it were going to rain.

I paid the driver and Dangerfield followed me up the three steps of the verandah. I pushed a button and I suppose that a bell rang somewhere in the house because the door was opened almost immediately by a Chinese man in a white jacket.

"I'm Mr. Cauthorne," I said. "Mrs. Sacchetti is expecting me."

We followed the man in the white jacket down a hall and despite the air conditioning the palms of my hands began to sweat and I felt drops of perspiration form in my armpits and trickle down my sides. I held out my right hand to admire its quiver. The pain came in short stabs with every step and breath, but the pain didn't cause the tremor or the perspiration. That came from my obsession, which was finding Angelo Sacchetti so that I could collect whatever it was that he owed me. The end of my obsession, I thought, lay just behind the door that the man in the white coat opened.

I went through the door first with Dangerfield following. "Don't be so eager, pal," he said. "He's not going to run away."

It was a living room and the furniture was ordinary, impersonal and utilitarian. There were a couple of sofas, some armchairs, a rug on the floor, and some pictures on the wall.

Several tables held vases filled with flowers, the only bright spots in the room. Angelo Sacchetti's wife sat in one of the armchairs, much as she had sat the night before, leaning slightly forward, her hands resting on the chair's arms, her knees together and her feet crossed at the ankles, as if it were a lesson she had learned in finishing school and she wanted to demonstrate how well she remembered it. A middle-aged Chinese in a white shirt and dark slacks, the island's universal business uniform, rose as we entered.

"Mr. Cauthorne, this is my father, Mr. Toh."

He bowed slightly, but did not offer to shake hands.

"My associate, Mr. Dangerfield," I said. "Mrs. Sacchetti and Mr. Toh."

Dangerfield wasn't much for formalities. "Where's your husband, Mrs. Sacchetti?"

She ignored him and directed her next remark at me. "You didn't mention that you were bringing an associate, Mr. Cauthorne."

"No, I didn't, did I? But Mr. Dangerfield has a rather personal interest in this matter. In fact, his interest runs almost as deep as mine."

"In what matter?"

"The matter of stolen property," I said. "I mentioned it last night. As soon as Angelo arrives, we can discuss it in detail."

"I'm afraid that you are going to be disappointed," Toh said in a curiously deep and resonant voice.

"Why?"

"Because, Mr. Cauthorne," Mrs. Sacchetti said as if mentioning her plans for next Tuesday's bridge game, "the police are looking for him."

"Why?" I said again.

"There was a murder last night. A woman was killed and the police say that they have found evidence that my husband committed the murder. Ridiculous, of course." Even then there was no emotion in her voice.

"And Angelo ran?" Dangerfield said.

"Not ran, Mr. Dangerfield," Toh said. "He simply thought it best to become incommunicado until he could clear the matter up to everyone's satisfaction."

"Who was the woman?" I said, but I didn't really have to ask.

"An American, I believe," Angelo Sacchetti's wife said. "Her name was Carla Lozupone."

CHAPTER XVIII

They found Carla Lozupone's body a long way from the Raffles Hotel. It had been dumped beside a road on the east coast of the island near Geylang, not far from a Malay *kampong* or village. She had been strangled with a cord or a rope and there was nothing to identify her, only a wallet that contained an American passport, an expired California driver's license, a Social Security card, and 176 Singapore dollars. The wallet was clutched in Carla Lozupone's right hand and the police had been forced to pry the fingers open. The name on the passport, the license, and the Social Security card was Angelo Sacchetti.

An early-rising Malay fisherman had stumbled across the body. He immediately summoned his neighbors from their thatched huts in the *kampong* and all of them, men, women and children, had squatted around the dead girl and palavered for a long time about what should be done. Finally, they dispatched a youth on a bicycle to find a policeman. He couldn't find one at first and it was not until well after nine in the morning that members of Singapore's Criminal Investigation Department arrived. It took another hour for them to check the major hotels and discover, through the help of a Raffles room clerk, that the dead girl was Carla Lozupone.

Dangerfield took over after Sacchetti's wife told us that Carla Lozupone was dead. His questions were direct, logical and curiously compelling and I decided that he was very good at his job. We learned most of the details later because Mrs. Sacchetti and her father didn't know much, other than that Carla Lozupone had been murdered and the police were looking for Angelo. Toh had his informants in the Singapore police and they had tipped him off that Angelo was the prime suspect. The tip came twenty minutes before the police arrived, but it seemed to have been plenty of time for Sacchetti to vanish.

"Where is he now?" Dangerfield asked.

"I don't know," Mrs. Sacchetti said. "I assume that he will be in touch with me."

"Do you know what time the police think that the girl was killed?"

"I don't know that either."

"Did they ask where your husband was last night?"

"Yes."

"What did you say?"

"That he was with me, on the yacht."

"Did they believe you?"

"No."

"Why?"

"Because they had already been to the yacht to question the crew."

"And the crew said that he hadn't been there?"

"Yes."

"All night?"

"Yes."

"Where was he?"

"I don't know. He had a business appointment last night. If it ran late, he probably stayed in the city. We have a *pied-à-terre* that he often uses."

"A what?"

"An apartment."

"Where did you first see Angelo today?"

"Here."

"When did he first get in touch with you?"

"Early this morning, by radio-telephone to the yacht."

"What did you talk about?"

"About Mr. Cauthorne. And what Mr. Cauthorne said last night."

"He didn't mention that his wallet was missing?"

"No."

158

"Why?"

"I don't know."

"What did he say about Cauthorne?"

"He said he wanted to see him. This morning. I suggested that we meet here and he agreed."

"The Lozupone girl saw your husband the day before yesterday," Dangerfield said. "She told Cauthorne that she did. You knew she saw him, didn't you?"

Toh stirred in his chair. "My daughter has answered enough of your questions," he said in his deep voice. "She will answer no more."

"Yes she will," Dangerfield said, turning to me. "Got a cigarette?" I handed him the pack and he shook one out and lighted it with a match from a folder. He looked around for an ashtray but couldn't find one so he stuck the used match behind the ones still in the folder.

Toh rose. "Since my son-in-law is not here, I suggest that there is no point to this conversation. It is a police matter and you, Mr. Dangerfield, are not of the police. At least, not of the Singapore police."

"Sit down," Dangerfield said. "We've got a long way to go."

"I'm sorry, but you leave me no choice," Toh said. He started towards the door.

"I said sit down," Dangerfield said and there was a hard edge to his voice that I hadn't heard before. Toh paused at the door. He stared thoughtfully at Dangerfield for several moments and then said, "Why?" and the way he said it indicated that there had better be a very good answer.

"Because your son-in-law has something that I want and unless I get it I'm going to the police with the information about why Carla Lozupone saw Angelo yesterday."

Toh turned from the door and crossed to an armchair. He sat down in it slowly. "What information?" he said softly.

"That Angelo was blackmailing Carla Lozupone's father and that she was carrying around a letter that would allow Angelo, or anyone else, to get his hands on one million U.S. dollars in a Panama bank, no questions asked. I think the police would be very interested in that letter."

Mrs. Sacchetti exchanged a glance with her father. Toh nodded slightly and I assumed that they had some private method of communicating. A lifted eyebrow might mean that cook had given notice again while Toh's nod perhaps served to inform his daughter that rain had cancelled the party rally at the culture center.

Regardless of how they managed it, the communication was there and Mrs. Sacchetti picked it up quickly enough. "What do you mean 'or anyone else,' Mr. Dangerfield?"

"Just that," Dangerfield said. "The letter was just like bearer bonds. Whoever has it collects the kitty—one million dollars' worth. The Panama banks adopted the system several years ago and it's a convenient way to transfer big sums anonymously. And it's also the best motive around for the death of the Lozupone girl."

"Why should my husband—"

Dangerfield interrupted her with an impatient wave of his cigarette and dropped some ashes on the rug. "You mean why should he kill her if he was going to get the letter anyway once Cauthorne here left town?"

Again the wife of Angelo Sacchetti glanced at her father and again he nodded slightly. "You have made an excellent point," she said.

"Then you knew about the letter?"

"I didn't know it was transferable."

"Whoever killed the girl knew."

"What you're saying, Mr. Dangerfield," Toh said, rolling his tones up from deep in his stomach, "is that whoever killed the young woman took the letter and then planted evidence to make it appear that my son-in-law murdered her?"

"You're right. That's what I'm saying. But it's not much help to Angelo, is it? I mean he's not going to the local cops and say, 'Look, I was blackmailing this guy in the States, but somebody else killed his daughter and then framed me for the job.' He's not going to say that, is he?"

Neither Toh nor his daughter said anything. They continued to stare at Dangerfield who looked around for something to put out his cigarette in. He spotted a dish on a table, rose and ground the butt into it. It didn't look like an ashtray to me. He turned to Mrs. Sacchetti again who sat in the chair, her back straight, her feet firmly on the floor, motionless except for her eyes which followed Dangerfield around.

"I bet I can tell you what Sacchetti's doing right now," Dangerfield said. "I bet he's finding himself two or three witnesses who are going to account for every minute of his time yesterday and last night. And I also bet that he's going to find two more who'll swear that his wallet was lost or stolen last week or the week before. And for all I know, maybe it was. So maybe he'll clear himself of the girl's murder. I don't know. I don't even care. All I'm interested in is one thing and that's the stuff that he was using to blackmail Joe Lozupone with and I have an idea that when I walk out of this house it's going to be in my hip pocket."

Toh's deep, bass voice rumbled again. "Your theories are most fanciful, Mr. Dangerfield, and your threats are equally empty."

Dangerfield laughed. It was a harsh laugh that had a sharp bite to it. "You like this house, don't you, friend, and you like that Rolls that's parked out in front, and from what Cauthorne here tells me, you like the money that Angelo cuts you in on every month. I hear you weren't doing too well before Angelo appeared on the scene. I mean there was no house and no car and no yacht and no money. All you had was a certain amount of political muscle which was hard to cash in on until Angelo showed you how. Well, it takes money, real money, to get an operation like Angelo's running." He paused and turned to me. "Give me another cigarette." I gave him one and he lit it and dropped the match on the rug this time.

"Now Angelo's in trouble, bad trouble. It's going to take him a while to get out of it, if he ever does. And what happens to the operation when he's not around? I don't think it's going to run itself. So when he gets clear of the murder charge—if he ever does—then he's going to need money. Lots of it. And if he doesn't get clear of the rap, he's going to need it even worse. And there's only one place he can get it and that's from Godfather Cole. You know about Angelo and his godfather, don't you?"

Once again father and daughter exchanged glances and nods and raised eyebrows and this time the daughter spoke. "We are familiar with my husband's operations, Mr. Dangerfield." She paused for a moment. "All of them; there are no secrets."

"Now that's just fine," Dangerfield said. "Because you're going to have to make a decision in about two minutes and it's going to be a decision that you can't check with Angelo so I sure hope that you've got the sense to make the right one."

"What decision?" Toh said.

"If I don't get that stuff on Joe Lozupone, then I'm going to cut off Angelo's source of money."

"I don't believe you," the woman said.

I sat there and watched Dangerfield operate and I was glad that it was them and not me. He ran a hand over his large white dome, brushed a few thick strands of hair into place, and grinned at Mrs. Sacchetti.

"Well, I'm going to tell you what I'm going to do unless I get that stuff, and then you can make up your mind about believing me. Unless I get the information that Angelo's been using on Lozupone, I'm going to get word to Joe Lozupone that Charles Cole has been an FBI informer for years. Now once I get that word to Joe, Charles Cole is going to have about two days of living left and Angelo's going to have a hell of a hard time blackmailing a dead man."

It was the Dangerfield Plan, the one that the rumpled man with the red bulb of a nose had thought up in the hotel in Washington, and its merit lay in its implacable simplicity. It didn't take Toh long to decide. "Get it," he said.

"How do we know—" she started to say, but her father interrupted. "Get it," he said again. The woman rose and crossed to an indifferent oil painting of Singapore's harbor. The sky was too blue and the sea was too green. She swung the painting open and there was a small safe. She spun the dial on the combination, opened the safe, and took out a small yellow box, not as large as a cigarette package. She closed the safe, spun the dial on the combination, and swung the painting back into place. She crossed the room to her father and handed the yellow cardboard box to him.

"Microfilm," Dangerfield said.

"Yes, microfilm," Toh said.

"I suppose there are other copies," Dangerfield said.

"But it doesn't matter, does it?" Toh said.

"Not really. Not to me, anyhow, and very soon it won't matter to anyone."

"I take it, Mr. Dangerfield, that you are some sort of a policeman."

"It shows that much, huh?"

"It's quite evident. And I also take it that you will use this information," and Toh made a slight gesture with the yellow box, "to indict this Lozupone person."

"What do you care what I do with it?" Dangerfield said.

Toh smiled for the first time since we had arrived. "You have a curious mind, a cunning one, even devious. Such a mind could easily find other uses for such information."

"What you're saying is that I might use it to black-mail Lozupone; that I might cut myself in on all the money we've been talking about."

"That occurred to me," Toh said.

"Do you really care?"

"Not really. I just want to make sure that Mr. Cole will continue to have a source of income. Some of the funds that he has transferred to my son-in-law have gone for most worthwhile causes."

"I don't want anything to happen to Charlie Cole," Dangerfield said.

"But you do want something to happen to the Lozupone person. You want it to happen so badly that you would sacrifice Cole, if necessary."

"That's right," Dangerfield said. "Now you can give me the box."

I rose and walked over to Toh and took the box out of his hand and put it into the pocket of my slacks. "I'll keep it, Sam."

Dangerfield was on his feet. "What do you mean, you'll keep it?"

"Just what I said. I'll keep it. I need some insurance."

"Look, kid, give me the—"

"Shut up," I said. "I've been sitting here for half an hour listening to you three. You've made your deal and everyone's happy. Sacchetti can keep the money coming in from Cole, and Toh can keep on making the payments on his house and buy gasoline for the Rolls, and beer for the Singapore version of the Red Guard. You're happy to trade the evidence on Lozupone for that, aren't you, Toh? And what about Dangerfield? He got what he came for, what he sent me for. The Dangerfield Plan worked, didn't it, Sam, and now you're happy. In fact, everybody's happy but me."

"Okay, kid, what do you want? Your fifty thousand from Cole?"

"What I came for. I want to see Angelo."

"What the hell difference would it make?" Dangerfield said. "Just because you get the nasties every night when Angelo falls overboard and gives you the big wink. You think just seeing him's going to cure that? You're crazier than I thought, Cauthorne."

"You're forgetting one thing," I said.

Dangerfield shook his head. "You're really nuts, kid."

"You're forgetting that I was supposed to look after Carla, but now she's dead, and I don't think her father's going to be too happy with me."

"Give me the box and I'll put him away so quick he won't have a chance to be unhappy," Dangerfield said.

Toh rose and faced Dangerfield. "I think that this discussion no longer concerns either my daughter or me. If you gentlemen will excuse us, I will have my driver take you back to your hotel."

"I'm sorry but it does concern you," I said. "I keep the box until I see Angelo. That's part of the price. Dangerfield just forgot to mention it, didn't you, Sam?"

Dangerfield stared at me. "I can get it away from you, Cauthorne, one way or another."

"Don't try it. Just tell them that it's part of the price."

"You're making a mistake," he said.

"As long as I make it."

Dangerfield turned to Toh. "Fix it up."

"I don't think it would be—"

"I don't care what you think. Fix it so that the kid can see Angelo. Like he said, it's part of the price."

Toh and his daughter once again exchanged glances. It was the daughter's turn. "Very well, Mr. Dangerfield. I will, as you say, fix it up. I'll probably send word by messenger as to the time and place."

"Just one thing more," I said.

"What?" she said.

"Make it soon."

We were halfway back to the hotel before Dangerfield spoke to me. "By God, you almost screwed it up, didn't you?"

"Screwed what up?"

"The whole thing."

"Angelo owes me something."

Dangerfield grunted. "He owes that wife and the father-in-law something, too."

"What?"

"You don't think Angelo actually killed the Lozupone girl?"

"I don't know," I said.

"You don't know," Dangerfield mimicked. "God, you are dumb, Cauthorne."

"Okay, I'm dumb."

"It's a frame like I said. You can smell it a mile off. And you know who hung it on him?"

"I know what you want me to say."

"What?"

"The father-in-law and the wife, right?"

Dangerfield looked at me and smiled. Then he leaned back in the Rolls and gazed out the window. "You got it right, pal," he said, but he seemed to be talking to himself.

CHAPTER XIX

The Chinese room clerk at the Raffles didn't give me his usual cheerful smile when I asked for my key and a large manila envelope.

"There are some persons to see you, Mr. Cauthorne," he said.

"Where?"

"In your room."

"Do you usually let just anyone into your guests' rooms?"

He smiled a little then, but there was more embarrassment than humor in it. "We usually let the police in, yes, sir."

"I see. Do you have that envelope?"

He found one and I put the yellow cardboard box inside, licked the flap and sealed it, wrote my name on the front, and handed it back to him. "You have a safe, don't you?"

"Of course."

"Put this in it, will you, please?"

He nodded and then added: "I was distressed to learn of Miss Lozupone's—"

"Yes," I said before he had to complete the polite and meaningless ritual of expressing sorrow over the death of a stranger. "Thank you. It was a terrible thing."

"A terrible thing," he agreed and headed back to

the safe with the envelope which contained the microfilmed evidence that could send Carla Lozupone's father to jail.

I thought about Carla as I walked down the hall to my room where the police waited with their questions about who she was and why she had died. I didn't think that they would ask about who would mourn her, but I wasn't sure that I could answer them if they did. Her father would mourn, I decided. Joe Lozupone, whom she had described as a fat little man with a bald head and an accent, would be not only the chief mourner, but also the chief seeker of vengeance, a role that he had played often enough before. Perhaps her lovers would mourn her for a while and I included myself among them, one in what probably was a long casual list of men who, hearing of her death, would feel a fleeting sense of personal loss, if not of grief; men who would remember something she had said or the way her hair had looked against a pillow or the way that she had once walked across a room. It wasn't so bad a way to be remembered if you had died for less than nothing.

There were two of them waiting for me. One stood by a window and the other sat in an armchair. The one by the window turned when I opened the door. He had a bony face and a high forehead that was topped by thick black hair that he wore fairly long and parted in the middle. He also wore glasses with wide, dark plastic rims and he had on a suit jacket which he may have thought succeeded in concealing the revolver that he carried in the holster on his belt. He nodded at me as I came in. "Mr. Cauthorne?"

"Yes."

"I am Detective-Sergeant Huang of the Criminal Investigation Department," he said with a certain measure of formality. "This is Detective-Sergeant Tan."

I tossed my key on the bureau. "The clerk told me you were here."

Sergeant Tan was the younger of the two, but neither of them was much over thirty. Tan also wore the jacket to his suit, unusual in Singapore during the day and not at all common at night. He rose when I entered and I guessed his height at around five-ten or -eleven, a little tall for a Chinese. Although he was wearing a polite smile there was nothing polite about his eyes, but then I have still to meet my first shy policeman.

"We would like to ask you several questions concerning the death of Carla Lozupone," Sergeant Huang said. "Is my pronunciation correct?"

"It's fine," I said.

"You knew that she was dead, of course," Sergeant Tan said.

"I heard it on the radio." I had. Dangerfield had told the driver to switch it on during the drive back from Toh's house. "The cops will be around," Dangerfield had said as I dropped him off at his hotel. "If you heard it on the radio then you won't have to act surprised when they tell you she's dead."

Huang nodded. "Yes, I believe it was on the eleven o'clock program."

"I heard it at twelve," I said. "If this is going to take a while, we may as well sit down. I'd also like some coffee. What would you care for, coffee or tea?"

"Tea, please," Sergeant Huang said.

I pushed the button and the houseboy made his usual miraculous appearance and took the order. Sergeant Tan resumed his seat in the chair, but Huang continued to stand by the window. I crossed over and sat on the couch to the left of Huang so that when I looked at him, I could avoid the glare from the window.

"You accompanied Miss Lozupone from the United States, I believe, Mr. Cauthorne?" Huang said.

"Yes."

"Were you very good friends?"

"No; in fact, I met her for the first time the day that I left."

"And you struck up your acquaintance during the flight?"

"Not really. Her father wanted someone to more or less

168

less look after her while she was in Singapore and a mutual friend suggested me. We met first in Los Angeles at her hotel."

"When did you last see Miss Lozupone?" Tan said.

"Yesterday. Just after noon. She dropped by and we had lunch and a couple of drinks."

"You did not see her again?" Huang said.

"No."

"Mr. Cauthorne," Tan said, "you called for a doctor last night. You were, according to his report, rather badly beaten."

"Yes. It happened in Chinatown; I'm not sure of the street."

"Were you robbed?"

"It was only a few dollars. I never carry much cash or even my wallet when I'm wandering around a strange city."

"That's wise," Huang said. "But you didn't report the robbery to the police?"

"As I said, it was only a few dollars."

"How many were there?" Huang said. "I mean assailants, of course, not dollars."

We all smiled at that a little and I had the feeling that they both knew that I was lying and that they knew that I knew. But we played it out; there was nothing else to be done.

"There were three of them," I said, adding one to the actual total out of pride.

"You must have put up some resistance," Tan said.

"A token amount, you might say. They didn't seem to care much for it."

"Had you been drinking?" Huang said, then added, "I'm sorry that we have to ask these personal questions, Mr. Cauthorne, but I'm sure you appreciate our reasons."

"It's all right," I said. "I'd had several drinks, perhaps enough to give me too much courage."

"Did you do your drinking at any one place?"

"Yes. At a place called Fat Annie's."

"Was this place recommended to you by a friend?" Tan said.

"No. By a trishaw driver."

"When did you arrive back at the hotel?"

"Shortly after eleven o'clock."

"But you didn't attempt to see Miss Lozupone."

"No."

"Why not, if you were hurt?"

"I needed a doctor more than sympathy."

There was a knock on the door and I crossed and opened it to admit the houseboy who served the coffee and tea. When we all had our cups and saucers, we made some comments about the weather because it suddenly had started to rain, and then we went back to questions and answers.

"You are acquainted with Mr. Angelo Sacchetti, are you not, Mr. Cauthorne?" Tan said.

"Yes."

"You were involved in an accident with him here almost two years ago, I believe."

"I think your records will show that," I said.

"Did Miss Lozupone know him?"

"Yes. At one time, they were engaged to be married."

"Have you seen Mr. Sacchetti?" Huang asked.

"No."

"Are you looking for him?"

"Yes."

"Why?"

"I thought I had caused his death and then I learned that he was alive. His death had bothered me so I wanted to make sure that he was really alive."

"And you traveled all the way to Singapore just for that?" Tan said.

"Just for that," I said.

"Have you seen Sacchetti?" Huang repeated, dropping the mister.

"No."

"Was Miss Lozupone also looking for him?" Tan said.

"Yes."

"Why?"

I shrugged. "As I said, they were once engaged."

"But Sacchetti is now married."

"So I hear."

"Why then should a young woman—"

I interrupted Tan. "As you say, she was a young woman. It's sometimes difficult to tell what a young woman of Carla Lozupone's temperament will do when she's been jilted."

"The woman scorned thing, you mean?" Huang said.

"She didn't talk to me about it."

Huang moved from the window and placed his cup and saucer on the coffee table. "Let me see if I have the correct picture of your relationship with Miss Lozupone," he said, as he returned to the window to take in the view again. "Both of you, through coincidence, came to Singapore at the same time to find Angelo Sacchetti. You, Mr. Cauthorne, for what seems to be some type of psychological reassurance that he was not dead. Miss Lozupone, perhaps for revenge. But you didn't discuss your reasons with each other. Tell me, did you discuss Angelo Sacchetti?"

"Yes."

"Tell us about that."

"There's not much to tell. We both agreed that he was a son of a bitch."

"In just those words?" Tan said.

"Those will do."

"Do you think that Miss Lozupone might have disliked, or even hated, Sacchetti enough to have tried to do something foolish?" Huang said.

"What's foolish?" I said.

"Try to kill him," Tan said.

"No," I said. "I don't think so."

"Did you know that we are looking for Angelo Sacchetti in connection with her death?" Huang said.

"No." That hadn't been on the radio.

"When we found Miss Lozupone, we found her holding Sacchetti's wallet."

"If he killed her, I doubt that he would have been thoughtful enough to leave his wallet in her hand," I said.

"That did occur to us, Mr. Cauthorne," Huang said and kept most of the sarcasm out of his voice.

"But you're still looking for him?" I said.

"Yes," Huang said. "We are."

They told me the rest of it then, at least as much as they felt I should know. Carla Lozupone had been murdered around midnight, give or take an hour, and had been driven to the Malay *kampong* or village near Geyland and dumped by the side of the road. She had not been sexually assaulted, as Tan put it, and they had wired her father in New York.

"Her purse and passport were missing," Tan said. "Did she carry large sums of cash?"

"Traveler's checks, I think. How did you know her father's address?"

"From the hotel registration and the immigration records at the airport."

There was a pause then. It stretched out for almost two minutes. Huang stared out the window and Tan was busy inspecting a button on his coat. Neither of them had taken notes and I felt that they really weren't too interested in the lies that I had to tell them.

It was Huang who broke the silence. "Are you familiar with Sacchetti's activities in Singapore, Mr. Cauthorne?" he said, still taking in the view.

"Yes."

"Lim Pang Sam informed us this morning that he had briefed you when you first arrived."

"Then you've talked to him?" I said.

"At length," Huang said. "If we hadn't, we'd probably be talking at headquarters rather than here." He turned from the window and gazed at me through his thick-rimmed glasses which almost gave him a professorial air. "The Singapore Police, Mr. Cauthorne, are under the control and direction of our Ministry of Defense and Security." Huang paused. "The Ministry's principal function is to deal with threats to Singapore's security—both internal and external threats and sometimes it's exceedingly difficult to differentiate the two. One could say this has been true in the case of Angelo Sacchetti and that is why he has been given a certain

172

amount of latitude. Although his operations could properly be defined as a threat to our internal security, their disruption could have proved to be an even greater threat to our external security."

"Because of his father-in-law?" I said.

Huang nodded. "Yes, because of his father-in-law. I see that Mr. Lim briefed you well."

"He told me that Toh could start a full-scale race riot almost at will," I said.

"That's true," Huang said. "And such a riot, of course, if serious enough, could prove disastrous. Although this was true more in the past than now, a riot possibly could lead to intervention by other countries."

"Malaysia?" I said.

"Or Indonesia, although our relations with it have improved since the confrontation ended and Sukarno was deposed."

"So you let Sacchetti operate in exchange for domestic peace," I said. "It's a logical trade. It might have a slightly gamey smell, but it's nothing unique."

"It's a humiliating trade, Mr. Cauthorne. Especially to a policeman."

"Yes, I can see that."

"But murder is something else," Huang said. "Murder cannot be overlooked."

"Or covered up?" I said.

"Or covered up."

"What if Sacchetti didn't do it?"

"The evidence is overwhelming," Huang said.

"Not to a policeman," I said.

"No," Huang said, "not to a policeman. Only to the public."

"You plan to hang it on him then?"

"Of course."

"Even if he's innocent?"

"He's not innocent, Mr. Cauthorne. There are at least six murders in our files that can be directly traced to the Sacchetti operations."

"But not to him?"

"No. We have never questioned him."

"But you know he was responsible?"

"We know."

"Don't you keep someone on him all the time?" I said.

"We watch his yacht," Tan said. "We keep it under observation twenty-four hours a day." He paused and looked at me and smiled, displaying some nicely even teeth. "He has most interesting visitors."

"Doesn't he ever leave the yacht?"

"Not recently," Huang said. "But that means nothing. A sampan could come by at night, without lights, on the side away from shore and he could easily go aboard and disappear once it went up the Singapore River."

"He used to give a lot of parties," I said. "Doesn't he give them anymore?"

"Not since he purchased the yacht," Huang said. "He's become quite the homebody."

"Except for last night," I said and immediately wished that I hadn't.

"What makes you think he wasn't there last night, Mr. Cauthorne?" Tan said.

This time it was my turn to smile. "He couldn't very well have murdered Carla Lozupone, driven her to the east side of the island, and then dumped her without leaving the yacht, could he?"

"Tell me, Mr. Cauthorne, would you have any objections if Sacchetti were convicted of the Lozupone woman's murder?" Tan said.

"Even if he weren't guilty?" I said.

"Even so."

I thought a moment before replying. "No," I said. "I wouldn't have any objections."

Tan nodded. "I didn't think that you would."

He rose and headed for the door, Sergeant Huang right behind him. "How long do you plan to remain in Singapore, Mr. Cauthorne?" Huang said.

"Until I see Angelo Sacchetti," I said.

"Forgive me if I sound inhospitable," Huang said, "but I hope that your stay will not be too long." Tan opened the door, nodded at me, and left. Huang paused. "Thank you for the tea, Mr. Cauthorne."

"My pleasure."

"And also for your answers to our questions," he said. "Some of them were most ingenious."

CHAPTER XX

The phone rang while I was trying to decide whether a drink would help to pass the time or ease the pain or both. The caller was Lim Pang Sam, the spymaster of Singapore's four-man counter-espionage network, and he wanted to know how I was feeling.

"Rotten," I said.

"That's what Detective Huang reports," Lim said. "He rang me up just a few minutes ago."

"Were they satisfied?"

"With what?"

"With my answers to their questions."

Lim chuckled. "I don't think they believed a word you said, but you're no longer their prime suspect."

"Was I?"

"At first, but there turned out to be too many witnesses to your movements last night."

"I did see a few people," I said.

"But not the one you were looking for," Lim said.

"No. I didn't see him."

There was a pause and then Lim said, "I think it might prove useful if you could drop by my office this afternoon, say around two-thirty? Would be that convenient?"

"Fine," I said.

"I have some news for you," Lim said. "And then I have something else, too."

"At two-thirty then."

After I hung up I mixed a drink and stood at the window and watched it rain a hard, tropical downpour, the kind that puts a wet chill into the air conditioning and gives even synthetic fabrics the clammy smell and feel of damp wool.

I thought about Carla Lozupone and who had killed her and why. Somewhere, just out of reach, a nebulous, unformed idea skittered around, saw that I was trying to sneak a glance at it, blushed, panicked, and disappeared. Having nothing better to do I stood there at the window and watched the rain and went back over it all, from Callese and Palmisano to Huang and Tan. No revelation burst through; no shining truth glimmered; there was only that something, small and elusive, that seemed to nag and snicker just over the next mental hill, just out of sight.

After a while I gave it up and rang the bell for the houseboy. He agreed to produce a plate of sandwiches and a pot of coffee and I reminded myself to increase the size of his tip if I were ever lucky enough to check out of the place. I ate the sandwiches slowly, chewing on the left side of my mouth because the right side still ached where the tall Chinese had slammed the edge of his hand against it. I refought last night's battle and remembered the times when I had taken on three and four and even five of them and had won handily before an admiring audience of cameramen, actors, grips, script girls and assorted hangers-on. Then, of course, there had been a couple of rehearsals and the script had called for me to win, but last night's performance had neither script nor rehearsal and the scene, as well as myself, had suffered because of it.

At two o'clock it was still raining and I went in search of the turbaned doorman to see whether he could find a cab. After five or ten minutes he whistled one to a stop and held a large umbrella over me while I climbed in. I gave the driver Lim's address and he sped off through the rain, apparently unaware that windshield wipers could have proved useful.

Lim Pang Sam smiled broadly as he walked around

his desk and extended his hand which I shook. "Except for right here," he said, touching his own right jaw, "you don't look bad at all. That's a nasty bruise."

"It feels nasty," I said.

Lim moved back to the chair behind his desk and picked up the phone. "I'll have some tea brought in," he said. "It has marvelous curative powers. As the British are so fond of saying, 'There's nothing like a nice cup of tea.'"

"Nothing," I agreed.

When the tea ritual was completed, Lim leaned back in his chair, holding his cup and saucer against his comfortable stomach. "Tell me about it," he said and smiled, adding, "and you can leave out the more obvious fabrications, if you like."

I told him what had happened from the time I had left his office the day before until Huang and Tan arrived. I didn't bother to tell him about Carla Lozupone and me; I don't think I ever told anyone about that.

When I was through Lim put his cup and saucer on the desk and spun his chair around to see how the ships in the harbor were doing in the rain. "So it would seem that someone is mounting a clumsy effort to make it look as though Sacchetti killed the Lozupone woman," he said. "A frame, as you say."

"That's the way it looks, but then I'm no expert."

"But your Mr. Dangerfield is."

"He's an FBI agent. That might make him an expert in some circles."

"But he is not in Singapore officially?"

"No."

"I can't say that I like the idea of an FBI agent running about, officially or otherwise, but I even less like his theory that Toh and his daughter are responsible for the death of the Lozupone woman."

"I don't think he likes it too much either," I said. "I just think he wants to like it."

"Why?"

"I don't know. Maybe he just wants everything tidy."

Lim brought out his Lucky Strikes and offered me

177

one. While I was accepting a light, he said, "This is a most untidy affair, Mr. Cauthorne. Assault, blackmail and murder. Most untidy. Yet there is the possibility that some good may come of it."

"You mean there's a chance to get rid of both Sacchetti and Toh."

Lim nodded. "A very good chance, I think, unless it's bungled badly."

"By outside amateurs such as myself."

Lim smiled. "Not at all, Mr. Cauthorne. If anything, your efforts have brought matters to a head. In fact, I was just going to make you a proposition. But first I must ask you a question. Satisfactory?"

"All right."

"Are you still determined to find or confront—I'm not sure which term to use, but nevertheless, do you still intend to find Angelo Sacchetti?"

"Yes."

"Good. Then you don't mind if we use you as a stalking horse."

"I don't know whether I mind or not," I said. "But there's probably not much I can do about it."

Lim smiled again as if delighted with my answer. "My proposition is this: we would like you to continue just as you are with one exception." He opened a desk drawer, took out a revolver, and placed it on his blotter. "We would like for you to have this."

"Why?"

"For protection," Lim said.

I leaned over and picked up the revolver. It was surprisingly light.

"Aluminum alloy frame," Lim said. "It's become very popular throughout Asia."

It was a Smith & Wesson Chief's Special that fired the .38 caliber Special cartridges and it didn't seem to weigh much more than half a pound, if that. I put it back on the desk.

"What would happen if I pulled the trigger and someone got shot?" I said.

"It depends," Lim said.

"On what?"

"On whom you shot."

"Let's say I shot Angelo Sacchetti."

"Then it would be self-defense, wouldn't it?" Lim said.

"No fuss, no bother?"

"None. I might not be able to convince the Prime Minister to strike a special medal for you, but I'm sure you understand."

"Perfectly," I said. "You wouldn't mind at all if I killed Angelo Sacchetti and saved you the trouble."

"In self-defense, of course."

"Of course."

I shook my head and pushed the revolver an inch towards Lim; he pushed it back an inch. "Mr. Cauthorne, let me say that we do not hand out firearms in Singapore lightly or without a great deal of thought. I hope you will believe me when I also say that you need this revolver. You need it very much. You already have been shot at once."

"That was only a warning."

"Possibly," Lim said and raised a cynical eyebrow. "You have been beaten severely. If you continue your search for Sacchetti, there will be a third, and probably final, incident."

"No more warnings?"

"None."

"All right," I said. "I'll take it, but what do you want me to do with it?"

"I beg your pardon?"

"I mean I'm not wearing a coat, so how do I carry it—by the barrel?"

"Oh, dear," Lim said, clucking his tongue. "I do believe I have a paper bag here somewhere." He rummaged through his desk and found one. I put the Smith & Wesson in it.

"Very handy," I said.

"I think you'll have to wear a coat," he said.

"I'll manage. You said over the phone that you had some news."

Lim took off his Ben Franklin glasses and polished

them with a handkerchief. "It's about Dickie," he said. "I talked to him today."

"To Trippet?"

"Yes. He called from Los Angeles. He's worried about you."

"Why?"

Lim put his glasses back on and they promptly slid halfway down his broad nose to where he habitually wore them. "Well, I believe that I mentioned you had been attacked."

"What else did you mention?"

"That the girl had been murdered."

"So what did he say?"

"I tried to dissuade him."

"From what?"

"From flying out, I'm afraid."

"Christ," I said. "May I use your phone? I'll call him collect."

"You're perfectly welcome to the phone, my dear chap, but it's probably useless."

"Not if I talk to him."

Lim looked at his watch. "That could prove rather difficult to do. I expect he's just leaving Honolulu now and he's due in tomorrow at 12:30 P.M."

"What in God's name am I going to do with Trippet?" I said.

"Well, you could meet him at the airport and then pass him over to me. I quite look forward to seeing him, you know."

I rose and walked around Lim's desk to take a look at the harbor. I rested my forehead against the window and it felt cool and somehow comforting. "Mr. Lim, you have given me a pistol in a paper sack and virtually declared open season on Angelo Sacchetti. You have upset my partner to the point where he's making a ten-thousand-mile wild goose chase out here when I would a hell of a lot rather have him back in Los Angeles running the business on which I depend for my livelihood. Now have we reached the bottom of today's surprise bag or do we have one more grab?"

"One more, I'm afraid, Mr. Cauthorne."

180

"What?"

"Look a little to your left and down."

"I don't see anything."

"That's because it's not there."

"What?"

"*The Chicago Belle*. She weighed anchor three hours ago."

I turned to look at Lim who had spun his chair around towards the window. "Was Sacchetti aboard?" I said.

Lim shook his head. "No. As soon as we learned that she was moving out, we had a marine police launch alongside. They boarded and made a thorough search. There was no one aboard except the crew."

"Where was she headed?"

"The captain wasn't sure. He was sailing under sealed orders."

"Who gave him the orders?"

"Mrs. Sacchetti."

I moved around the desk to my chair and sank into it. "Anything else?"

"Only the suggestion that we might well have a drink."

"At least we can agree on that," I said.

Lim rummaged through his desk once more and produced a bottle of Ballantine's and two glasses. He poured us both a generous measure and we toasted each other's health, although he put a little more feeling into his because he seemed to think that I could use it. After that we talked for a while longer, but about nothing consequential, and then we shook hands and I headed towards the door.

"Mr. Cauthorne," Lim said.

I turned. "Yes."

"I think you forgot something."

"So I did." I went back and got it and then went down the elevator, out to the street, into a cab, and back through the rain to the hotel carrying my Smith & Wesson .38 caliber Chief's Special in its convenient brown paper bag.

CHAPTER XXI

I was talking to myself when the phone rang. I had waited in silence from half-past three until seven when I suffered through my usual evening horrors that were no better or worse than usual. By seven-thirty I was well launched into a silent monologue that proved to be a pitiless self-examination of character—weak, it seemed—with occasional witty asides of brilliant insight. When the call came just after eight I snatched up the phone. I was ready to talk to the devil himself, but had to settle for Dangerfield.

"What's the good word, Cauthorne?" he said. "Hear anything?"

"Nothing."

"Didn't figure you would. Sacchetti probably wants to make you sweat a little."

"He's succeeding."

"I've been out nosing around."

"And?"

"I think I've got something."

"What?"

"I got wet."

"Must be the rain," I said.

"So I went into this tailor shop to see if they could dry my suit and press it. I was sitting there and I noticed that the guy was taking numbers."

"So?"

"So about the time I was ready to go another guy comes in and makes what looks like the pickup. I followed him."

"To where?"

"To Chinatown. It's some dive on Fish Street."

"And you're still waiting?"

"That's right."

"Why?"

"Because if my guess is right, this place on Fish Street is just a substation. Once they count it and check the slips they'll move it to the main headquarters."

"And that's where Angelo will be?"

"You got it right, Cauthorne."

"What if he is?"

I could hear Dangerfield sigh over the telephone. "Sometimes, Cauthorne, I don't think you've got the brains God gave a crabapple tree. Sacchetti doesn't much want to see you, does he?"

"Not especially."

"Well, when his wife sends you the word, you'll get in to see him all right, but what about getting out?"

"What about it?" I said.

"What about it?" Dangerfield mimicked me and did a fair imitation. "Angelo's hot, Cauthorne. Red hot. He might just decide to disappear and take you with him. So you'd better have somebody on the outside when you go inside."

"And that's you."

"You got it right, Cauthorne."

"Sounds like cops and robbers. Why so noble, Dangerfield?"

"I want that microfilm," Dangerfield said.

"You'll get it."

"But not until you see Angelo. And if anything happened to you while you were seeing Angelo, I'd never get it."

I started to tell him that he could come to the hotel and get the microfilm then, but he said, "The guy's coming out now. I've got to go." The phone went dead. There was nothing to do but wait for it to ring again or for someone to knock on the door. I decided to do it comfortably. I sent the houseboy down for dinner and after that I went to bed and stared up at the ceiling for a long time before I fell asleep. The next morning I waited until almost noon, but nobody called, so I caught a cab and headed for Paya Lebar International to meet my partner who seemed to think that I needed someone to help me sit around and wait for the phone to ring.

Trippet, dressed in a medium blue tropical weight suit that had scarcely a wrinkle in it, was the fourth person through health and immigration. The fifth person in the line looked at me, frowned, and then turned to the sixth person, a man with eyes that were too close together, a nose that was too pointed, a mouth that was too thin, and a chin that was too sharp and needed a shave. The man behind Trippet had long, black wavy hair and an acne-scarred face. Carla Lozupone had called him Tony and I decided that he and his fox-faced friend had made excellent time from New York.

Trippet spotted me and waved. At customs, he collected the last of his papers and I walked over to meet him. "Edward," he said. "It was good of you to come all the way out here."

We shook hands and I said: "Why the trip, Dick?"

"Didn't Sammy tell you?" he said.

"He told me that you were worried about my health or something."

Trippet's face acquired a surprised look. "Did he now?"

"He did."

"I wasn't in the least worried," Trippet said. "He rang me at four in the morning to tell me that you were involved in some kind of jiggery-pokery and that it would be most wise for me to fly out and lend a hand."

"Doing what?" I said.

Before Trippet could answer, a voice said: "What happened, Cauthorne?" I knew the voice; the last time I'd heard it was in front of the Los Angeles airport and it had been advising me to take good care of Carla Lozupone. Now it wanted to know why I hadn't.

I turned and said, "Hello, Tony."

He was dressed for the tropics. He wore a persimmon-colored double-breasted linen jacket with white buttons, dark green slacks, a yellow shirt with inch-wide green stripes, and brown loafers. I decided that he had packed his Miami Beach wardrobe. His fox-faced friend wore a light-weight dark suit and his only concession to the climate was a tie that was loosened and pulled down an inch or so from his unbuttoned collar.

"This is him," Tony said to fox-face. "Cauthorne. The guy I was telling you about." Fox-face nodded and put on a pair of dark glasses, the better to see me with, I thought. "This is Terilizzi. He wants to know what happened, too. That's why the boss sent him."

"This is my partner, Mr. Trippet," I said. "Mr. Teri-lizzi—and I don't think I ever got your last name, Tony."

"Cea," he said to me and "hiyah" to Trippet. No-body seemed to want to shake hands. "What happened to Carla, Cauthorne?" Cea said. "The boss wants to know bad."

"She was strangled."

Terilizzi took off his glasses and slipped them into his breast pocket. He nodded his head slightly, as if encouraging me to go on with the story, and then I looked fully into his eyes and I wished that he had kept his sunglasses on. His eyes had the color and warmth of chilled oysters and I had the feeling that if I looked into them long enough, I would discover something that was better left unknown.

"Where were you?" Tony Cea asked.

"I was getting beat up."

"Who did it?"

"Who beat me up or who killed Carla?"

"I don't give a shit who beat you up," Cea said. "Who killed Carla?"

"The cops are looking for Sacchetti."

"Sacchetti, huh?" Cea searched his pockets for a cigarette, found one, and lit it with a small leather-covered lighter. "He do it?"

"How should I know?"

"Well, here's something you should know, Cauthorne," Cea said and his mouth twisted into a crooked grin. "You should know why Terilizzi and me are here. We're here because we're going to find who killed Carla and then I'm going to turn him over to Terilizzi who's just a little nuts. Not much; just enough. You follow me?"

"It's not hard," I said.

"Quite simple, really," Trippet said.

"Who'd you say he was?" Cea said, jerking a thumb at Trippet.

"My partner."

"Tell him to shut up."

"You tell him."

Cea glared at Trippet who gave him a polite, even friendly smile. "Now if we or the cops don't find whoever made Carla dead in forty-eight hours, you know what I'm supposed to do?"

"Something perfectly wretched," Trippet said.

"You," Terilizzi said to Trippet, and made a sharp horizontal motion with his left hand.

"He can talk after all," I said.

"Sure, he can talk," Cea said. "He's just a little nuts, like I said, but he can talk all right when he wants to. I was looking to tell you what I'm going to do if whoever killed Carla's not caught."

"All right," I said. "What?"

"We're going to find a reasonable facsimile," he said, pronouncing the phrase carefully, as if he had just learned it. "We're going to find the guy who was supposed to look after Carla but didn't and that's you, Cauthorne."

"You," Terilizzi said.

"A little screwy, but good at his job," Cea said. "Does beautiful work; all hand carved." Cea laughed at that and Terilizzi smiled and gave me a careful appraisal with his oystery-grey eyes. "You," Terilizzi said again.

"I'm afraid you don't understand the situation, Mr. Cea," Trippet said.

"Will you get him off my back?" Cea said to me.

"You might learn something," I said.

"You see, you are not in New York or New Jersey or even Los Angeles," Trippet said smoothly. "At a word from either Mr. Cauthorne or myself to the proper authorities, the pair of you will be clapped into the local jail—for safekeeping, of course. The civil servants who run the Singapore prison system are most forgetful, I believe, and they might forget about you for one or even two years. It's been known to happen."

"Who is this crumb?" Cea said.

"His father used to own half of Singapore," I lied. "Now Trippet does."

My partner smiled modestly. "Only a third, Edward."

"I don't care what he owns," Cea said to me. "You're the one who'd better be worried because I'm going to be right on your ass from now on. Me and Terilizzi."

I shrugged. "You can reach me at the Raffles."

"They told me that was a real crummy old place."

"Old anyway."

"Did you book me a room?" Trippet said.

"You've got the one that Carla had."

"Fine," Trippet said.

"You going to stay in it?" Cea said and he seemed a little shocked.

"Well, I never really knew the lady, you understand."

"Yeah. I guess that's right. Me and Terilizzi are at the Hilton."

"Where else?" I said.

"What's that, some kind of a crack?"

"Forget it," I said. "If you want to talk to the cops, the ones to see are Detective-Sergeants Huang and Tan."

"Write 'em down, will you?"

I wrote the names down on the back of Cea's airline ticket.

"Thanks," he said. "I'll go see 'em. Just remember, Cauthorne, I don't care how much pull your partner here has, me and Terilizzi are going to be right on your ass. The boss didn't take it too good about Carla.

In fact, he took to the bed when the telegram came. He don't feel so good and finding who got to Carla might make him feel better."

"Should cheer him up tremendously," Trippet said.

Cea gave him a sour look. "Just remember what I told you, Cauthorne."

"Right on my ass," I said.

"You," Terilizzi said again.

"You better believe it," Cea said, turned, and went to pick up his luggage.

"Pompous bastard, isn't he?" Trippet said.

"You know something?"

"What?"

"That must be the first time he's ever been described in just those terms."

We collected Trippet's bag, a bleached pigskin affair that seemed to have solid silver fittings, found a porter who laughed when Trippet said something to him in Malay, and located a bearded Sikh cab driver who agreed to take us to the Raffles in his prewar Jowett-Jupiter that was a marvel to us both.

"Just what did Lim say to you exactly?" I said, once the cab was rolling.

"First, he told me that you had been rather badly beaten and from the bruise on your jaw I'd say he was telling the truth—as he usually does, of course."

"What else?"

"That the Lozupone girl had been killed and that you were getting in over your head and had refused any offer of assistance. He strongly recommended that I come out and lend a hand."

"Doing what?"

"Well, I must confess he was rather vague about that."

"Dangerfield's here," I said.

"The FBI man?"

"Yes."

"What's he doing?"

"Lending a hand."

"Oh," Trippet said and gazed out the window at the

188

Singapore scene as we threaded our way through the Indian section that lined Serangoon Road. "It hasn't changed," he said as we rolled slowly through the treeless, grubby neighborhood, entire sections of which could have been transplanted intact from Bombay or Calcutta or Jubbulpore. *Ghee* and *tal* cooked in pans over cow dung fires and their odors mingled with those of oil and urine and incense and rose water. Men in white dhotis chewed betel and stared at nothing and everything. Women in bright, even brilliant, saris rattled their gold bangles and a Hindu wise man, his arms smeared with ashes, wandered through the crowd. A Parsee leaned against a post, picked his teeth with a sharp knife, and sneered at the Hindu. An old man hobbled by with the aid of a malacca cane, his mouth wrapped in gauze, his eyes fixed on the ground.

"What's the one with the gauze over his mouth?" I said.

"Must be a Jain," Trippet said.

"Afraid of germs?"

"Not at all. He's probably orthodox. The gauze keeps insects from committing suicide by flying into his mouth. Notice how carefully he walks; he doesn't want to step on any of them either."

Just past Balestier Road which takes you to the Singapore Island Country Club, if you can afford the dues, the traffic became spotty and the driver urged his aged car on to new efforts. We must have been making forty when the black, four-door Chevelle pulled up alongside and stayed there. Our driver slowed, but the Chevelle dropped back with us. When the Chevelle's rear window started to roll down, I caught Trippet by the shoulder and gave him a hard, abrupt shove towards the floor. I dropped flat on the seat and one of the two shots plunked into the far door about eight inches from my head while the second one, fired at an angle as the Chevelle pulled ahead, knocked out the taxi's rear window. The glass wasn't shatterpoof and a few shards fell on the seat.

Our driver shouted something and then slammed on his brakes. I rolled off the seat onto Trippet. He squirmed under me and I managed to get back to a sitting position and noticed that a crowd was gathering.

"The neighbors are here," I said.

Trippet raised up to look around. "So they are. Any damage?"

"The rear window and my nerves."

"Do you have any money?"

"Sure."

"Give me fifty dollars."

The driver was now outside of the car, explaining to the interested bystanders how it had happened and his gestures were a pleasure to watch. Trippet got out the left door and walked up to the driver and said something into his ear while pressing the bills into a hand that momentarily was not in flight. The driver peeked at the denominations, smiled, and hurried around to open the door for Trippet. The crowd watched us drive away. A four- or five-year-old boy waved for no good reason and I waved back.

"It was an accident, sir," the driver said.

"I'm sure of it," Trippet said.

"But the rear window."

"A sad loss, but fortunately replaceable."

"Perhaps after all one should inform the police."

"It would only inconvenience them," Trippet said.

"If only I could be certain it was indeed an accident," the driver said.

Trippet stretched his hand out to me, palm up, and I laid two Singapore twenty-dollar bills across it. Trippet folded them and tapped the driver on the shoulder. "Perhaps this will give you the certainty you seek," he said.

The driver's right hand came up over his right shoulder and his fingers closed over the bills. He didn't turn his head. He glanced down at the numerals on the bills and then tucked them into his shirt pocket. "Truly," he said, "it was a most regrettable accident."

CHAPTER XXII

Trippet knocked on my door after he had unpacked, showered, and changed clothes. The temperature outside was pushing ninety and the humidity was even higher. Both of us had been sopping by the time we reached the hotel.

"Gin and tonic?" I said. "My boy brought some fresh limes."

"Anything," Trippet said.

I mixed the drink and handed it to him.

"We'll drink to your first Singapore shoot-'em-up," I said.

"I still expect to go into shock any moment," Trippet said. "I must say that it didn't seem to bother you much; but perhaps you're used to it by now."

"It scared the shit out of me. I thought you were the one who wasn't bothered."

"I nearly panicked," he said, "and I must confess that I also noticed a slight looseness of the bowels. Any idea who it was?"

"It looked like the same car that one of Sacchetti's men used on Raffles Place the other day. It could have been the same car, but I don't know if it was the same man."

"Perhaps I should call Sammy," Trippet said.

"Lim?" I said.

"Yes. Any objections?"

"He bothers me."

"You mean it bothers you that Sammy said that I called him and I say that he called me. I wouldn't worry about it."

"Why?"

"He simply told you what you wanted to hear, Edward. It was a face-saving gesture. It would have embarrassed him to tell you that he thought you needed help."

"Sorry. I forgot how sensitive I am."

"Tell me about it."

"What?" I said.

"Everything."

"You mean the Dragon Lady and all?"

"Good Lord, is there another woman mixed up in it?"

"Sacchetti's Chinese wife. I think she steals her lines from old Charlie Chan movies."

"Extraordinary."

"Who's minding the store?" I said.

"I shipped both Sydney and my wife off to her parents in Topeka. In fact, their plane left just a few minutes before mine. Jack and Ramón are sharing management responsibilities, if you can call it that."

"Who sits in the front office?"

"They take turns."

"Ramón should be useful, providing the customers speak Spanish."

"What's what I thought."

"Where did you learn Malay?" I said.

"Here and in Malaya," Trippet said. "I spent a year out here in thirty-eight and I also did a turn here after the war."

"Doing what?"

Trippet smiled. "This and that."

"Lim said you were in British Intelligence during the war."

"For a while."

"And afterwards?"

"For a while."

"It's none of my business."

"You're right, Edward, it isn't. Tell me about the Dragon Lady. She sounds much more interesting."

I told him the same story that I had told first to Dangerfield and later to Lim, but the third time around the account grew thin and stale and it seemed

192

as if I were describing by rote something that had happened a long time ago to some other persons in another place. Trippet listened carefully, not interrupting once, but nodding occasionally at times to show that he understood when the tale grew complicated. He was, as always, a very good listener and I wondered if he had learned the art while in British Intelligence.

When I was through Trippet gazed up at the ceiling and then ran both hands through his long grey hair. "The pistol," he said. "I don't like the pistol."

"Why?"

"It's not like Sammy."

"That's what he said."

"What?"

"That he didn't hand them out lightly."

"Where do you keep it?"

"In a brown paper bag. The bag is in my suitcase."

"That fellow Nash," Trippet said. "Can you describe him?"

"Medium height, around fifty or fifty-five in a harsh light, compact build, deep tan, blond hair going grey. Rolls his own cigarettes."

"Green eyes? I mean really green?"

"Right. You know him?"

"I can't say, but I think so. It's been a long time."

"He came in handy," I said.

"So it would seem."

"But after all, Nash and I are fellow Americans."

"A true bond."

I yawned and stretched. "What do you say to some lunch?"

"I say it's a good suggestion."

We had lunch in the room and Trippet helped me to listen for the phone to ring. We listened until four o'clock but nobody called, knocked, or slipped a note under the door. I rang the bell and the houseboy came for the dishes and both Trippet and I beamed at him and Trippet inquired about his family which I thought was polite.

We carried on a vague kind of conversation made up of half-phrases, grunts, long silences, and old jokes;

the kind of verbal shorthand that is used by two persons who know each other well or have been married for a long time. The hamburger king had called again and was shipping his Stutz DV-32 Bearcat down from San Francisco next week or the week after. The plumber had brought his wife in to look at the Cadillac; the wife had been unimpressed. Two young ladies had phoned for me; one gave her name as Judy and the other had refused to leave either her name or number and I spent a few moments trying unsuccessfully to think who it might have been. I knew who Judy was.

The phone finally rang at a quarter to five. It had been a long afternoon and the sound was welcome so I let it ring three times. "Damned if I'm going to seem anxious," I said and picked it up on the fourth ring.

"A man will come to your hotel at seven this evening, Mr. Cauthorne." Once again Angelo Sacchetti's wife didn't think it was necessary to identify herself so I said: "Who's this?"

"Make sure you're not followed," she said.

"Who's the man?"

"You'll recognize him," she said and hung up.

I replaced the phone and went back to the divan where I'd been doing my waiting with my head propped up on two pillows from the bed. "The Dragon Lady," I said. "A man's going to pick us up at seven o'clock here."

"Us?"

"Don't you want to sit in? We just play for matches."

"I mean, did she say 'us' or 'you'?"

"She said 'you' but I interpreted it as 'us' which reminds me; I'd better call Dangerfield."

I crossed the room again, looked up the number of the Strand Hotel, and asked its operator for Dangerfield's room. She rang the room for at least two minutes and then said she was sorry, but Mr. Dangerfield did not seem to be in and would I like to leave a message. I told her to tell him to call Cauthorne.

"Not there?" Trippet said.

"No."

194

"What do you think of his numbers racket head-quarters theory?"

"Not much."

"Neither do I, but it's probably better than sitting around some hotel room."

"What isn't?"

Trippet went back to his own room to write a letter to his wife and to call Lim Pang Sam, he said. I continued to lie on the couch and count the cracks in the ceiling. I could have spent the time more profitably by reading a newspaper or studying Chinese or working on my bird calls, but I didn't. I just lay there and stared at the ceiling and counted fifteen major cracks and six probables which actually were hairlines. I was waiting, I told myself, for the man who was going to take me to Angelo Sacchetti. But that wasn't true. What I really waited for was Sacchetti to fall off the Chinese junk for the last time. I was waiting for that final grotesque, obscene wink and it arrived at a quarter past six along with the usual measure of shakes and shivers and a river of cold sweat. When it was over I headed for the bathroom and my third shower for the day. I dressed slowly, killing more time. I wore a white Egyptian cotton shirt with a button-down collar, a striped tie from some long-disbanded regiment, a dark blue poplin suit, black socks and loafers and a .38 caliber Smith & Wesson Chief's Special which I stuck in the left-hand waistband of my trousers so that it could remind me of how much my stomach hurt. By fifteen to seven I was sitting on the edge of a chair, neat if not natty, waiting for someone to guide me to the man who the Singapore police thought would do for the prime suspect in the Carla Lozupone murder case until a better one came along.

Trippet knocked on my door at ten till seven and joined me in a final gin and tonic. "Did you talk to Lim?" I said.

"For a few minutes."

"Did you tell him about tonight?"

"I mentioned it."

"What did he say?"

"Nothing," Trippet said. "Nothing at all."

The knock on the door came promptly at seven and I didn't jump as much as I thought I would. I put my drink down, crossed the room, and opened the door. Mrs. Angelo Sacchetti had been right when she had said that I would know him. I did. It was Captain Jack Nash.

"I don't have any choice in this thing, Cauthorne," he said as he moved quickly into the room, flicking a brief glance at Trippet.

"What do you mean?" I said.

"Just what I said."

"How much did she offer, since you and Angelo are both Americans and all?"

"Who's he?" Nash said, jerking his chin at Trippet.

"I haven't changed that much, have I, Jack?" Trippet said.

Nash turned for another look. A long one. "Hey, I know you."

"You should."

"Sure, I know you," Nash said, more slowly this time. "It was a long time ago up in North Borneo. Jesselton. You're—let me think a moment—you're Trippet, that's it. Major Trippet." He turned to me again. "How come you brought in British Intelligence, Cauthorne?"

"He didn't," Trippet said.

"I think it's nice that you two know each other," I said.

"Your friend, Captain Nash, was Colonel Nash when I knew him," Trippet said. "Actually lieutenant-colonel in the Philippine Guerrilla Army until he was court-martialed."

"They wiped that out, friend," Nash said.

"He was using his good office to run guns to North Borneo when I knew him," Trippet said.

"You never proved it."

"He was buying them on the black market in the Philippines, or so he said. Actually, we had quite a bit of evidence that he stole them from various American Army installations. It was just after the war, in 1946."

196

"Ancient history," Nash said.

"During the war," Trippet went on, "Nash captured a Japanese vice-admiral and then set him free. That was on Cebu, wasn't it, Jack?"

"You know why I turned him loose."

"For one hundred thousand dollars, according to my information."

"Bullshit," Nash said. "I turned him loose because the Japs were going to wipe out every Filipino on the entire island."

"It was an excellent story; even most of the Filipinos believed it," Trippet said. "Jack was quite the hero. It seems that the admiral's seaplane was forced down by engine trouble and he and nine top-ranking staff officers walked right into Jack's arms carrying with them, curiously enough, a complete set of plans for the defense of the islands. So Jack made a deal with the admiral. In exchange for the defense plans and one hundred thousand dollars, the admiral could go free providing he arranged for the phony massacre threat."

"It wasn't phony and there wasn't any hundred grand," Nash said. He produced his tin box and began to roll a cigarette. "What the hell," he said after he got his cigarette lit, "it all happened more than twenty-five years ago anyway."

"Go on," I said to Trippet.

"All right. It seems that when the American command in Australia learned that Jack was planning to release the admiral, they ordered him to ignore the alleged Japanese threat. But Jack disobeyed orders, managed to get the defense plans to Australia, somehow collected the hundred thousand, released the admiral, and got a citation from the Philippine government for gallantry, and a court-martial from the Americans."

"You want a drink?" I said to Nash.

"Sure," he said.

"Gin all right?"

"On the rocks."

I poured the drink and handed it to him. "That's a

phony story," he said. "The Flip government gave me a medal, not any citation."

"Why tell it now?" I asked Trippet.

"Because I don't trust the good ex-colonel," Trippet said.

"They gave me my rank back," Nash said. "They only busted me to major anyhow."

"Back up to my first question, Nash," I said. "How much is she paying you?"

He looked into his drink as if the amount were written on one of the ice cubes. "Five thousand bucks. American."

"For what?"

"For letting Sacchetti cool off."

"Where?"

"On my *kumpit*. That's where I'm going to take you."

"And Sacchetti's there?" I said.

"He was an hour ago."

"Where's your *kumpit?*"

"Across the island south of the naval base just off Seletar in the Johore Strait."

"Why there?" Trippet asked.

"Look, this limey isn't coming along, is he?" Nash said.

"He's an American and all now," I said. "He's coming along."

"Sammy was right," Trippet said. "A hand does need to be lent."

"What kind of crack is that?" Nash said.

I told him it was a private joke and he said that his *kumpit*, the *Wilfreda Maria*, was anchored in the strait because it had been "moving around."

"Where'd she find you?" I said.

"Sacchetti's wife?"

"Yes."

"At Fat Annie's."

"When?"

"Yesterday morning."

"And they're paying you five thousand just to give him bed and board for a few days?"

198

Nash ground his cigarette out in an ashtray and then glanced at his watch. "Them? Not hardly. As soon as he's through with you I've got to rendezvous with his yacht."

"Where?" I said.

"They're paying me five thousand to do it. It'll cost you five thousand to find out where."

"Seeing as how we're both Americans and all," I said.

"Yeah," Nash said. "There's that, too."

CHAPTER XXIII

A small herd of middle-aged sweaty-looking American tourists, necks festooned with cameras, were being channeled towards the registration desk in the lobby by their leader, a fussy man in an electric blue shirt, who stamped his foot when one of his charges wanted to know why they weren't staying at the Singapura like her sister, Wanda, did last year.

Trippet and I followed Nash through the crowd and out the door where he turned towards the trishaw stand. "I thought we were going to the other side of the Island," I said.

"Just do it my way," Nash said. "You take the second trishaw in line and tell him to follow mine."

"To where?" I said.

"To Fat Annie's."

I said "Fat Annie's" to our Chinese pumper and he grinned wickedly.

"Why didn't you say 'follow that trishaw?' " Trippet said, as we climbed in. "Would have lent some atmosphere, don't you think?"

"I thought it was your line."

We had traveled about a hundred yards when I poked my head around the canvas top of the trishaw and looked back. There was another trishaw about fifty feet behind us, but I couldn't make out either of its occupants.

"I think we're being followed," I said. "Which is a pretty fair line itself."

"Who?"

"Can't tell."

"Difficult to request more speed."

"We might as well enjoy the ride."

Fat Annie's still didn't look like much and Trippet said so when we arrived right behind Nash's trishaw. "It's got a nice parlor," I said, and paid off our driver.

Nash was waiting at the door. "Let's go," he said.

The old woman with the long-stemmed pipe was still sitting on the low bench in the cubicle of an entrance. She ignored us as we went into the room with the rattan bar which held the new National cash register and the abacus. Fat Annie sat on her stool, three hundred pounds of joy, and called, "Hello, Snooky," at Nash.

"He ready?" Nash said.

"He's waiting," she said and looked at me. "You were here the other night. Got time for a quickie?"

"Not tonight," I said.

"How about your goodlooking friend?"

"Thank you, no," Trippet said and smiled politely.

Nash was moving towards a door that led to the rear and we followed. "You boys come back," Fat Annie called.

The door led to a dingy hall. We went down that and through another door and found ourselves in a narrow cul-de-sac that was just wide enough for the waiting trishaw whose thin-faced driver was perched on the bicycle seat smoking a cigarette.

"Somebody's going to have to sit on somebody's lap," Nash said. "I didn't know there was going to be three of us."

"I'll sit on yours," Trippet said to me.

"Who's following us, Nash?" I said.

"Cops, I guess."

"Think this will fool them?"

"Annie will stall," he said and climbed into the trishaw and said something to the driver in Chinese. I got in next to Nash and Trippet gingerly crawled onto my lap and his rear pushed the Smith & Wesson against my taped stomach and I bit my lip so that I wouldn't yell. The driver said something to Nash who barked back in Chinese and we were off, the driver's thin leg muscles bunching into hard knots as he pushed at the bicycle pedals.

He turned left at the entrance to the cul-de-sac and wound his way through packed streets. A few people tittered at the sight of three in a trishaw and Nash muttered something about how goddamned ridiculous it was for Trippet to be along anyhow. Some ten minutes later the trishaw turned down a street that I remembered led to the Singapore River. At the quay the driver stopped and Nash jumped out.

"Any time," I said to Trippet.

"Sorry," he said as he eased himself off my knees.

After a few moments of debate Nash paid off the trishaw driver and walked down the steps of the quay and kicked the sleeping Indian with the yellow teeth. He woke up smiling and began to untie the line that ran from his big toe to the runabout.

"Get in," Nash said.

We got in, the Indian, too, and Nash started the motor and backed out into the river. He turned the boat upriver this time and wove in and out of the anchored *tonkangs*. We were well over fifty yards upriver when I looked back at the quay. Two men stood on its bottom step and they seemed to be staring at us, but I couldn't tell who they were in the dusk.

We must have gone a mile upriver before Nash headed the runabout towards the right bank. He pulled up to the steps of the quay and the Indian jumped out and fastened one line to a metal rung and another, smaller one, to his big toe. He grinned his yellow teeth at us once, then curled up and went to sleep.

We went up the steps of the quay, crossed the loading area, and moved down another narrow alley. At the end of the alley Nash stopped at a building that looked like a garage, took out a key, and felt in the dark for the lock. He twisted the key, put it back in his pocket, and then slid the door open. It was a wide, high door and he grunted when he pushed at it. Neither Trippet nor I offered to help.

Inside the garage was a fairly new Jaguar 240 sedan. "Yours?" I said.

"Mine."

"The smuggling business must be good."

"It's okay," Nash said. He handed me the key to the garage door. "Close it and lock up when I drive out."

He started the Jaguar and backed it slowly out of the garage. I closed the door, locked it, and climbed into the back seat. Trippet sat in front. Nash switched on his lights and turned into a one-way street, traveled three blocks, and turned right. He was a rotten driver.

We wound our way through the commercial section of Singapore until we hit Upper Thomson Road. Nash made a left turn, barely missed a Volkswagen, and kept the Jaguar in second gear too long.

"How far?" I said.

"About eleven, maybe twelve miles to where we're going," he said.

We drove in silence for fifteen or twenty minutes except for when Nash cursed at fellow motorists who invariably were in the right. After fifteen minutes or so I looked back for the fourth time and noticed that the lights of the car behind us had still not moved any closer or any farther behind for a good quarter of an hour. I shifted the revolver in my waistband to what I hoped would be a more comfortable position and when that didn't work out, I shifted it back.

At Yio Chu Kang Road a black Chevelle sedan cut in front of us, momentarily illuminated by the lights of the Jaguar. For once Nash didn't curse.

"Friend of yours?" I said.

"Not mine."

"How about the one behind us?"

"Who?"

"We've had a tail for the last twenty minutes," I said. "Mrs. Sacchetti said she didn't want any tails."

Nash looked into his rear view mirror, probably for the first time that night, and the Jaguar veered to the left. Trippet grabbed for the wheel and got it back into line.

"I'll lose him," Nash said.

"Let me out first," Trippet said.

"Think you can do any better?"

"Anyone could."

"Well, just watch, fellah."

Nash pressed down on the accelerator and the Jaguar jumped ahead. He pulled up until he was only thirty or forty feet behind the black Chevelle, then blinked his lights three times in rapid succession. The Chevelle lights blinked twice. Nash cut the Jaguar lights completely and slammed on his brakes and the car skidded to a stop on the left-hand verge of the highway. He turned off the ignition.

"That doesn't make you invisible," Trippet said.

"Watch," Nash said.

The only thing that I could tell about the car that had been following us was that it was painted a dark color and it had two men in the front seat. Neither of them wore hats and I couldn't see their faces because they turned their heads as they sped past the parked Jaguar. Another car, also containing two men, roared by a few moments later. It looked like a Ford, but I wasn't sure.

Nash started the engine again, switched on his lights, and pulled back onto the highway. "They didn't stop, you notice," he said. "They didn't want us to think they were tailing us."

"You can follow from the front as well as from the rear," I said.

"Watch," Nash said.

Ahead of us we could see the taillights of the two cars that had passed while we were parked. The taillights of the lead car flashed as its brakes came on and the lights veered to the right, crossed the center line, then skittered to the left. The brake warning lights went off and suddenly the regular taillights rose up in the air, turned over three times, and went out. The car that was following pulled sharply to the right, slowed, and then sped on. The four-door black Chevelle was nowhere in sight.

"See what I mean," Nash said.

We were almost abreast of the car that had gone off the road. It had rolled three times and it had come to rest on its top, prevented from rolling any farther by the splintered palm tree that it had crunched into. A crowd was beginning to gather. "Stop," I told Nash.

"I'm not stopping," he said. "We're late now; you want to see Sacchetti or not?"

"Stop or I'll break your goddamned neck," I said.

"Don't tell me what to do, Cauthorne."

I leaned forward, slipped my right arm around his neck, and pressed my wrist against his adam's apple. "Stop," I said again, and eased off the pressure.

Nash stopped the car and I got out and hurried back towards the wreck. Trippet was close behind. It was almost a fifty-yard walk back to the car and by the time we got there the occupants had been pulled from the wreckage. The car was a Rover sedan and it looked to be a total loss. Gasoline trickled from its tank. The crowd chattered away in Chinese and Malay and one bystander shined a flashlight on the faces of the two occupants of the car who had been carried or dragged to the side of the road. One was Detective-Sergeant Huang who had lost an eye somehow. The other was Detective-Sergeant Tan whose legs were folded under him in an impossible position. Both of them were dead.

"Know who they are?" Trippet said.

"Singapore police. They were the ones who talked to me."

"Could you tell how it happened?" he said.

"No," I said. "Could you?"

"I'm not sure, but I think that the Chevelle forced them to swerve. It came out of nowhere from the left. Then a tire must have blown."

"Or someone shot it out."

204

"I didn't hear anything," Trippet said, "and that's a amned difficult shot."

"So were the ones that missed us this afternoon and didn't hear those either."

"Wasn't that some kind of signal that Nash gave the hevelle when he blinked his lights?" Trippet said.

"It was a signal."

"They had it worked out in advance."

"Not all the way," I said. "It must have been a con-ngency plan."

"Now they'll be looking for Sacchetti because of two ead policemen."

"They'll never prove it," I said. "Did you see any-hing that you can swear to?"

"No."

"Neither did I."

There wasn't anything to be done for Tan and Huang so we went back to the Jaguar and got in.

"They're both dead," Trippet told Nash.

"Too bad. You ready now?"

"We're ready," I said.

Two miles from the wreck Nash turned right onto a dirt road and bounced past houses that were built on stilts over swamp and water. It seemed to grow hotter. Nobody said anything until he pulled the car up at what was apparently the end of the road. "From here on, we walk," he said.

We got out and followed him down a path that led to a crude dock.

"This the strait?" I said.

"This is it."

"Now what?"

"We wait," Nash said. "Somebody'll be along."

We waited five minutes and then I could hear the oar-locks of a rowboat. Nash said something in Chinese and a voice answered. It sounded familiar.

"This way," Nash said. He headed out to the end of the dock and Trippet and I followed. A rowboat was drawn up alongside and a man was standing up, hold-ing onto the dock. "You two into the stern," Nash said.

The man in the boat turned on a flashlight and Trip pet and I crawled down into the boat. "Let them hol the light for me," Nash said. The man who was stand ing up passed the flashlight to Trippet and he shined on the bow of the boat. Nash got in. Trippet flashe the light over the man who was standing up in the boa and I understood why his voice seemed familiar. H was the tall, lean Chinese who had once shot at me o Raffles Place and later had clubbed me unconsciou with a revolver in the saloon of *The Chicago Belle*. H looked almost naked without his pistol.

The Chinese shoved us off from the dock and ther sat down and unshipped the oars. He rowed for fiftee minutes. Then we bumped against a large dim bull and Nash said, "Okay, up the ladder. Use the flash light."

Trippet shined the flashlight around until he found a rope ladder with wooden steps. "You guys first," Nash said.

"This your *kumpit?*" I said.

"This is it."

From its running lights the *Wilfreda Maria* seemed to be about sixty or seventy feet long. I climbed up the ladder and then helped Trippet onto the deck. We let Nash manage by himself. The deck was lighted by five or six haphazardly placed naked bulbs and by the glow from the windows of what seemed to be a cabin and a wheelhouse that was aft. Nash headed for it. "This way," he said and I noticed that the Chinese who had rowed the boat was right behind us.

"You sure Sacchetti is here?" I said, and my voice cracked like a thirteen-year-old adolescent's.

Nash grinned. "You're really eager, aren't you, Cauthorne?"

"I've waited long enough."

"The great man is just inside," he said. "Right through that door."

I put my hand on the knob, then stopped, because it seemed for a moment that the shakes and the horrors were due, but that passed, and I opened the door. In side there were two bunks, some chairs, and a deal table that held a gin bottle and a glass. The man in the blue shirt who sat behind the table stared at me curiously for what seemed to be a long time. Then he said, "Hello, Cauthorne," but neither his face nor his voice belonged to Angelo Sacchetti.

They belonged to Sam Dangerfield.

CHAPTER XXIV

Trippet, Nash and the lean Chinese had followed me into the cabin whose stifling small space reeked of stale sweat, mingled with the odor of rotting copra that had the sweet and sour locker room smell of old jock straps and dirty sneakers.

"Hello, Sam," I said.

"Sit down," Dangerfield said. "Want a drink? Don't think I ever offered you a drink before, did I?"

"Not of your own booze."

"Well?"

"No thanks."

"This your partner?" he said, nodding his head at Trippet.

"That's right."

"Trippet, isn't it?"

"Yes," I said.

"Sit down, Mr. Trippet."

We all sat down, except for the Chinese who stood by the door, his arms folded across his chest. "You were getting too close, Cauthorne," Dangerfield said as he burrowed his blue eyes into me. "You're dumb, but you were getting too close."

"Most of the pieces were missing," I said. "They still are."

"You're Dangerfield," Trippet said.

The heavy man behind the desk nodded his white domed head slowly. "That's right, Mr. Trippet. Sam Dangerfield of the FBI as your partner here sometimes calls me. Special Agent Dangerfield with twenty-seven years in the bureau."

"It's a lot of money, isn't it, Sam?" I said. "More than enough to pay off the mortgage at Bowie."

"You don't know how much, kid." He looked at Nash. "Any trouble?"

Nash finished rolling a cigarette before he answered. "Two cops. They had a wreck."

"Dead?"

"Dead."

"That makes three," I said.

Dangerfield smiled and he didn't bother to make it a pleasant one. "You figured out the Lozupone girl, huh?"

"About two minutes ago. But you're right, Sam, I'm a little dumb. I should have tumbled when we were at Toh's house and you knew too much about the letter to the Panama bank. I didn't know as much about it as you did and the only way you could have known was to have seen it. So you must have seen Carla. In fact, you must have been the last one to see her."

"One of the last, Cauthorne," he said. "One of the last."

"Okay," I said. "Now for the kicker. Where's Sacchetti?"

"Tell him, Cousin Jack," Dangerfield said.

I looked at Nash. "Sacchetti's in Cebu," he said.

"Doing what?"

"Being dead."

"Been dead for almost twenty months, hasn't he?" Dangerfield said to Nash.

Nash looked up at the ceiling as if counting the months. "About that."

Dangerfield poured gin into a glass. "I'm going to tell you about it, Cauthorne. I'm going to tell you because you got mixed up in it all accidental-like and I'm going to tell you because I like you, kid. I really do. You're just not too bright."

"I'm not much on keeping secrets either," I said.

He took a swallow of his drink and stared at me over the rim of the glass. Then he put it down, belched, and reached for a cigarette. "You'll keep this one," he said and looked at Nash. "How much time we got?"

Nash glanced at his watch. "About a half hour."

"Good a way to kill time as any," Dangerfield said. He motioned to the Chinese by the door. "Open it up; it's too goddamned hot in here."

The Chinese opened the door and leaned against the sill again, his arms still folded across his chest.

"You were going to tell me what happened to Sacchetti," I said. "I'm still interested."

Dangerfield nodded. "I know you are, kid. I know you are. Well, it seems when Sacchetti went over the side of that junk he had a sampan close by and swam underwater to it and then lit out for the Philippines. He didn't know anyone there, but it seemed like as good a place as any to operate out of."

"With Cole's microfilm," I said.

"That's right. With Charlie's microfilm. The only trouble was he ran out of money so he nosed around and learned that Cousin Jack here was loansharking it so he made the approach. Well, Jack loaned him—what was it, five thousand?"

"Six," Nash said.

"Six. Jack loaned him six and was supposed to get back seven, but Angelo dropped the whole bundle on the ponies and then couldn't pay up. Jack naturally got impatient and he took Angelo by the hand and showed him a couple of ex-gamblers who'd been customers until they couldn't pay. They were scooting around Cebu on platforms built on roller skates because their legs wouldn't work any more."

"Nash told me about the baseball bats," I said. "Only it was Angelo who was supposed to have used them."

"Jack tells a good story," Dangerfield said comfortably.

"Very good," I said.

"Since he couldn't pay, Angelo decided to cut Jack in. Angelo had always wanted his own shop. You know how he'd been around New York and Los Angeles, always on the fringe, always for peanuts. Well, his idea was to blackmail Godfather Cole for the nut and then set up an operation in Singapore. Except he didn't think he could swing it by himself, so he cut in Jack, like I said, because Jack knew the territory which sounds like something out of a song, doesn't it?"

"Not much," I said.

"Yeah. Well, Angelo told Jack about how he could blackmail Cole and Jack told him about how to set up the fix in Singapore. So together they started the blackmail on Cole. Then Jack got a good look at all of the microfilm that Angelo had and it looked like a goldmine and I'm afraid that Jack got greedy."

"Not too greedy," Nash said. "I cut you in."

"I'm your cousin," Dangerfield said. "We just kept it in the family."

"What happened to Sacchetti?" I said.

"He had an accident," Dangerfield said.

"What kind?"

"A fatal one. He got run over by a jeep taxi while crossing the street; it could happen to anyone."

"Only his name wasn't Angelo Sacchetti then."

"No; I'm afraid that the papers they found on his body said he was someone called Jerry Caldwell."

"You and Nash are really cousins?" I said.

"Grew up together," Dangerfield said.

"In Baltimore," Nash said.

"How much time now?" Dangerfield said to Nash.

"Twenty minutes."

"Going to have to cut this short, Cauthorne. We have to catch the tide."

"You're going someplace?" I said.

"All of us are," he said. "A short cruise."

"I won't keep you then."

"You've been plenty of laughs, Cauthorne."

"You're sure Sacchetti's dead?" I said.

"Sure."

"Then who married Toh's daughter?"

"My second cousin," Dangerfield said. "Jack's kid. With a mustache and longer hair who was to say that he wasn't Angelo Sacchetti? Nobody in Singapore knew Angelo anyway."

"Where's he now?"

"Jack's kid? In Panama City."

"Picking up the Lozupone million from the bank?"

"You got it right, Cauthorne."

"I'm sorry that I don't," Trippet said.

Dangerfield gave us another unpleasant smile. "Okay, I'll tell it quick. Jack and I grew up together, like he said, in Baltimore. He got in a little trouble in thirty-nine and caught a boat to Manila and then did this and that until he wound up in Cebu. I went to law school. I was always the goody-goody. *You* believe that, Cauthorne, don't you?"

"Sure," I said.

"We kept in touch by letter and after the war, I helped him on a few things. Information from the bureau that he could use."

"And you split whatever you made?" I said.

"It wasn't much. So when he got Cole's microfilm dumped into his hands, after Angelo had his accident, Jack got in touch with me. He needed somebody in the States who knew how Lozupone, Cole, and the rest of the boys operated, and how much they could be tapped for. That's me. He also needed somebody who knew how numbers and the rest of it were set up, and again, that's me. Jack's part was to put the fix in at Singapore which he did through Toh for three hundred grand and didn't make any secret about the fact that he'd bought protection."

"Toh and his daughter know that Nash's son isn't really Sacchetti?"

"They know," Dangerfield said. "But they don't give a damn. The marriage was nothing but one of convenience anyway; Jack's son doesn't go for girls much."

"He likes boys," Nash said. "His goddamned mother ruined him."

"That was Jack's first wife," Dangerfield said. "Now he's married to a nice Chinese girl."

"I heard."

"So everything was going along smooth in Singapore. The numbers were making money, the loansharking was taking hold, the protection was paying off, and Toh kept everyone in line by threatening to call a race riot if anything happened to his son-in-law. Everybody played ball and then Charlie Cole got dicey and called Callese in L.A. without checking with me."

"And that's how I got in," I said.

"Cole panicked and there wasn't anybody else he could think of."

"Or trust."

"That's right. Or trust."

"And Callese was just a messenger boy," I said.

"A high-priced one, but that's all," Dangerfield said. "I had it all worked out, but Cole screwed it up. I was going to squeeze a million out of Lozupone and then put him away. If he was out of the way in Atlanta, then the rest of them would ease up on Cole and he'd keep on paying."

"What happened to Carla?" I said. "Why kill her?"

"I didn't kill her," Dangerfield said. "I never killed anybody."

"Your friend at the door then."

"Like the cops say," Nash said. "Angelo Sacchetti killed her."

"All right," I said. "That was clever, but why kill her?"

"Carla turned bad when she found out that me and Jack were running the thing and that Sacchetti was dead. She threatened to tell her old man; blow the whole thing. She also had a soft spot for you, Cauthorne."

"Carla was okay," I said and somehow it seemed that I could have said more than that.

"So we set up another meeting with her; she brought the letter along; we took it, and then turned her over to the gentleman standing behind you. We just made sure that Angelo's billfold was in her hand."

"It looked like a frame," I said.

"We wanted it to. It'll keep them guessing for years.

Angelo Sacchetti disappeared that same night. Jack's kid cut his hair, shaved off his mustache, flew to Panama under his real name, and that's it."

"Extraordinary," Trippet said.

"He used to be with British Intelligence," Nash said to Dangerfield.

"Are you still, Mr. Trippet?"

"No, I'm in the used-car business."

"Just like Cauthorne, huh?"

"There're a couple of more loose ends," I said.

"Afraid they'll have to wait," Dangerfield said. "We're due to move out. Take the gentlemen's coats," he added, nodding to the Chinese. "They look all hot and sweaty."

"I'll keep mine," I said.

Dangerfield shook his head. "I'm disappointed in you, kid. That suit's got a nice cut, but that gun in your belt spoils the hang. If you'll look under the desk, you'll find that something's pointing at you and has been since you walked in."

The Chinese came over and I let him take my coat. He also took the Chief's Special. My stomach, at least, was happy to get rid of it.

"Now what?" I said.

"Now? Well, we take a trip and rendezvous with the yacht. Toh and his daughter should be aboard by now and I'm sorry you won't get to see them."

"You mean you're going to make us walk back?"

"That's the way it cuts out. Toh gets the yacht and a few more bucks and we shut down operations in Singapore. It's been one sweet deal, I can tell you. But if you know when to close the store, well, hell, you know what I mean."

"You can always work the big con, Sam," I said. "You worked it on me; you had the store and everything."

"You're a mark, Cauthorne," Dangerfield said. "You'll always be a mark, but always won't be a hell of a lot longer for you."

"I don't know," I said. "I was getting to—" I never finished it. The same stunt had worked in three pictures and I thought I knew exactly what to do. So I yelled, "Trippet!" and kicked the deal table over into Dangerfield's lap. He had a gun underneath it after all and it went off, but the bullet went into the floor and by then I was sailing across the table and both feet slammed into Dangerfield's chest. He yelled and fired the gun again, but it didn't seem to hit anyone. I kicked his hand and he dropped the gun and I scooped it up, noticed that it was a .38 caliber automatic and thought that an FBI agent should know better. Trippet seemed to be tangling nicely with Nash and the Chinese by the door was trying to get a clear shot at me so I shot him instead. He grabbed his stomach and amazement spread slowly over his face, the first real emotion that I had ever seen him display. He still wanted to pull the trigger of the Chief's Special so I tried to shoot him again, but the automatic jammed. I threw it at him and missed as he folded slowly. His knees bent first, then his head dropped as if he were trying to take a close look at his stomach. Finally, he curled up on the floor and started to groan.

From behind Dangerfield brought the gin bottle down on my left shoulder. He ran out the cabin door and I got up after a while and started to follow. I tried to pick up the Chief's Special that the Chinese had dropped, but Nash broke away from Trippet and kicked it under the bunk. Both of them dived for it and I went after Dangerfield.

He was moving towards the stern of the *kumpit* and shouting something. He stopped near what appeared to be a bale of copra, snatched up a wicked looking machete, and turned, his face red and dripping with sweat. "Don't come any closer, kid, or I'll cut your gizzard out."

I looked around for something to hit him with. I would have settled for a bottle or even a small rock. There was a short, thick stick with a hook in one end lying on the deck next to the copra bale. I bent down slowly, my eyes on Dangerfield, and picked it up, talking all the time. "You're too old for that, Sam," I said.

"Too old and fat." The stick and its hook were about two feet long and looked something like the kind that longshoremen use.

Dangerfield moved towards me, shuffling, the machete raised high in his right hand. I didn't bother to tell him that it wasn't a particularly good position. I feinted with the stick and he tried to slash it and I poked him in the stomach. He said "oof," or something like it, and moved back; he was quicker than I thought.

Dangerfield waved the machete around some more as he shuffled flatfooted backward towards the stern. A yellow light that hung just above him rippled highlights off his white dome as the bulb glowed by fits and starts on the erratic current that came from the *kumpit*'s generator.

Dangerfield changed his mind, stopped backing, and came in fast, the machete slashing and hacking in front of him. As in fencing, I lost any sense of space and time. All that existed was a kinetic image of the machete. The stick with the hook went to meet the machete when needed, but it was guided by intuition, not thought. Dangerfield's moves fed information into my brain and my right hand responded automatically. I thought about something else. I thought about how much I hated Dangerfield and found, to my surprise, that the intensity of the hate was most comforting.

It was no formal fencing match on a six-foot-wide, forty-foot-long white strip. It was not even good theatrical sword-play with lots of leaping about from balcony to stairs and swinging around on the drapes. It was only a man with machete in his hand who wanted to kill me and I let my reflexes take over completely. The only conscious thoughts I had were about how much I hated him. I liked those thoughts; they helped.

Dangerfield began to tire, but not much, and I forced him back, shuffle by shuffle. His machete still made no pattern; there was no *corps-à-corps* with our wrists locked and straining and our faces an inch apart while we sneered our dialogue at each other. He

215

hacked and I parried. He had no *riposte,* just one wild swing after another and each one threatened to take off my head.

As he reached the stern his right hand dropped an inch and it was the inch I needed when he made another vicious hacking lunge. I drove the round edge of the hook deep into his stomach. His arms flew out and he waved them around as he tried to keep his balance, but the back of his knees caught the low rail and for a long moment he teetered there, his arms swinging wildly, his right hand still clutching the machete. I poked him in the stomach again, not too hard, just enough, and his arms flailed at the air some more, but it didn't help and then he knew he would fall. His eyes fastened on mine and he said, "Goddamn it, kid," and just before he fell I thought his left eye closed and his mouth went up at the corner and together they formed a knowing, grotesque, and perfectly obscene wink.

CHAPTER XXV

I knelt at the low rail and stared down at the black water and the tricky current of the Johore Strait, but there was nothing to see, not even a bubble or two. I yelled, "Goddamn you, Dangerfield, come up!" I must have yelled it five or six times, but it did no good. Sam Dangerfield no longer paid attention to me or to anyone else.

Two shots came from the cabin and I spun around, holding the hooked stick before me. Trippet came out of the lighted doorway, standing not so straight as usual, the Chief's Special dangling at his right side. I moved towards him and he brought the revolver up until its muzzle was even with my belt buckle. "I believe you borrowed this from Sammy," he said and handed me the pistol.

"What happened?" I said.

He turned and gazed at the open doorway. "We were scuffling around underneath the bunk. I found the revolver; Nash tried to take it from me, so I shot him. Twice. I think he's dead."

"So's Dangerfield."

"Oh?"

"Drowned."

"I heard you shouting at him, but I couldn't make out what you said."

"I told him to stop being drowned."

A rowboat bumped against the side of the *kumpit* and a man's voice muttered something, but nothing I could understand. I handed the pistol back to Trippet and motioned him to one side of the rope ladder that hung down to the water's edge. I crouched on the other side, the hooked stick ready to push somebody else overboard. I could hear the labored breathing of whoever was coming up the ladder. There was a gasp when a hand or a foot slipped, a curse upon recovery, and then a head stuck up above the railing. The head was topped by a mass of dark wavy hair, decorated with old acne scars, and belonged to Tony Cea.

I stood up. "You're late," I said.

Cea stared at me and then at the pistol that Trippet aimed at him. "Up yours, Cauthorne," he said and swung his legs over the rail. He was followed by Terilizzi whose grey eyes, even in the dim light, looked just a little mad.

"How'd you find us?" I said.

"We just followed the cops all night until that Chevelle run them off the road," Cea said, "and then we followed the Chevelle. Then we waited some more and you guys showed up with somebody else and then took a boat. We spent all the rest of the time looking for a boat to steal. Where's Sacchetti?"

"Dead," I said.

"Let me see," Cea said. "I want to make sure."

"He's been dead for almost two years," Trippet said.

217

"But there are two other corpses in the cabin if you care to examine them."

"Who?"

"The ones you're looking for," I said. "The ones who killed Carla."

"You sure?"

"We're sure," I said.

"Come on, Terilizzi, let's look," Cea said.

They entered the cabin and stayed for two or three minutes. Then they came out, Cea first, with Terilizzi following as he wrapped something carefully into a large white handkerchief.

"You're sure those are the two who got Carla?" Cea said.

"That's right," I said.

"Well, Terilizzi took their ears along to show the boss. We got to have something to show when we get back, you understand. Terilizzi wanted to work on them a little more, but I told him it didn't make no sense seeing as how they were already dead."

"Seeing as how," Trippet murmured.

"The ears will cheer the boss up anyway," Cea said.

"Make him feel better," I said.

"That's right," Cea said. "They'll make him feel better." He looked around the *kumpit* and sniffed as if he didn't care much for the smell of rotting copra. "Hot, ain't it?" he said.

"Rather warm," Trippet said.

"Well, I guess there's nothing else for us to hang around here for," Cea said. "Thanks for taking care of things for us, Cauthorne."

"Don't mention it," I said.

"Well," Cea said, and nodded at both of us, "it's been nice talking to you. Let's go, Terilizzi."

Terilizzi stared at me with his wet oyster eyes and then made an abrupt, flat slashing movement with his hand. "You," he said and giggled as he patted the pocket that held the handkerchief-wrapped ears. He seemed quite mad.

At two in the afternoon the following day Trippet

218

and I walked into Lim Pang Sam's office. I took the Chief's Special out of the brown paper bag and placed it on Lim's blotter.

"It came in handy after all," I said.

Lim smiled. "So I understand."

"Anything new since last night?" I said.

"There was an emergency cabinet meeting," Lim said. "It was decided to put Toh in jail."

"They had a cabinet meeting about that?"

"Well, to be frank, it wasn't so much about whether they should put Toh in jail; it was more concerned about who should be let out."

"I don't follow you," I said.

"The party does need *some* opposition, you understand, Mr. Cauthorne, and except for Toh, all of them seem to be in jail. So it was decided that two should be released."

The Chinese secretary came in with the tea tray and we went through the ritual which Lim so thoroughly enjoyed and appreciated. He settled himself into his high-backed executive chair and rested the cup and saucer on his stomach.

"The fantastic part about it, of course," he said, "is the discipline that they displayed throughout. Amazing discipline along with what can only be described as consummate acting."

"Not really," Trippet said. "Not when you think of who they were and the size of the stakes that they played for. They were all pros—Dangerfield and Nash especially. As Edward told Dangerfield, it was simply an expanded variation of the big con. All they had to do to make it pay off was to keep Angelo Sacchetti officially alive. When that no longer proved practical, they decided to let him disappear, taking with him all the responsibility for every major and minor crime that's been committed in Singapore for the last year and a half. He was a perfect whipping boy and there was nothing to tie either Dangerfield or Nash to him."

Lim placed his cup and saucer on the blotter next to the revolver. He picked up some three-by-five index cards and thumbed through them. "There are a few things that have happened since we picked up Toh and his daughter this morning," he said. "I wasn't quite sure what to do about Nash's son in Panama City so I got in touch with the British and they flew a man down from Mexico City."

"The British?" I said.

"Well, as I told you, Mr. Cauthorne, we're not on the best terms with your CIA."

"So what happened?"

"He found the young Mr. Nash and relieved him of a million dollars in currency. The only thing now is what to do with it. The British agent is quite concerned." He looked at me over his Ben Franklin glasses. "It would be rather difficult to return it to Mr. Lozupone, wouldn't it?"

"Rather," I said.

"Any suggestions?"

I shrugged. "Do you have a favorite charity?"

"Several most worthwhile ones."

"Divide it among them."

"Done," he said and shifted the card to the bottom of the pile.

"Oh, yes. We talked—or rather, some friends of Detective-Sergeants Huang and Tan talked to Toh at length. He was most cooperative."

"I can imagine," Trippet said.

"About that information you were interested in, Mr. Cauthorne. The microfilm?"

"Yes," I said. "I looked at the box that Toh gave me. It was just blank film."

"I'm not surprised. We found the original material in his safe. Toh swears that there were no copies—only the ones that Sacchetti stole from his godfather. Although they intended to do so, they simply never got around to making copies. Under the circumstances, I must believe what Toh says."

"Where are they now?" I said.

"The microfilm?"

"Yes."

"As I said, they were in Toh's safe." Lim opened a drawer in his desk and brought out a wrapped package, not quite as large as a cigar box. "He even gave us the combination to his safe. More tea?"

"Thank you, no."

"I think that this information would prove more valuable to you than to us, Mr. Cauthorne," he said. "Please," and he moved the wrapped package towards me, three inches past the Chief's Special. I picked it up and put it in my lap. "Thanks," I said.

"Not at all," Lim said and leaned back in his chair with what seemed to be a real sense of accomplishment. "It has been a most rewarding venture, don't you think so, Dickie?"

"I have discovered a truth," Dickie said, "and the truth is that I'm far too old for such adventures. I find I crave the quiet and honest chicanery of a used-car emporium."

"Nonsense," Lim said. "You're in your prime. In fact, I feel so smug and self-satisfied that I think we should have a drink."

Nobody objected so Lim poured three drinks and then toasted our health. Once again he seemed to think it was necessary to put a little extra feeling into the toast that he proposed to me.

CHAPTER XXVI

When our flight landed at Los Angeles, Trippet and I went in search of a stamp machine. We fed dimes and nickels and quarters into it until we had almost three dollars' worth. He helped me lick them and we pasted them on the carefully wrapped package that Lim had pushed across his desk.

I borrowed Trippet's broad-nibbed fountain pen and printed the address on the package of microfilm. It read: "Mr. J. Edgar Hoover, Federal Bureau of Investigation, Washington, D.C."

"You have the zip code?" Trippet said.

"No."

"What about the sender's address?"

"I'm coming to that."

I printed it carefully in the upper left-hand corner and then showed it to Trippet. It read: "Samuel C. Dangerfield, Bowie, Maryland."

CHAPTER XXVII

Ten days later I was sitting in my glass cubicle with my feet on the desk trying to remember exactly what Angelo Sacchetti looked like and rejoicing a little over the blank that I almost drew. They came in together and once again the big man paused at the 1932 Cadillac and gave it a lingering glance of mild adoration.

They didn't stop long at the car, this time. Callese walked into my office, gave it a quick appraisal with his dusty eyes, and said, "What happened, Cauthorne?"

"Angelo Sacchetti finally died," I said. "That's all."

"That isn't all."

"What else?"

"They got Charlie Cole."

"Who?"

"The FBI picked him up yesterday."

Palmisano was staring at the Cadillac through the glass walls of the office. "They got Joe, too," he said. "Tell him about Joe."

"They picked up Lozupone. In Jersey."

"That's your problem," I said.

"And about six others," Palmisano said. "Maybe seven."

"I figure it ties in to you," Callese said.

"You figure wrong."

"You better hope I'm wrong."

"I'll have to think about that," I said. "Sometime."

His lips turned up at the corners again in what he passed off to the world as a smile. Then he took out his gold cigarette case and lit one of his oval cigarettes. When he was through with that he sat down and crossed his legs so that I could admire his pearl grey spats. "We're checking it out, Cauthorne. I just thought I'd let you know."

"What happens when you're through checking?"

"We might drop around again."

"I'll be here."

Palmisano was still staring through the glass at the Cadillac when the two men came in. They were in their middle thirties and wore plain dark suits. They looked at the Cadillac, but not long, and then headed towards my office.

"Get rid of them," Callese said.

"They're the first customers I've had all day."

"Get rid of them," he said again. "We're not through talking."

"I think we are."

The two men came into the office and looked at Callese and then at Palmisano. "FBI," one of them said and they both whipped out their folding identification cases and showed them to Callese and Palmisano. They didn't bother to let me look.

"What's this?" Callese said.

"You'll have to come downtown with us, Mr. Callese," one of them said.

Callese shrugged, dropped his cigarette on the floor, and ground it out with his neat black, shiny shoe. He stood and looked at me. "I'll be back," he said.

"I'll be waiting."

At the door Palmisano turned quickly. "That Caddy out there," he said. "What's your last price?"

"Still six grand," I said.

He nodded and smiled as if remembering something pleasant that had happened a long time ago. "I had one like that once. You know what color it was?"

"Green," I said. "Real dark green."